EEK DAAN – THE OTHER SIDE

KRUNG THEP BOOK 2

MARIA KUHN

To the City of Angels

Officially known as
Krung Thep Mahanakhon Amon Rattanakosin Mahinthara
Ayuthaya Mahadilok Phop Noppharat Ratchathani Burirom
Udomratchaniwet Mahasathan Amon Piman Awatan Sathit
Sakkathattiya Witsanukam Prasit.

Or simply
Bangkok

CHARACTERS

Taylor Family
Luna – 16 year old American expat
Luke – Luna's 12 year old brother
Mark – Luna's dad/Khun Mark
Susan – Luna's mom/Khun Susan
Apichart Family
Nui (Benjawan) – 16 year old Thai
Duen (Duenswang) – Nui's 13 year old sister
Krit – Nui's 18 year old brother
Tum – Nui's 11 year old brother
Mae – Nui's mom
Paa – Nui's dad
Khun Yaa – Nui's grandmother
Khun Bpoo – Nui's grandfather
Khun Varaporn – Nui's aunt (sister of her dad)
Khun Karl – Varaporn's husband
Eve – Nui's 6 year old cousin
Jenny – Nui's 6 year old cousin
Others
Khun Pak – Taylor family driver
Khun Bo – Taylor family helper/cook
Mom Luang Teerawat – Khun Mark's boss
Thanpuying Wassana – Mom Luang's wife
Channon – Veterinary Assistant
Chone – Channon's husky
Pi'Ohm – street food stall owner
Yumi Wilson – Luna's 16 year old friend from Shanghai
Jake Wilson – Yumi's dad
Toey and Dearn – Nui's friends

EEK DAAN – อีกด้าน

THE OTHER SIDE

Idiom: A different way of considering a situation, making it seem either better or worse than it did originally; another aspect or version of something, especially its reverse.

Happiness does not depend on what you have or who you are.
It solely relies on what you think.
—Buddha

1

Bangkok, Wat Phatum
January

NUI

"So, this was a hoax?" Ajaarn Anurak didn't raise his voice, but the underlying anger was unmistakable and hit me like a punch in the gut. I almost fell backwards, my knees jerking out of my half-lotus position. I didn't dare look at Ajaarn. Monks were supposed to be serene, not angry. Shivers of guilt rippled through my body. I had only myself to blame. And Luna, of course.

"No, no, Ajaarn kha! It really happened, I promise!" I bit my lips trying to come up with something else to say. If we were to need his help in the future, Luna and I had to convince him that our reason for being here was legit.

"You said you wanted to switch back, and you were ready for it. I know you both had an out-of-body experience; I sensed the change of vibration in the air," Ajaarn Anurak insisted. "What happened? You mean to tell me you changed your mind?"

I glanced at Luna, silently begging her to help explain our conundrum.

A month earlier, she and I had taken meditation classes here at Wat Pathum Temple with Ajaarn Anurak to test our hare-brained theory of astral projection while pretending the sessions were for a school project. The principle seemed simple enough: if you can meditate to an out-of-body state, theoretically you should be able to switch bodies with someone who wants the same thing. I was keen to experience Luna's unrestricted expat lifestyle, while she wanted to see what it was like living with my traditional family in a settled environment.

We weren't one hundred percent convinced a mind swap was possible, but our experiment succeeded, mostly by accident. For two weeks, we had been living in each other's body and with each other's family. Each time I looked in the mirror, I saw Luna's face, and she saw mine. Confusing? Definitely. Sustainable? Definitely not.

Our previous attempts at reversing the change had been unsuccessful, hence today's session with Ajaarn Anurak, which allowed us to connect again in the astral space. We never predicted, though, that we would agree to postpone the swap back for a few extra days. Ajaarn Anurak's anger with us was justified.

Luna cleared her throat a few times but her voice still sounded rusty. "You're right, Ajaarn. We had an out-of-body experience, and Nui and I linked up through the energy stream exactly as you explained, but we realized we need more time to resolve a few issues first." She looked up at the Buddha behind Ajaarn. "Neither of us expected that; we only discovered this while we were connected. We honestly didn't mean to deceive you, and we're very sorry." She wai'ed to Ajaarn in apology, then looked at me, eyebrows drawn together. "But what I don't understand is why we can leave our bodies so easily when you lead the meditation, but not when we try it ourselves. Is there something you do differently, Ajaarn kha?"

I doubted Luna intended to flatter, but her apology and question worked. Ajaarn's voice sounded more mellow again.

"No, there's nothing I do differently. It's all about your own expectations. You assume my voice is more powerful, therefore it is." He continued, gravely. "So, we're back at the beginning? You are asking me to accept that you switched bodies by mistake, but now you say you don't want to switch back?" He rose from his lotus position, adjusted his orange robe and looked down at us, a deep frown line between his eyes. "I am disappointed you are treating meditation like a game. I suggest you figure out what you want. If you are not absolutely clear about that, don't waste my time." He shook his head, wai'ed to the Buddha, and walked away.

2

LUNA

"Damn!" I whispered. "I didn't mean to make him angry. We might still need his help."

"Don't swear Luna. We're in a temple," Nui objected.

We were still sitting on mats in front of the Buddha statue, trying to come to grips with this unexpected development. It wasn't the outcome we'd envisioned when we walked into the temple an hour earlier.

"What did you think of the session? It was pretty amazing how we communicated, wasn't it?" Nui grinned wide, slowly shaking her head.

My brain wasn't quite up to speed yet after the intense experience. "Can we talk about it later? I need to digest it first. Let's go home. We can discuss it there."

We rolled up the mats and left them near the pavilion entrance, where we picked up our sandals. Walking through the lush gardens, I hoped this wouldn't be the last time I got to enjoy this oasis. It was a peaceful retreat. *Even if Ajaarn is angry with us, he can't prevent us from visiting, can he?*

Outside the gates, the Bangkok rush-hour traffic jarred after the quiet of the temple grounds. People were bustling back and forth along the elevated skywalk that connected several malls in the central shopping district. Wat Pathum sat between two mega malls, and though the side-by-side placement of commerce and worshipping wasn't uncommon in Bangkok, I still found it peculiar.

Nui and I made our way to Siam station to take the Skytrain to my family's apartment on Sukhumvit, soi twenty-one. It was four-thirty, so schoolkids and early commuters packed every train, and we had to push and shove to get inside one for the short ride. Millions of questions bounced around in my head, but we were both quiet out of necessity. A mind-switch wasn't a topic to be discussed amid curious ears, regardless of the language we used.

Nui and I had met at Bangkok International School, or BIS, when my family moved to Thailand in August. I had resigned myself to coasting through the last two years of high-school without getting attached to anyone or anything. After moving eight times in sixteen years, I was tired of having to start afresh yet again.

Nui and I got off to a rocky start, but eventually we became friends, and when our ridiculous idea to switch bodies actually worked, life suddenly became a lot more complicated, but equally, a lot more interesting.

We had survived most situations, more through luck than know-how, but some complications had cropped up in the last week. I, as Nui, now unofficially owned a rescued husky, Chone. I had met Channon, the husky's official owner, on my first day as Nui. He interned at the local pet hospital and shelter and was due to start veterinarian school in March. I had wanted to adopt Chone for myself but because I was in Nui's body, that didn't work since she already had a dog,

Joey. Instead, I now volunteered at the shelter, partly to be closer to Channon, but also because Chone was there during the day. I really liked Channon, and we had gone on our first date the night before, which, unfortunately, had ended in shambles, mainly because I withheld the truth about my identity, expecting to reverse the switch in today's session with Ajaarn. I wanted him to know me as Luna, but I didn't know if he would consider dating a foreigner. Right now, he assumed he was hanging out with Nui, his friend Krit's younger sister.

Meanwhile, my parents were talking about moving back to the States much sooner than originally planned, to be closer to Mom's sick sister and to give me time to prepare for college. Nui was keen to study in the US, but didn't have the financial means, so moving there with my family, as me, would solve that problem.

Clearly, we were both confused about what we wanted.

Nui nudged me out of my reverie as we arrived at Asok station. "Let's go."

3

—

NUI

WE USUALLY MET AT LUNA'S HOME RATHER THAN MINE. HER apartment was always quiet, with only four people living here. Luna's mom was in Chicago supporting her sister, her dad was at work at his hotel, and her brother Luke was probably playing video games in his room. Khun Bo, their helper, brought us some water and fresh-cut guava as a snack.

"I can't stay long. Your grandma is expecting me home around six and I still want to check on Chone." Luna plopped down on the bed.

I walked into the bathroom to wash my hands. By now, it seemed almost normal to look at my blonde, blue-eyed alter-ego, although I still didn't have a handle on styling her longer hair the Luna way.

"I'm pretty sure you can miss one afternoon with the dogs, no? This is much more important. We need to sort out our stuff." I shouted through the open door watching her in the mirror.

Luna sighed and laid back on the bed but didn't respond.

"Hey, no time for a nap." I walked back into the room, nudging her legs. "So, what did you think of the session?" Sitting down on the ottoman facing Luna, I repeated my earlier question.

"That was pretty intense, wasn't it?" Luna grinned, pushing herself up on her elbows. "I still don't understand how this works, but I picked up on your feelings, or at least I think I did." She looked at me for confirmation.

I agreed. "Yeah, it was like you didn't have to say anything, but I could sense you didn't want to switch back yet, and I suppose you got the same vibe from me."

It was mysterious just how effortlessly our sentiments ran along the threads connecting our minds, almost like Morse code.

Luna nodded. "Hmm, perhaps it didn't work previously because we were so freaked out about the whole thing and assumed we had to reverse it immediately. But, if we both agree to a limited extension, maybe we can experience it more deliberately before we make the switch back. At least now we know we can do it. What do you think?"

"I guess, though, we should agree on a time frame. I mean, you know we can't do this indefinitely," I reminded her.

School was back in session after the winter holidays and we needed to figure out a way to get around the mind swap, as we had different aptitudes in several subjects. Getting poor grades a year before graduation wouldn't help either of us with our college applications.

"I suppose it all hinges on what your mom says when she's back on Saturday, and what's happening with your Aunt Jane. Who knows, maybe your parents have already decided to move but haven't told Luke and me yet?"

Luna frowned. "Yeah, I wondered about that, too. I hope

they haven't. Ok, so why don't we wait until the weekend and go from there? I want to see Mom when she's back, so maybe I'll come over on Saturday?"

"I'll find out what time she gets in. But, let me ask you something. What exactly *do* you need the time for?" That part hadn't been clear to me during our trance.

Luna blushed. "Well, hmm…" she trailed off.

Her dithering could only mean one thing: Channon.

"Luna, don't tell me you want to continue this thing you got going with Channon? I thought we talked about that already? You can't keep leading him on."

I was adamant she put a stop to the budding romance. After all, Channon thought he was talking to me, Nui, his friend's sister, when in fact, he was talking to Luna. I had no romantic interest in Channon and didn't want my family to become too used to seeing him around. It was a totally unnecessary complication for when we switched back. I couldn't understand why Luna refused to see the issue and do something about it.

She crossed her arms and blew out a noisy breath. "Stop telling me what to do! Why do you assume you have all the answers, Nui?"

"I don't have all the answers, but the problem here is so obvious I don't understand why you can't see it." It annoyed me having to repeat myself over and over again, but Luna refused to listen. To make my point crystal clear, I added, "Just promise you won't sleep with him, ok?"

"Eww, Nui! I wouldn't do that. That's sick."

"Exactly. Don't forget, it's my body and I'm saving that for myself." I was dead serious.

Luna wiggled her hands in front of my face. "Stop it. You're being gross. I want to be in my body too when I sleep with someone, so don't worry about it, ok?"

"Ok, but what are you going to do about Chone now? Isn't he with Channon's mom?" I was relentless, trying to make Luna see my point.

"He'll stay there eventually, but until next week he'll be at the shelter during the day, so he can play with the other dogs. I'll see him tomorrow after school." Luna dismissed the issue.

"You know you're playing with fire, don't you? At some point, you will have to explain to Channon and his mom what the deal is. Don't you think it's better to come clean now?"

I meant she needed to back away from Channon, but Luna misunderstood.

"What? You're the one who said I shouldn't complicate things further, and now you want me to tell Channon it's me in your body? Yeah, that'll go over really well."

At times, Luna's thought processes were so confusing they made my head hurt. Or maybe she did it deliberately, trying to justify her choices to me.

"Of course I don't want you to tell him *that,* but you gotta get us out of this mess somehow. You have to explain that you can't see him anymore. Maybe your date made you realize it wasn't meant to be, or something," I clarified.

"Come on Nui. I can't let Channon think it was his fault. That wouldn't be fair to him. I'll figure something out."

4

LUNA

I had to get Nui off the Channon subject. She was right. Channon and I had grown close in the past few weeks, and while our date hadn't gone quite as I'd expected, I hoped I could make up for it. How was still unclear to me, but I had promised him an explanation for my weird behaviour.

"So Nui, why didn't *you* want to switch back yet?" After her badgering, I thought it was only fair to turn the tables.

Nui looked down, twisting her hands. "You know I never got to live your normal life since your mom left right after we switched, and then we went to Bali. I'd just like to know what it's like day-to-day."

"But you already had almost two weeks. Same as me. What more do you want?"

"But your mom wasn't here, so it wasn't the same." Nui lifted her head.

"Your brothers weren't around either, but whatever." I thought her explanation was kind of flimsy, but another thought occurred to me. "By the way, you never explained why you told Dad you're ok with the move back to the States. I told you I want to stay here." As soon as I said it, I realized there was one plausible reason for her to encourage my parents about the move. Had Nui planned to go back home in my place, as me? I dismissed the idea immediately. The implications were too huge.

Nui's posture stiffened. "I only said that to get him off my back. I mean, I was daydreaming about what it would be like to study there, but I know it can't happen." She slouched down, her earlier belligerence gone. Now she just sounded sad. I could afford to be magnanimous and let her off the hook.

"You know, even if you can't go to study abroad, you can always go afterwards to work there, can't you?"

"Ha. If only it was that easy. Do you have any idea how difficult it is to get a work permit for America? Almost impossible for us Thais."

"Hmm, I didn't think of that. Ok then, let's just give it a few days until Mom's back and then we'll swap back, ok? But what are we going to do about school?"

Nui shrugged. "I don't know. Maybe we just need to study harder. Or maybe we can actually switch our test papers? We didn't even check our handwriting. Do you write like me now?"

"Hmm, don't know. Let's try it."

We both grabbed a piece of paper and wrote our names a few times in English.

"Nope, that won't work. I can't write English Lit for you, it'll be in Nui's handwriting. Damn."

"Arghh, why does this have to be so difficult?" Nui huffed. "What about Thai? Can you write Thai?" One of the side benefits of the switch was that we were both fluent in Thai and English now, but we hadn't tested the writing part.

I had to think for a moment, trying to envision the sound for my name before I put the pen to paper. The first few characters looked crooked, like a child's scribbling. But Nui's skills took over, just as they had with the speaking.

"Give me something else to test!" I demanded.

"How about this?" Nui grinned and started a song in Thai, which sounded goofy to me. She cracked herself up, almost falling off the ottoman, laughing.

"Ha, ha! Hilarious." I had to grin, despite myself, but trying to write in Thai was a bit more challenging.

"How does this look?"

เรามีตาไว้ดู
เรามีหูไว้ฟัง
คุณครูท่านสอนท่านสั่ง
ต้องตั้งใจฟัง
ต้องตั้งใจดู

"Not bad. Not bad at all." Nui gave me a thumbs up. "Glad you can do both now."

"What is that song?"

"It's called 'Looking Eyes'. Everyone knows it." She sang it again, this time in English. "We have eyes for looking. We have ears for listening. When the teacher is teaching. You have to listen. You have to pay attention and look." Nui was wiping her eyes. "Doesn't sound so good in English but it's all about paying attention in school."

"Great, thanks Nui. Now I'll have that in my head all day. But at least that's one less thing to worry about. Let's just get through the rest of the week and we'll regroup," I suggested.

"By the way, are we seeing Toey and Dearn on Friday?" Nui asked. The girls had been her best friends since kindergarten, but they were going to a local high school instead of BIS.

"Yep, Toey confirmed they'll meet us at that café on soi eight at four on Friday. That should work, right?"

"Sure, your mom won't be back, and your dad will be at work. We just need to get Luke on the bus home."

"Right, I better go, or I'll be late for Khun Yaa." I picked up my backpack and walked to the door, then backtracked to the dresser to grab some of the money I had stashed away. My occasional breakfast and dinner with Channon had left me short, and I had to buy my coffee every day since Nui's family only drank tea or water for breakfast. Nui's comparatively small allowance didn't cover those expenses.

Still seated, Nui casually asked, "How is Grandma? Is she ok? She had some heart problems a few months ago and is supposed to take it easier."

I flipped around, alarmed.

"What? Why didn't you tell me before? I'll check and let you know. Or you could come to the house on Friday after we meet the girls."

"Good idea. Bye Luna."

"Bye Nui. Let's text later."

5

NUI

As soon as Luna left, I picked up my journal. I had started it when we first went to the temple for our meditation class, to keep track of our progress. My notes recorded the process itself, and any feelings or random thoughts that flashed into my head during meditation. Originally, I thought we could use the comments for the essay we had to write, but after our mind swap, the detailed emotions had become way too personal.

I also wanted to compare our situation to the astral travel described in a book I had stumbled across at my favourite bookstore. As far as I'd read, it only covered out-of-body experiences, not actual swaps. I wondered if there was anything else about the mechanics of projection beyond what Ajaarn had explained.

I felt twitchy, and writing things down always helped me to clarify my thoughts, but right then I felt more confused than ever. On one hand, our swap was a huge accomplishment, but I felt uneasy about the way things were speeding up. Instead of simply experiencing our different lifestyles, we both had begun to shape them to our own preferences without consulting each other. I felt Luna was the primary culprit, making important decisions on her own that would affect us both long term. Yet, I had agreed to extend our switch. Why? The annoying little voice in my head reminded me. *In case you get to study abroad like you always wanted.*

I put the journal aside and stood up, too agitated to sit still. Pacing in circles, my thoughts bounced around my head like ping-pong balls. The prospect of moving still excited me, but could I leave my family behind for good? I had always dreamed of travelling, but with the assumption I could come home whenever I wanted. It was scary to think that not only would I have to pretend to be someone else, but I would also leave everything I knew behind, if only temporarily. *Sometimes you just have to take some risks, Nui!* I snorted at my feeble attempt to pep talk myself.

If I couldn't go abroad as Luna, the chances were slim to none that I'd be able to travel at all. The biggest obstacle was money. I knew my parents couldn't afford to send me to a university in the US unless I earned a scholarship, and even then, they probably wouldn't agree to it. Besides, I doubted my grades were good enough for a free ride and we didn't have any family living in the US who could sponsor or support me. So, my college education abroad remained out of reach. Crucially, I couldn't imagine Luna simply stepping aside and letting me leave Thailand in her place, even if she was quite happy living my life right now. Sure, I could encourage her friendship with Channon so she might consider staying, but the thought of them taking their relationship to the next level felt unacceptable to me. It just wasn't fair. Luna had a multitude of options lined up for her and didn't even particularly care about them while I was stuck.

Annoyed with my pathetic brooding, I picked up the tray that Khun Bo had brought us and marched off to the kitchen.

"Nong Luna, you don't have to bring. I come and get later," Khun Bo grabbed the tray and hustled me out of her domain. She was preparing dinner already and though I would have loved to help, as I did with Grandma, I knew she wouldn't let me. I felt useless.

Resigned, I went back to my room, figuring I could at least research some colleges in the US that have communication and journalism departments, just in case. Maybe I could use some of my old essays for a college application. Or better yet, I could do a more current story on the political climate in Thailand. After a series of election and corruption debacles, the military had stepped in and established a council to run the country. Not much had changed in daily life, but the military was tightening quite a few rules. No Thai paper would touch such a piece, but if I submitted it to a foreign newspaper as an op-ed piece, it might even get published. I'd have to be careful and not use my name as it was too dangerous and could draw the attention of the authorities. The more I thought I about it, the more excited I became, and already saw my by-line in the New York Times. I realized I had a big grin on my face.

I jumped up again, on fire. *Let's think this through, Nui.* Catching my reflection in the mirror, I froze. Inspiration struck me like a lightning bolt. *Nui, you are soooo stupid! You don't have to invent anything; you* are *already someone different! Why not start a blog using Luna's digital fingerprint and post all your writings there? Then, you won't have to worry about repercussions or censoring.* I had Luna's laptop, her log-in information, and she wouldn't have to know about it unless I told her.

As if I had just won a big victory, I raised my arms and

started laughing. *Ok Nui, settle down and think this through.* Energized, I started another to-do list:

- Come up with a catchy name for the blog
- Research options for how to build the site
- Start building an audience
- Use Luna's contact list from her social media profiles? My own? The alumni page of BIS?
- Decide on subjects. Check if you can use some of your old story ideas
- Current political situation—maybe I could ask Mom Luang Teerawat (what was his position at the Palace before he became Luna's dad's boss?) for an interview. (Need to come up with a reasonable request though, otherwise he'll say no)
- Luna's Third Culture status? (Could be interesting for other expat teens?)
- Thai habits and culture through the eyes of expats living here?
- How many posts do I need? How often do I need to update it?

I needed to do a lot of research, but I enjoyed that part and it made me feel productive. The beauty of the blog was I could change everything over to my name if I got to the States on my own somehow, and I would already have a portfolio. It would be a good writing exercise too, and I could test audience reaction to the articles I had in mind.

Nui, you're crazy! My more reasonable inner voice spoke up. *Shouldn't you be thinking about how to get through this week instead of ghost-writing stories?*

I was so engrossed in my list that I jumped when someone knocked on my door.

"Luna, Dad's here. Dinner's ready. Come on!" Luke called. Luna's brother was twelve, the same age as mine, but he somehow seemed more mature than Tum. Maybe travelling had given him more self-confidence.

"Coming. Give me a sec."

6

LUNA

IT FELT STRANGE TO LEAVE MY BEDROOM TO GO BACK TO Nui's home, but I hoped if I was early enough and caught the train right, I would have time to swing by the pet hospital on the way.

Maybe you should give that a miss until you know what to tell Channon. But I want to see Chone. Get your act together first Luna! Why did the voices in my head always have to argue with each other? Wouldn't it be nice if someone could just tell me what to do, so I didn't have to think about it?

The timing didn't quite work out, which was both a relief and disappointment. On the way, I texted Channon to say I was running late but would definitely come over to the shelter after school the next day.

He replied saying he hoped my project at the temple had gone well, and all was ok. How sweet of him to remember. *You probably scared him the way you behaved last night.* I had been too nervous about our impending switch-back attempt that I jumped around different subjects arbitrarily. *So, what am I going to tell him now?* I knew Nui wanted me to end our relationship without giving our secret away. How I was going to do that was beyond me.

As soon as I opened the front door, my stomach started rumbling, triggered by the delicious smells coming from the kitchen. Nui's family was just about to sit down for dinner. Khun Yaa had outdone herself again. Morning Glory, Thai Basil Tofu stir-fry, steamed rice and a catfish curry plus some chicken satay. Enough veggie options for me. *Whatever happens next, I'm definitely going to miss her cooking.* I looked around the kitchen, which was tiny compared to our own, but I had become quite used to sharing the house with Nui's parents, grandparents, three siblings and Joey, her dog.

"How was school Nui, and the temple?" Khun Yaa asked as we filled our plates.

"All good, thank you, Khun Yaa. Ajaarn Anurak gave us a few more things to think about." And remembering Nui's comment, "How are you feeling, Khun Yaa? Everything alright with you?"

"I'm fine Nui. I have my next check-up in a few weeks, but I'm feeling good. Nothing to worry about," she said.

Dinner was a noisy affair, as usual, with everyone talking over each other. At one point, I sat back to take it all in. I felt sad that I would have to give up this easy family camaraderie soon. But for now, I let it distract me from my other worries.

"Mae, when are Krit and Tum coming home?" Krit was Nui's older brother and Channon's friend, soon finishing up his military service. Tum was Luke's age and temporarily living as a novice monk in the local temple, a common tradition for Thai boys and men. I attended his ordination on my first day as Nui.

Mae raised an eyebrow. "You know, Tum will be home by

the end of the month. And Krit should be back by then as well. Why are you asking?"

"Just curious." It would get more crowded in the house when both brothers were back.

"It's nice not having to share the bathroom with the boys, right?" Duen, Nui's younger sister, grinned at me. "Mae, we definitely need another bathroom. It's impossible for us to share with the boys in future," she pleaded.

"And where do you think we could add another bathroom for you princesses?" Mae teased her. "We can't just build one into the backyard, and besides, Krit will leave for university in Chiang Mai soon. Then next year it will be Nui's turn. I think you can handle this for a little while longer, don't you?"

Duen shrugged. "If we have to. Where are you going to university, Nui? Still want to go to America?"

"I don't know. I guess it depends on what I want to study."

"It depends on what we can afford Nui," Paa interjected. "Universities in America are too expensive. You should look at universities here like Krit. And if you're going to become a lawyer, it makes more sense anyway to study here." He made it sound like it was a done deal, but I knew Nui had other ideas.

"Erm, I haven't looked into that yet, but they just assigned us college advisors, so I'm sure we'll talk about it in school soon." I tried to avoid the issue as I didn't know how much Nui had told her parents about the fact she had no intention of studying law or enrolling in a Thai uni. Knowing her, I was pretty sure she'd find a way to get her wish.

7

NUI

IT WAS UNUSUAL FOR LUNA'S DAD TO BE HOME FOR DINNER. As the General Manager of a five-star hotel he had to do a lot of business entertaining, but with Luna's mom, Khun Susan, in Chicago, he had made a special effort over the last few days.

"Hi honey, how was your day?" he asked as we sat down at the dining table. Khun Bo had prepared a green chicken curry with rice and a simple salad. I glanced around, but she must have forgotten to make a meat-free version for me. Bored with Luna's vegetarian diet, I was hoping to sneak in a few bites of chicken. In the past week, I had already indulged in a few pieces of meat here and there, even if she didn't like it. Luckily, so far, her body hadn't rebelled against the unfamiliar food.

"It was fine, thank you. They asked us to work with college advisors to decide what we want to study and where to apply."

"That seems early, no?" Khun Mark looked surprised.

"Yeah, but they have to do this for the entire grade, and we have to apply by the end of the year or early next year. I guess they thought it best to get the ball rolling. Plus, a lot of families are planning to look at colleges during summer break." I took a bite. Delicious, although, of course, not as good as Khun Yaa's.

"Yes, that makes sense," he agreed. "What are you thinking? Still interested in hospitality?" We had talked about that on New Year's Eve, which had planted the idea in my head. While journalism was my first choice, the hotel industry would also give me an opportunity to travel for work. Luna hadn't decided yet, as far as I knew, so I was free to experiment with all the options open to her.

"Yeah, that's one possibility, but I'm also thinking of communication or journalism. You know, Mom Luang and I spoke about it when we were at the barbeque last week, and he made a good point. I could combine both if I were to become a travel writer or editor. What do you think?"

"Hmm, I hadn't thought about it like that, but yes, I can see it. Although, it's not so easy anymore to make a living in travel writing. I know it looks like a dream job, but there are so many freelance writers now, and a lot of print publications, especially in the travel sector, have reduced staff or closed altogether because most media is digital now. Plus, many people write their own travel stories on social media nowadays," he cautioned.

"She just wants to stay for free and not have to make beds or work in the kitchen," Luke laughed. We also had *that* discussion before, so I ignored him.

"I know, Dad, but I'm more interested in focus stories about the countries, not just hotel reviews. You know, maybe something about how travel affects the local infrastructure, ecosystem and people, and maybe even politics. Thailand is a prime example of how tourism influences all aspects of life, don't you think? I wondered if it's ok to speak with Mom Luang about this sometime. He would know better than anyone the history and changes that have happened here over the years."

"Luna, I told you before that Mom Luang can't talk about anything sensitive with you, and has to stay away from political or controversial topics." Khun Mark shook his head. "And why this sudden interest? You never cared for politics or social issues before."

"I've been talking to Nui about it, and now I'm curious. It's not supposed to be anything controversial. I just want to get his input as a senior government person and hi-so. I wouldn't even mention his name. But I'm sure he has an opinion on this. After all, tourism in Thailand is huge, and he represents the hotel owners."

"I don't think so, Luna. You know he's my boss, and I don't feel comfortable asking him."

"But it wouldn't hurt to ask. All he can say is no, right? Maybe I can send him a card thanking him for the barbeque last week and see if he has half an hour to talk to me. I don't think he would mind, do you?"

"A thank you card would be nice, but I don't want you to bother him about politics."

"But Dad…"

"No Luna. Do your own research, and don't bother Mom Luang." Khun Mark said, putting an end to my argument.

"Fine." I felt grumpy and a bit guilty too, for considering to interview Mom Luang under a pretext. He had been exceptionally kind to me. His insights as an ex-Palace official would have been more than I hoped to get from talking to others, and it could have been the basis for a scoop that even foreign media might pick up. Now I needed to find another way to approach this subject.

"Write the card, and I'll have my secretary forward it to him, or hold it for his next visit. He'll be at the hotel staff party on Saturday. Speaking of, I want you and Luke there, ok? Even if it's just for half an hour."

"Sure Dad. Anything we need to do? Is it formal?" Luna had forewarned me she and Luke needed to attend hotel functions occasionally.

"No, not really, there will be a short reception followed by dinner, then most of the departments are doing some kind of performance they have been practising for. From what I've heard, it can become quite wild." He smiled. "You can just come for the reception part, then leave or have dinner in the hotel, ok? It starts at six."

"No problem Dad."

Yes! So there was still a slim chance I would be able to talk to Mom Luang then, as long as I could get around Luna's dad. I excused myself right after dinner, itching to get started on the blog.

8

LUNA

Walking Nui's dog had become routine for me. I didn't mind, as I quite enjoyed having some time away from the family. Joey was used to me by now, although I was pretty sure he knew I wasn't his Nui, even if I smelled like her. At least he couldn't tell anyone. We walked further than our regular stop at the little park in soi ten. If I was going to be here for a while longer, I wanted to get to know the neighbourhood better.

I was still pondering what to tell Channon when a sharp bark followed by yelping and more barking snapped me back to reality. Joey's hackles rose, and he stood still, sniffing the air.

"What's going on there Joey? Can you see anything? Let's turn around. This doesn't sound good." The streetlights were fairly far apart, leaving pockets of grey zones. I didn't see any people on the street. Lost in thought, I must have walked further than planned and was now in a residential area with no shops or bars. At seven o'clock, people were probably having dinner.

I turned around, but Joey refused to come with me. He took a few tentative steps forward. The barking had become more sporadic but still continued, and it sounded pretty aggressive to me.

"Come on Joey, we can't go that way. I don't know what's happening up there, and I don't want you to get into a fight."

He glanced at me, but turned back, taking a few more steps towards the commotion. It surprised me that people had not come outside to see what the ruckus was about.

Suddenly, Joey started barking himself and running towards the noise. "Joey, come back here! Shit, shit, shit!" There was nothing I could do but follow him. Nui would never forgive me if he got into some kind of trouble.

Just beyond the next streetlight I could see three medium-sized soi dogs circling a smaller dog, who was lying on the ground, tail tucked and whining. The bigger dogs kept snapping at him and the poor little fellow didn't know which way to turn to avoid the bites. Joey, bless him or curse him, ran forward and started barking at the three dogs. I wasn't sure why he felt protective of the little one—he was either fearless or dumb. I had no choice but to go after him to make sure he didn't get hurt. The soi dogs saw me coming, but didn't seem too concerned about a human. I finally saw that the little one was a scrawny pup, probably a soi dog too, but definitely not fully grown.

"Hey! Leave him alone!" I shouted and waved my arms. I realized I had lapsed into English. "Poh laew. Ploi khao dai laew!" I repeated in Thai for good measure, though why I thought the dogs would understand Thai better than English was beyond me. Chone had also been a lonely puppy when a restaurant owner found him living behind a trashcan in a parking lot. I was furious just thinking about that, or maybe it was the pent-up frustration of the past few days. In the back of my head, I knew I was being stupid as I didn't know how dangerous these dogs were, but if Joey could take a stand, so could I.

The bigger dogs just glanced at me but didn't back off. Nui's small figure probably didn't pose much of a threat to them. One dog advanced on Joey instead. I couldn't let him get hurt, so I ran to get in between them. The soi dog growled and bared his teeth, but at this point I was beyond caring. I wasn't proud of it, but I aimed a kick at him since he seemed ready to jump and bite. Thank God I was wearing trainers instead of flip-flops, otherwise I wouldn't have had any leverage. I caught him in the middle and he yelped, but seemed more surprised than hurt. As he retreated a few steps, I advanced further to get to the puppy, Joey right on my heels. The other two dogs had ignored what was happening and were still snapping alternately. I was now facing three dogs. *Luna, you're completely mad.* My inner voice cautioned me. *You can't take on three dogs.* For a moment, I completely disassociated from the situation and let adrenaline take over. Still advancing, I aimed another kick at one of the other dogs. He snapped at me, but I was out of reach. I was still shouting, with Joey barking his head off when I sensed, more than heard, someone behind me.

"What's going on here? What is all this noise?" A middle-aged man appeared in my peripheral vision, but he didn't seem inclined to take any action.

The dogs, however, must have sensed that two humans were not worth the trouble and retreated a bit. I bent down to pick up the puppy when one of the older dogs darted forward again and nipped at my left hand. It didn't even fully register, as I was so focused on getting the pup out of harm's way. The three dogs finally gave up the attack, then turned and wandered off.

The little dog was shivering and whining. I finally got my hands under him and picked him up, cooing and petting him, while Joey watched over us.

The man came closer. "Are you crazy to get into a dogfight like that?" He shook his head. "Don't you know that those damn dogs are probably rabid?"

"What was I supposed to do?" I snapped back. "Let them kill the little one?"

"Would have been one less nuisance," the man grumbled, and turned around to leave. "Someone has to do something about those stupid dogs. It's outrageous how they take over the streets. It's not safe to walk out here anymore."

"Thanks for nothing!" I shouted at his back, and for good measure, mentally added, "Idiot!" Walking back to the street-light, I could see the little one had bite marks all over his body. "You poor thing. You need to go to the hospital, but don't worry, I know just the place! Come on Joey. Thanks for being so brave."

I cuddled the puppy close as we retraced our walk. He finally stopped shivering and started licking my arm. Joey stayed close instead of forging ahead like he normally did. We passed our little park and continued on to the animal hospital on soi nine. Channon would have left by now with Chone as it was past his shift time, but the vets would handle it.

9

NUI

I WAS TYPING FURIOUSLY. POTENTIAL BLOG NAMES:

- ~~TheBigMango~~—*nah, overdone! Everyone calls Bangkok The Big Mango*
- ~~MindTales~~—*nope, too close to mind swap*
- GlobeNotes—*maybe. Would tie in with Luna's expat life*
- AllAbout—*too vague?*
- ~~Thaizilla~~—*silly!*
- PinkElephant or white or..? —*hmm not bad. Check availability*

Darn, I realised this was going to be much harder than I thought. I needed a name that hinted at the type of stories I wanted to publish—heavyweight, like an elephant, which was also our national symbol. Pink would show that a female wrote it but not give anything else away. So far, so good! *Now check that it's available.* Yes! It was for Thailand. There were a few 'pinkelelephants' in other countries but nothing under the .th domain. *Ok, keep that in mind, but don't do anything else until you've made a plan.* There was so much information online about blogging and building websites that my head was spinning. How do I know which is the best option? And how much does it cost to maintain a site?

I lost track of time again and jumped when Luna's dad poked his head into my room. I hadn't even heard him knock.

"Are you almost finished with your work Luna? Don't go to bed too late. I have to leave early for work tomorrow morning and you have to make sure Luke is ready, ok?"

"Sure Dad. I'm almost done here, anyway." My eyes felt gritty from staring at the screen for too long. Time to give it a rest. I quickly hit the screensaver as Khun Mark came to my desk to say goodnight. He kissed the top of my head.

"Night honey. Sleep well, I'll see you tomorrow evening. I'll try to be home in time for dinner."

"Ok, great. Night Dad."

At the door, he turned around again. "By the way, I was thinking. If Mom is only coming back on Saturday morning, she might be too tired to attend the staff party. She can decide when she gets here, but you and Luke should definitely show up for a short time, ok?"

"Sure Dad."

Originally, I had thought of asking Luna to come over that afternoon. She said she was keen to see her mom as soon as she was back. But her dad was right, she might be too tired for visitors, and if we had to go to the hotel at six anyway, it wouldn't make sense. *Are you sure you don't just want to keep Luna away for now, Nui?* Damn, I hated it when my conscience mocked me.

10

LUNA

ALTHOUGH STILL SMALL, THE PUPPY WAS GETTING HEAVY BY the time we reached the pet hospital. It would have been much easier if I had been in my own body, since I was a lot stronger and more athletic than Nui. He had settled in my arms, eyes half closed as if he was taking a nap. Joey balked at the entrance, but I didn't dare leave him on the sidewalk in front.

"This is not about you, Joey. Come on, don't be scared. You're not getting any shots. This is about our friend here. You were so brave back there, so you can be brave a bit longer, ok?" He probably thought I was talking gibberish, but he followed me anyway.

We walked through the emergency entrance and I was glad to see one of my favourite colleagues behind the counter.

"Nong Nui, what are you doing here? And who do you have there?" Khun Ning asked, rushing forward. "Oh, you poor little fellow. What happened to you? You look like you got into a fight," she cooed.

"He was attacked by some soi dogs and Joey and I got there just in time. I think they would have killed him," I explained.

Khun Ning pointed at my hand. "Those street dogs can be a real menace. Looks like they got you, too, huh? You need to have this checked."

My left hand was seeping blood. Too concerned with the puppy, I had completely forgotten about the bite and the guy's comment about rabies. A flash of fear shot through me. I felt dizzy and wobbled on my feet.

"I think I need to sit down for a moment. Can you take him? And do you have any bandages or tissues I could use?"

"Let me get Channon to help you."

"Channon? He's still here?" I definitely needed to sit down now.

"He's working a double shift today. Let me get him."

Khun Ning took the pup from my arms and pressed a button on the console. Then she handed me a couple of sterile bandages.

I made it to a chair in the waiting area, covered the bite marks, and put my head down on my knees. *Just breathe Luna. Everything is going to be alright.* Joey pressed his body against me and whined softly. "I'm alright Joey, I just need a minute."

"Nui, what happened? Are you ok?" Channon was kneeling down in front of me and took my hands in his. *He really has the most gorgeous eyes. Stop, Luna, this is not why you're here.*

"Hi Channon, you're still here," I giggled. I was really close to losing it. Whether from the dogfight, potential rabies, or the unexpected sight of Channon, I couldn't tell. Probably a combination of all three.

"And a good thing too, I'd say. What happened?"

"Some soi dogs attacked this little puppy. Joey and I stopped them. I think Khun Ning is taking care of him. Can you check on him?"

"Never mind the puppy. You know, he's in excellent hands. What about you?"

"I'm just tired. I better get home. Grandma will be worried about me." I looked down at my hand and saw spots of blood soaked through the cotton. *Eww.*

I tried to stand up, but couldn't really muster the energy. The adrenaline must have completely drained out of my system, and I felt weak as a kitten.

"Hm, any chance you can help me get home? I'm a bit off right now. And sorry about last night." I didn't know why I had to throw that in, but my mind was all messed up.

"Don't worry about it." Channon brushed aside my apology and stood up. "We need to have a doctor look at that bite, and you probably need some rabies shots. Stay here. I'm going to get the car out front. We'll drive by your house to get your mom and go to the hospital."

"But…" I tried to interject.

"No but. You need to see a doctor for this. At the very least, it needs to be cleaned up properly. Wait right here."

I was too tired to argue, so I just closed my eyes and rested my head against the wall. Joey put his head on my knee, offering his support.

I must have fallen asleep immediately. The next thing I knew, my head was against Channon's chest as he carried me out the front door. *Mmm, this feels so good. I'm going to stay here.* I snuggled closer in his arms and kept my eyes closed. *He smells delicious.* My insides became all tingly. Channon was my hero! Not only had he rescued me on New Year's Eve from a guy who spiked my drinks, but he also adopted Chone on my behalf to make sure he didn't go to someone else. And now he had come to my rescue yet again.

Unfortunately, it was only a few steps to the front entrance. Channon settled me into the passenger seat but I kept my eyes closed, pretending I was still in his arms. A wet tongue in my ear woke me up, rudely. I turned around to see Chone, my own husky, standing on the middle console, his face inches from mine.

"Hi Chone. So happy to see you. I missed you today." I was babbling, but I felt so much better having my favourite boys with me. The rest I would figure out.

I must have dozed off again on the way home. Channon parked in front of the house, then took Joey up the front step. I'd just mustered the energy to get out when Khun Yaa answered the door.

"Hello Channon, what brings you here? Nui is not back yet. Do you want to wait? But, why is Joey with you?" I saw her frowning.

"Actually, Auntie, I have Nui in the car. She got into an accident while walking with Joey and I think she needs to go to the hospital to get checked. I wanted to get her mom to come with us. Is she here?" Channon asked.

"Heavens help, is she ok?" I saw Khun Yaa clutching her chest, which instantly blew away my drowsiness. *Please don't have a heart attack!* Nui's comment about her grandma's heart condition was still fresh in my mind.

I kept holding on to the door just in case I became dizzy again, but called out to her. "I'm fine Khun Yaa. It's just a scratch that needs to be looked at. Is Mae home?"

"She went with your dad to a community meeting. Let me get my bag. I'm coming with you. I'll call your mom on the way. Channon, can you take us to Samitivej?"

"Yes, of course, I want to make sure Nui is ok. She was a

hero today." He turned and winked at me. I smiled back at him, goofily.

"Hero might be a bit much. More like really stupid," I corrected him.

"You rescued that dog, didn't you? So that makes you a hero in our eyes, right Chone?"

Chone's nose nudged my hand. I was definitely feeling better now.

Khun Yaa returned to the door, and I saw Khun Bpoo and Duen behind her. I waved, wanting to reassure them I was alright, in case they talked to Mae before I could. I moved to the backseat so Khun Yaa wouldn't have to sit with Chone. He licked my face until I buried my head in his fur.

The hospital was only a short drive away. My family used Bumrungrad hospital but a lot of Thais and the so called hi-so, high-society, preferred Samitivej. From what I heard, they were equally good.

We drove up to the emergency entrance, and Khun Yaa escorted me in while Channon went to park the car. Khun Yaa made straight for the front desk and explained what had happened. Within five minutes, I was sitting on a bed in one of the treatment bays with a nurse taking my blood pressure, pulse, temperature, and oxygen levels. All seemed to be within the norms. I avoided looking at the bite wound though, as I had always been squeamish about blood, and even though it wasn't my body bleeding, I still didn't want to risk fainting. A young doctor showed up a few minutes later. She asked a few questions and looked at my hand. The wound wasn't too deep, but there were three puncture marks that had to be cleaned and covered. Since it came from a street dog, she highly recommended a course of four rabies shots. A simple band-aid was enough to cover the marks, but I wasn't looking forward to the shots. I would get one that evening, then I'd have to go back again after two days, one week, and two weeks to complete the course. The doctor said the shots were not as painful as they used to be, and I would be fine, but she recommended I stay home from school the next day just in case I had any adverse reaction. The whole thing took less than half an hour, and by the time we were leaving, I saw Mae and Paa come in through the front door and Channon waiting in the lobby.

Mae looked me over critically and shook her head, but I could tell she was relieved I was none the worse for wear. I wished my own mom was there. She would have fussed over me, which was always nice. At least I had Khun Yaa, who had held my hand while the doctor injected the first dose into my upper left arm.

Paa patted my shoulder awkwardly.

"What were you thinking Nui? You know better than to get in the middle of a dogfight."

"It was that or risk Joey getting hurt," I said, in my defence, although I had to admit in hindsight, it was pretty reckless. Perhaps it was better that I didn't have the time to think.

Paa went to settle the bill and Mae thanked Channon for driving us and being there when I needed help. We all left together to walk to the garage. I felt awkward with the family there, but I hugged Channon anyway.

"Thanks so much for everything. I don't know what I would have done without you."

Mae coughed dramatically. She probably disapproved of me hugging Channon, but I didn't care. He had been my saviour yet again.

"Just promise me you won't get in the middle of any more dogfights, ok? You scared me." Channon tried to look disapproving, but his concern made my knees go wobbly.

"I'll check on the puppy and maybe you can come to see him tomorrow if you're not going to school. Just take it easy tonight and we'll talk tomorrow, ok?"

"Night Channon. Night Chone, I'll see you tomorrow." Chone stuck his nose out the window. He seemed confused when I didn't get in the car.

Paa shook Channon's hand and thanked him again for his help. I was pretty sure I hadn't heard the last from the parents about my adventure, but I hoped for tonight they would let it slide, relieved that nothing more serious had happened. At home, I took a quick shower with my hand wrapped in a plastic bag, and then called it a night. I needed to let Nui know I would miss school tomorrow, but I fell asleep trying to think how to downplay a fresh scar on her hand.

11

NUI

LIKE EVERY MORNING, I HAD TO HUSTLE LUKE OUT THE DOOR at the last minute to catch the school van. One of these days I would reset all the clocks, including his cell phone, an hour fast so he would have to get up earlier. I didn't see Luna anywhere when I got to class. My phone vibrated just as I sat down.

'Won't make it to school today. Minor accident last night. All ok, will explain. Come over after school?'

Accident? What has she done now? I'll kill her if I'm going to have scars or broken bones.

Just then, our teacher walked in, giving me only enough time to type a quick 'Ok'. I barely paid attention in class while I went over our new semester schedule and the adjustments we would have to make if we didn't switch back soon.

Mostly, Luna and I had the same basic and elective classes. It must have been part of the reason the school had put us together as buddies initially. We both hated math and were equal in 'Social bases of behaviour', so those would be easy. The biggest difference was Luna had registered for an IB Diploma, while I was only taking the course programme without the certification. I was still hoping my parents would agree to the diploma fees if I performed well.

Other subjects could become trip wires, especially our language classes, as they required substantial background reading, which neither of us had done. I don't know how we were going to find the time, as we still had to perform community services too. Maybe Luna's volunteering at the shelter would count towards my grade? I grinned. *That would be too ironic after I've given her such a hard time about it.* My grin dissolved when I realized that I would have to volunteer for something in her place. At least we'd be able to pick our own TOK—Theory of Knowledge—subjects. It all boiled down to the fact that we both had to put in some serious study time to keep up until we switched back.

All this meant nothing though compared to the sheer terror of having to take part in Luna's 'Lifeguard certification course'. I knew she was a strong swimmer, and it made perfect sense for her, but the thought of voluntarily jumping into the water to rescue a drowning person scared me to death, especially after my narrow escape during our rafting trip in Bali.

Luckily, there were no tests today, but this was likely to change in the next day or two. We might be able to flunk one, but more than that would destroy our grades and jeopardize college admissions. Not only would we run into problems at school, but the consequences at home would be even worse. My parents had threatened more than once they would withdraw me from BIS if my grades dropped. I was too ambitious to admit defeat so easily and would have to make it work somehow.

12

LUNA

Despite all the excitement of the night before, I woke up at my usual time. When had six o'clock become the new normal for me? At home, I would have hit the snooze button at least four times.

Though I could have slept in, it seemed Duen was banging about more than strictly necessary—her revenge for me having a day off. I gave her an evil look, but as I had to take Joey out for a walk anyway, I got up. Khun Yaa was making breakfast in the kitchen.

"Morning Nui, how is your hand? Did you sleep well?"

"Morning Khun Yaa, actually not bad. The hand doesn't really hurt that much. I wonder if I shouldn't go to school, anyway?"

"You heard the doctor. It's best to give it a day, so don't push yourself. I'm sure it'll be fine to miss one day. Do you want breakfast now?"

"I'm just going to take Joey for a quick walk, is that ok?"

She waved a spatula at me. "Stay away from soi dogs and

be back here in twenty minutes. Tum is coming for his alms round this morning."

Tum, Nui's younger brother, had ordained as a novice monk a couple of weeks earlier, and all monks depended on the generosity of the population for goods and services. Each morning, they walked the neighbourhoods with alms bowls, receiving food and money donations from the locals. I still hadn't figured out if they had assigned routes or if they picked them randomly. There must have been some kind of system behind it, as people had to prepare the food early enough. Dad's hotel offered breakfast to the monks on special days like anniversaries in exchange for their blessings.

Joey and I walked our usual route to the little park, just two streets down Thong Lo Road. I didn't see any dogs at all along our path.

Pi' Ohm was already busy with customers at her street food stall when we arrived. Channon and I had met at Pi' Ohm's the morning after the mind swap. While Joey wandered off to the park to do his business, I walked to the food stall to say hello.

"What do you want for breakfast this morning?" Pi' Ohm asked.

"I can't stay Pi' Ohm. Sorry. Khun Yaa wants me back in half an hour."

"She needs to rest today, Pi' Ohm. She was a hero last night rescuing a little dog. See? She got injured too." Why was I even surprised that Channon had snuck up on me? He had a knack for surprising me this way. I grinned up at him.

"What happened, Nong Nui?" Despite being gruff with me most of the time, Pi' Ohm actually sounded concerned.

"I was kinda stupid and got in the middle of a dogfight, then I got bitten and had to go to the hospital to get a shot." I tried to downplay the incident.

"See, I always said those soi dogs are bad." Pi' Ohm shook her head and mumbled something I couldn't hear.

"Yes, but they were attacking a puppy. I couldn't just leave him there."

"Aiyah, those dogs are the bane of my life. I wish someone would do something about them," she grumbled, but for a second I thought she was nodding approval at me. I probably imagined it. More likely, she didn't want to say anything negative about me while Channon was listening. She adored him, and he knew how to charm her.

I had been getting grief about our close friendship not only from Nui but also her parents, and recently Channon's mom had also added her misgivings. I'm not sure what everyone suspected we were doing, but apparently, they thought I was too young to date a guy and should concentrate on my studies instead. My parents wouldn't have had an issue with me dating at my age, especially a nice guy like Channon, who was the most considerate—not to mention handsome— guy ever. But given that I wasn't even in my body, it was way more complicated than everyone assumed, except Nui, of course.

"Are you coming to the hospital, Nui?" Channon asked, after he placed his order with Pi' Ohm. "You can check on your little guy there and see how he's doing."

"I'll definitely try. I'm not allowed to go to school today, so I have time. Gotta go now, Khun Yaa is waiting for me and then Tum is coming around. See you later."

I collected Joey and headed back.

I had breakfast with the family. The parents briefly asked how I was feeling, but then mostly talked about plans for their kitchenware shop. I didn't really pay attention. After Duen left for school, we got ready for the monks' visit. I enjoyed seeing twenty plus monks in their bright orange robes coming down the sidewalk in a long line. Together with the neighbours, we had set up tables in front of the house, and every family member put one piece of food in each bowl with a wai as a show of respect. I winked at Tum, though I wasn't supposed to make eye contact with any monk out of respect. He barely suppressed a grin. Guess he still had to work on his own proper composure.

Afterwards, we cleaned up and then Mae and Paa left for their shop on soi eight. Suddenly, the house was quiet. Khun Yaa and Khun Bpoo were going to the temple and then the market for a short while. I picked up my phone and saw Nui's reply to my earlier text.

With the whole day ahead of me and not much to do, I decided it would be a good time to meditate. I always felt calm afterwards. We had recorded all the sessions with Ajaarn at the temple, so it was easy to fall into the rhythm. I felt pretty relaxed, although I didn't achieve what we called an OBE—an out-of-body experience. *Don't worry, Luna. You've done it before, and you can do it again. Meanwhile, think about what to tell Channon.*

I had promised Nui not to tell Channon about our mind swap, yet how could I keep pretending to be Nui when I, Luna, was attracted to him? I had also promised Channon to explain my weird behaviour during our date. But what could I say that would make him believe me in the first place, or worse, what if he wasn't interested in foreigners? I'd lose a friend and would look like a nutcase. But it also wasn't fair to string him along, especially as Nui and I were planning to reverse the swap soon. Would he still want to see me afterwards as Luna? Or would that be the end of it? So many questions and not a single answer.

I needed a distraction. Going to the hospital to check on the puppy and say hello to Chone would give me a good excuse. And maybe I could invite Channon for lunch to thank him for his help. Khun Yaa walked in just as I was leaving. She offered to cook lunch for Channon, but I needed to see him on my own this time. I told her I'd come right back afterwards.

13

NUI

DURING LUNCH BREAK, I SETTLED INTO A CORNER OF THE cafeteria with a sandwich, planning to draft the note to Mom Luang to give to Luna's dad. I also wanted to continue my research for the blog.

I jerked upright when I heard a loud, high-pitched screech. Conversations stopped as everyone craned their necks to see who had caused the commotion.

"LUNA?! OH! MY! GOD! Is that really you?" A tiny Japanese-looking girl came barrelling down the aisle and threw herself at me, nearly falling into my lap.

"I can't believe you're here!" She burst with excitement, almost bouncing off her feet. "This is soooo cool! I'm so glad you're here. I had no idea you were at BIS. We just got here. I'm so happy to see you." Every sentence seemed to be a major statement in complete contrast to her small stature. I almost grinned, although the attention was slightly embarrassing. Around me I saw students shaking their heads, some smiling, some glaring. There was no particular dress code for the senior classes at BIS, but her outfit definitely stood out. It was as if she had voluntarily adopted some sort of high school uniform, only with a much shorter skirt, a white shirt with a loose purple tie and slouchy socks over… combat boots? In this heat? Despite her size, she sure looked like she would kick butt if someone got in her way, or maybe just steamroll over them with her non-stop chatter. Her black hair had streaks of vivid pink tied in two braids hanging past her shoulders with a purple ribbon running through each. It amazed me she had gotten away with that look at school. It probably wouldn't take long before the younger ones would try to copy her.

She finally paused, realizing I hadn't responded. I was absolutely clueless who she was and just stared at her, probably with a big question mark on my face.

She frowned. "Don't tell me you've forgotten me? I don't believe it. That is so mean. Remember? Shanghai? YKPS?"

Shit!

"Err…" I stalled.

Luckily, she just carried on. "Remember? Yumi. And Leslie and Sara."

Help! There are more of you? I quickly peeked over her head to check, but didn't see anyone else new.

I slapped my hand to my forehead, pretending a delayed recall.

"Duh, of course! I'm so sorry Yumi. I just didn't expect to see you here. It was so out of context that I spaced out." Unwittingly, I mimicked her exaggerated speech pattern.

She grinned. "I know, right? Isn't this cool? Dad just got transferred to the embassy here. I wasn't sure I wanted to come, but now I'm glad I did. I thought you had gone to Hong Kong when you left. We have so much catching up to do. When can we meet? And what classes are you in now?

Maybe we're in the same? You can show me around. Did you hear from John and have you been in touch with Ellie?"

I didn't see her take one breath during the barrage of questions, and her hands were in constant motion, punctuating everything she said. Luna always told me I was fidgety, but Yumi's energy put me to shame. She was exhausting me, and I didn't know what to say. The end-of-break bell rang, interrupting her. I had never been more glad to go back to class.

"I have to go, Yumi. I'll see you around, ok?"

"Here, take my number. It's +66 82 720 2259. Send me yours and we'll talk. So great to see you, Luna. Can't wait to catch up." She hugged me again, then turned around and marched off, probably to overwhelm her poor teacher.

I had just enough time to jot down the number before the bell rang again. Great. Another complication we didn't need. I rolled my shoulders to relieve some of the tension. It sounded like Yumi and Luna had been close in Shanghai. I definitely needed to see Luna to get the details before school tomorrow. Would Yumi expect to join our duo now?

14

LUNA

THE PET HOSPITAL WAS ON SOI NINE, A TEN-MINUTE WALK from the house. The building was brand new, and included an adoption centre for pets, a recreation area, and a pool for the dogs. My volunteer pass meant I could walk straight through to the adoption area, but I wanted to stop at the emergency intake first to check on my rescue from last night.

The attendee recognized me and must have heard about the incident.

"Nong Nui, are you here to check on your puppy? We got him in the recovery area. He had some bites that needed to be treated and he hasn't had any shots at all, so he's now getting the first round."

"Yes, I'd love to. Can I go back there? And then I want to see Chone."

"Ah yes, Mak-ku-tet, the guide!" Khun Nan smiled.

"The guide?" I asked. Yes, Chone was special to me, but I didn't think anyone else felt the same way about him.

"Hahaha, yes, that's what we call him now. He seems to

welcome all the newcomers and makes sure they don't get picked on by the other dogs. It's interesting to watch. He must have a very protective gene."

I beamed with pride. "That's Chone! I knew there was something special about him."

The recovery section was right behind the emergency area, and one of the other volunteers showed me where the puppy was resting. He couldn't have been older than six or seven months, by my estimate. His fur was the colour of wheat, with some white patches along the front, and it was much longer than the normal short-haired soi dogs. He was definitely a mix and looked to have a bit of retriever in him. When I stood in front of the cage, he lifted his head briefly and wagged his tail, but didn't get up. He seemed pretty groggy.

"You ready to adopt another dog?" Channon said behind me.

I turned around and laughed. "One day, you'll have to explain how you always manage to sneak up on me. How did you know I was here?" I playfully swatted his arm.

"The grapevine here works as well as everywhere else," Channon grinned. "So, what do you think of your latest rescue? He's cute, no?"

"Very cute. Is he going to go into the adoption programme?"

"He definitely doesn't belong to anyone, no tag or chip, so let's see how he recovers and how sociable he is. I'm pretty sure he'll be up for adoption soon. You acted just in time before the dogs could do any real damage to him."

"So glad that worked out then. Worth the hassle."

"Speaking of, how's your hand?"

"It's fine. The wounds aren't deep, and I don't feel

anything from the shot. Good as new. Can I invite you to lunch to thank you for your help last night?"

"Glad to hear that. You don't have to invite me for lunch, but yes, I'll join you. Want to see Chone now?"

"You mean Mak-ku-tet?"

"Huh?"

"Just heard that's what they call him now, as he's apparently become the guardian of all newcomers," I grinned.

"Ok then, let's see our guide dog," Channon laughed. "I have five minutes before I need to get back."

We walked through to the running area where about twenty dogs were having a blast chasing each other over the grass and around the trees. *This is what dog heaven must look like.*

Chone was in the middle of the pack, but he immediately broke away to come and say hello.

"Hello Chone, I hear you're helping all the newbies here. You're such a good boy." I bent to pet him and scratch under his chin, which I knew he liked. "Does that mean you want a job here?"

"Hey, that's not a bad idea," Channon jumped at the suggestion. "It would definitely help to have a sort of go-between here for the new arrivals. Let's see if that's really what he does and I can talk to the head of the department about it."

"That would be fantastic, and I would get to see him more often when I work here."

"You're not working today, are you?"

"No, I was supposed to be in school, so I'm not scheduled, and it's probably not a good idea with my scratches. I want to make sure there's no infection first."

"Ok, I have to get back. Why don't you meet me at the café at noon and you can bring Chone?"

"Sounds good. I'll hang around here for a bit. Missed him yesterday."

"Ok, see you later," Channon said, then walked away.

I sat on a bench under a tree to watch the dogs play. My stomach was churning, thinking about the upcoming conversation and the potential consequences.

15

NUI

At three, I made sure Luke was on the van home, then hopped on the Skytrain to find out about Luna's accident and Yumi. It had been more than a week since I'd seen my family and Joey. I missed them all and was glad to finally have a good reason to visit home. It was weird to live in the same city, but not with them. *Is this what homesickness feels like?* I knew it was too early for Mae and Paa to be home, but I would at least get to see Khun Yaa, Khun Bpoo and Duen.

Holding on to the grab rail, I absently glanced at the overhead monitors with their ridiculous ads for skin whitening creams and energy drinks. Mentally, I was preparing another to-do list. I needed to update Luna on school assignments and check she had 'The Pearl' by Steinbeck for English class. She would have to ask one of the other girls about her Thai lesson since I couldn't be in two places at the same time. Then, I needed to find out about Yumi, and of course, the accident. But mostly, I was eager to start on my blog. Soon, I'd have to record my list to keep track.

A sharp elbow in my side brought me back to the present. Ouch! I looked down, angrily, primed to give the person a sharp rebuke. Yumi was grinning up at me. *Yikes! Where did she come from?*

"Surprise! I saw you get on the train. Where are you going? Are you on your way home? What station are you getting off at? I have to go to Chidlom to meet Dad. When are we catching up? You haven't texted me yet!"

She finally took a breath, and I quickly jumped in. "Actually, if you're going to Chidlom, then you're on the wrong train. You need to go the other direction." I was hoping she'd take the cue, but she merely shrugged.

"No problem, I still have some time before I meet him. So, I'll come with you and we can catch up. Tell me, how long have you been here? Have you spoken to John at all? He asked me about you a few times, but I didn't know what to tell him. You never really stayed in touch. Why not? Did you have a fight with him? Sara and Ellie are still in Shanghai, but Leslie went back to the States. How's your mom and Luke? Is your dad still in hotels? Which one?"

Why does she ask all these questions but never waits for an answer? At least it saved me from making up some kind of story.

Sure enough, she just rattled on, "Did I tell you my parents finally got divorced? My mom wanted me to come back with her and Kiko to Tokyo, but I thought Bangkok would be more fun, and Dad was ok with it. Then next year he'll probably have to go back to Washington anyway, and I can go with him."

"That's interesting. What does your dad do?" I squeezed one question in.

"Huh? You know he's at the embassy. He just got promoted and is now some attaché or something."

"Which embassy, the Japanese?" I was slightly confused.

Yumi frowned at me. "No, of course not. Why would he be there? You've met him."

Hmm, that didn't really explain why he wouldn't work at the Japanese Embassy, but I let it be. Luna could fill in the gaps. I glanced out the window. One more stop to go.

Yumi had gone quiet, which somehow was more disturbing than when she chatted non-stop. She was still looking at me, but with uncertainty and maybe even hurt.

"You really have forgotten me, haven't you?" Her voice had lost its sparkle. *Damn!* It wasn't her fault that I knew nothing about her. I felt guilty for no good reason.

"I'm so sorry Yumi, I really haven't thought about Shanghai in a while. It's been over three years, you know, and then there was Hong Kong and now Bangkok. It's really tough sometimes to keep everything straight." *Especially if you don't have the slightest clue,* I added mentally.

That seemed to perk her up. "Right, so we definitely have to meet soon." We pulled into Thong Lo station.

"Yes, we will for sure. And I'll definitely see you at school tomorrow, right?" I felt better being able to offer her the reassurance. "I have to get off here and you need to take the train on the other side of the track, ok?"

We walked down the stairs together and I pointed her to the right platform, waving goodbye before I left the station to get some much needed answers from Luna.

16

LUNA

I PICKED A TABLE NEAR THE WINDOW AND WAITED FOR Channon to arrive. Chone stretched out on the floor and I rubbed his back with my foot. Just having him here as moral support for the forthcoming conversation was a godsend.

"Everything ok at home? Did they give you a hard time about last night?" Channon asked, as he sat down with a sandwich and a bottle of water. He gave Chone a quick pat on the head. I had been so preoccupied I hadn't even seen him enter the café. *Pay attention, Luna!*

"No, actually they were pretty calm about it, but I'm sure I haven't heard the last of it yet. They probably felt I learned my lesson." I winced. "Thank you so much again for your help. I'm not sure what I would have done if you hadn't been here."

Channon waved off my gratitude. "That's what friends are for. Don't mention it."

He took a sip of water and changed the subject. "So, how

did it go at the temple yesterday? You seemed so nervous about it on Tuesday."

And here it is Luna. What do I do?

"It's pretty complicated, Channon. Luna and I needed to talk to the monk about something that happened to us during meditation."

"That sounds serious, or rather mysterious." Channon raised his eyebrows. "What did you do? I thought you were there just for lessons, weren't you?"

"Yes, we were, and we meditated, but we went farther than either of us expected and even Ajaarn doesn't really know what to make of it." I didn't like that I was sounding so evasive.

"So, what did you do that went beyond meditation? It wasn't anything illegal, was it?" Channon winked.

"No, of course not, but it's something that affected both Luna and me, and I'm not sure I can talk about it without her permission." I stumbled along.

Channon looked at me with his big brown eyes, probably trying to figure out why I was being so cryptic. "I take it you've asked her and she said no?"

"Channon, I know you think I'm completely crazy, but even if I told you, you wouldn't believe me."

"Try me!"

"I can't, not without Luna's ok." I wanted to tear my hair out for having manoeuvred myself into this dilemma.

Channon pushed his lunch away, looking hurt. "I thought we were friends and... never mind. You said you would explain why you were so anxious on Tuesday, and now you won't?"

Against my best intentions, I felt myself tearing up, swallowing hard to not fall apart completely. This was exactly the reaction I had wanted to avoid. Though I had only known

Channon for ten days, he was the most genuine and caring person I had ever met. He'd never asked for anything in return for all the favours he had done for me and was always there when I needed him. Sure, I had a major crush on him, but he was also the first guy who had shown any genuine interest in me. Did that justify betraying Nui's confidence? No matter what I did, I'd be breaking a promise. I wished there was some sort of sliding scale to tell me which action would leave me feeling less guilty.

Channon apparently decided my silence was my answer and got up.

"I'm disappointed, Nui. I thought we could trust each other. But if you feel that way, I'd better go." He picked up the lunch tray to drop it off at the clearing station.

"No, wait!" I panicked. I couldn't let him leave this way. "I'll try to explain, but you need to promise that you won't tell another person, even if you don't believe me."

"You know I won't." Channon put the tray back down.

Chone sat up and rested his head on my knee. I stroked his head to calm down and took a deep breath, "Ok, this is what happened. You remember me saying that when Nui and I meditated, we both had out-of-body experiences, right?"

"Right, I remember. Sounds pretty cool," Channon replied.

"But what I didn't tell you is that while we were in that state, we, by accident, did a mind swap." I held my breath.

"A mind swap? What does that mean?" Channon looked confused for a second, but then grinned. "Yeah, right. Good one, Nui!" He obviously thought I was playing a joke on him.

"No seriously, it means that Nui and I exchanged spirits, or I guess you could say, we swapped bodies. I'm actually Luna in Nui's body and Nui is in my body as Luna." Saying it out loud sounded crazy even to me.

Channon stared at me. "Say that again. You swapped bodies?" He started laughing. "Nice try Nui."

"See, I knew you were going to say that, and Ajaarn thought the same at first too, but now he believes us, sort of. Yesterday, we tried to reverse it. That's what the session was about. But it didn't work." I didn't want to explain why Nui and I had given ourselves a bit more time.

"Hang on a minute. You're saying that I'm actually talking to Luna while I'm looking at Nui?" Channon was shaking his head.

"Exactly!" I exhaled. The secret was out. "You can't tell anyone about this. Of course, we'll keep trying to swap back, but it's more difficult than we thought it would be."

Channon frowned. "And when did all this happen?"

"Just before New Year's. I know it sounds totally nuts, but it happened, and for the past two weeks I've been pretending to be Nui, and Nui has been living with my family."

"If that is true, and I'm not convinced it is, how in the world did you keep this up for two weeks?"

"It wasn't easy, but we managed. But now we're back in school and it's getting more difficult and…" I left it open at that.

Channon shook his head as if to clear water from his ears. "And your Ajaarn doesn't know how it happened, either?" He sounded incredulous.

"He had some ideas, and it's something Nui and I have to work on, but…" I trailed off again.

Channon was sceptical but quick on the uptake, faster than I expected. "Hang on, you said it was an accident, or did you do this on purpose?"

Shit! I really didn't want to get into the details, but I knew I should probably come clean.

"When we started, we had this fantasy that we could switch for a little while. I wanted to see what it's like to live in a big, normal family. and Nui wanted a taste of my life, you know, travelling, no big family obligations, more freedom. We never thought it would be a full body swap. We thought we might experience it, I guess you could say, virtually."

"I can't get my head around this. So, do I call you Nui or Luna?"

"Nui of course."

"Why should I believe any of this? Admit it, you are just playing a big practical joke on me!" Channon tried to call my bluff.

"No Channon, I promise, it's not a joke. Nui and I have been freaking out and especially yesterday when the reversal didn't work." He didn't need to know we had given ourselves a short extension for the swap. Now that the secret was out, I felt better, even knowing I would have to tell Nui about it. The crucial question was what Channon would do with the bombshell I had dropped on him.

"Can you prove any of this?" Channon challenged.

I glanced down at Chone, who seemed to sense something weird was going on. He kept his head on my leg, eyes glued to my face.

"Do you remember when Luna came to Tum's ceremony and Joey went ballistic about her?"

"Yeah, so what?"

"Joey knew right away that I wasn't Nui when I walked in the door the first time. You can ask Khun Yaa or the family about it. He barked and growled and behaved as if he'd never met me before. But when Nui walked in, Joey recognized her immediately. You and Krit both commented on how strange that was. I think dogs have that kind of instinct."

"Hmm."

"There are tons of other things I could tell you. I know, Channon, it sounds fantastical, but it's real and we're stuck right now until we can reverse it."

"Okaaay. But what about us? Are you saying you've been lying to me the whole time, pretending to be someone else?" Channon hit the nail on the head. More hurt than angry, I sensed. I couldn't look at him. My face was burning. I had to bite my lips and swallow hard to keep my stomach from revolting.

"I honestly didn't mean to deceive you Channon. But once we started hanging out and then you got Chone for me, I didn't know what to do." I pleaded, sounding whiny even to myself. "I didn't know if you would like me as Luna or only because I look like Nui?" I realized I had made it sound like a question, which wasn't really fair.

Channon took his time to respond. "How am I supposed to answer that? Even if you're Luna in Nui's body, how am I supposed to separate that? For me, you're the same."

He paused again. "I need to think about this, and I don't have the time right now. I need to get back to work."

There was nothing else I could say. I'm not sure I would have taken this as calmly as Channon had. He appeared fairly stoic, or maybe he didn't care enough one way or another? That thought hit me like a wrecking ball in the stomach, but I tried to match his composure.

"I understand, Channon, but please remember not to tell anyone."

"I promised already, didn't I, Nui or Luna or...?" For the first time, his response was brusque.

"Chone, come!" Channon grabbed the lead.

"I'll take him back before I leave," I offered.

"That's ok, I'll take him. Bye."

Chone looked from me to Channon, clearly not sure what was going on. *Join the club.* I knew Channon would be upset or confused, but I hadn't expected his reaction to hurt so much.

I grabbed a bunch of napkins to wipe my tears as Channon and Chone walked away. *Had I just lost both of them?*

17

NUI

Leaving the station, I stopped at Swenson's Ice Cream Shop to buy a tub of Durian ice-cream for Khun Yaa who rarely treated herself to it. She was the only one in the family who liked the taste of the smelly fruit, and even though the ice-cream was less intense, I couldn't get that awful stink out of my nose. I was too lazy to walk, and with the ice-cream I had a good excuse to take a moto-taxi to get home quickly. I still felt bad about hurting Yumi's feelings, but didn't know what I could have done differently without further information from Luna.

Joey was already yipping excitedly as I walked up the steps to the house. As soon as Luna opened the door, he shot out, twisting himself around my legs and almost tripping me. I knelt to pet him and he leaped into my arms, licking my face.

"Hello my little puppy. Did you miss me?" I laughed at his excitement. It felt good to be home.

Looking up at Luna, I flinched. My eyes were red and

glassy. I never looked like that, even after eating some seriously hot chillies. *What's happened to her? The accident? Is she hurt more badly than she let on?* I scanned my body to see what was off but noticed only a small band-aid on the left hand. Not big enough to justify her look of gloom.

"Luna, are you ok? What happened?" I whispered quickly in English as I saw Khun Yaa peeking out of the kitchen to see who was at the door.

Luna nodded. "I'll explain later." Her tone was soft, almost frail.

I wasn't sure what to make of that, but Khun Yaa had joined Luna with a big smile. "Noo Luna, sawasdee kha. Sabai di mai kha?" She spoke Thai of course and I automatically wai'ed and responded without even thinking. "Sabai di kha, Khun Yaa!"

Her smile widened, surprised and delighted with my 'new' language skills. It was the first time I'd actually talked with her directly as 'Luna' and I realized how much I had missed our daily chats. I offered her the ice-cream and her face lit up. Luna rolled her eyes, as if I had shown her up deliberately. *Should have thought of that yourself.*

Khun Yaa ushered us into the kitchen, insisting we sit down and eat some snacks. I knew it would upset her routine for dinner preparation, but I was selfish enough to enjoy her company and talk a bit more. Rummaging around the fridge and firing up the stove, she magically produced some leftover Khanom Khrok, both sweet and savoury, Kluai thot, Green mango with nam pla wan and the ingredients for Miang Kham. It never ceased to amaze me how she could whip up something so tasty so easily.

All the while she chatted, asking about school, Luna's parents and the trip to Bali. Luna herself sat quietly at the table, not contributing to the conversation or eating, just

taking small sips of water. Joey had made himself comfortable on my feet and I occasionally rubbed his head, tempted
to sneak him a bite or two, but I knew Khun Yaa had an issue
with that. I was almost embarrassed by how much I ate, but it
all was too delicious and I knew my grandmother appreciated
someone enjoying her food.

It was Khun Yaa who told me about Luna's accident and
how she had to go to the hospital and get rabies shots. I
looked at Luna, annoyed at what she had done to my body,
but still there was hardly any reaction, just a sheepish shrug.
Finally, I had enough.

"Khun Yaa, thank you so much for all this wonderful
food. I'm quite full and I think I better tell Nui about school
and homework." My grandmother nodded and asked if I
wanted to take some food home with me later. I grinned and
happily accepted.

Turning to Luna, I switched to English. "Shall we?"

18

LUNA

I HOPED THE FOOD HAD PUT NUI INTO A SOMEWHAT MELLOW mood. I didn't even care that she'd stuffed herself, though I was sure it would put a few pounds on my body. She'd be mad about the rabies shots for sure, but I was wavering about whether I should tell her about my conversation with Channon. I seriously considered omitting it, at least for now, unsure if I could handle the fight that was bound to follow. But eventually, I would have to come clean, and the longer I waited, the worse it would get.

I tried to pre-empt her. "I'm really sorry about the bite, Nui. It happened so fast and I know I probably should have backed away, but Joey was ready to jump into the fight and I had to do something." I could tell Nui had been about to launch into some kind of tirade, but she clamped her mouth shut and swallowed whatever she had planned to say. Instead, she bent to stroke Joey's head while shaking her own.

"Joey, Joey, Joey, what were you thinking? You know you can't fight with the soi dogs. They are too dangerous."

Turning to me she said, "Ok, I get that, and thanks for making sure he didn't get hurt, but…"

I interrupted her. "Don't worry, the shots are really not bad and there will be only a tiny scar, the doctor said. So how was school today?"

I wasn't sure if she'd buy the distraction, but amazingly, it worked. "You won't believe what happened today, Luna. It was so bizarre. Do you know someone called Yumi?"

Huh? That wasn't what I had expected.

"I knew a Yumi in Shanghai, why?"

"Guess what? She's here. At BIS!"

"She's what? No way! You serious? How come I haven't seen her? She should be in our grade."

Nui shrugged. "I don't know. She found me in the cafeteria and made a big scene in front of everyone. How happy she was to see me, how we have to get together, blah, blah, blah. It was surreal. I had absolutely no clue who she was."

"Wow, that's a surprise. Hahaha, yes, I remember Yumi can be a bit much, but she's fun. She always turned everything into a big production. But what is she doing here? I thought they were still in Shanghai."

"Get this, I ran into her again on the Skytrain. Actually, I think she followed me. It was slightly creepy. She said her parents got divorced, and she's here with her dad who works at the embassy, and her mom and Kiko went back to Japan? Who's Kiko?"

"Oh no. Poor Yumi. Kiko is her little sister. I knew her parents were having some issues. I think it had something to do with her mom's parents refusing to accept Yumi's dad because he's American or something like that."

"Really? Why?" Nui asked.

"I don't know all the details but Yumi said her grandparents were very traditional Japanese and expected their daughter to come back to Japan. But her dad was working for the American Embassy and they kept sending him to different places. To be honest, I wasn't paying much attention, I just know that Yumi only met her grandparents once." I tried to recall more of our conversations, but it all seemed too grown-up for us then.

Nui looked embarrassed. "Yikes, no wonder Yumi thought I was being mean."

"Huh? Why would she think that?"

"I asked if her dad worked at the Japanese embassy and she got upset that I remembered nothing. Da man! Damn it! How was I supposed to know that?"

I brushed it off. "Nah, you couldn't have known that. But yeah, she's half American, half Japanese. I know she looks more Japanese, though. I think her parents met in college in the States. Oh man, this is going to become really tricky. I mean, I lost touch with her, but I knew her for a few years and we used to hang out a lot. How the heck are we going to manage this? Do you know if she's in any of our classes?"

Nui shrugged. "I saw her for the first time today, so maybe she just started. No idea if we overlap, but I don't want to meet her again by myself. It's too difficult. Oh, and what's YKPS? Was that your school?"

"Yeah, Yue-Kong Pao School. Sounds Chinese, but it was actually international. I liked it there."

"She also mentioned some other names, a Leslie, and I forgot the rest." Nui said.

I grinned. "We had a fun little group. Seems like ages ago."

"How are we going to handle this when she wants to talk with me and I have no clue?" Nui asked. "By the way, she gave me her phone number, but I can't really text her or call her until I know more."

"I guess the same way I dealt with Toey and Dearn when you weren't here. I'll jump in when I can and pretend you told me about Yumi, and the rest you'll have to fake. And you can always forward her texts to me if you need to. Just pretend it was so long ago that you can't remember some things," I suggested.

Yumi's arrival would complicate things, but at least it had distracted Nui from asking about my misery.

19

NUI

Luna looked a bit more animated now, but I still wanted to know why she had been so miserable and clearly crying. Her attempt to distract me didn't fool me, and I wanted to get to the bottom of what was bothering her.

"Ok Luna, what's really going on with you? You look like you ate a whole prik jinda by mistake." I meant it as a joke, remembering how my hot chilli eating contest with Krit had left me in tears for hours.

Luna's face crumbled, and she burst into tears, taking me by surprise. *What now?* Judging by the dramatic outburst, it probably had something to do with Channon or Chone or both.

"I did something really stupid, Nui. I am so sorry. I didn't mean to, but I had to tell him something." Luna started hiccupping in her distress.

"Telling who? You mean Channon? Okaaay, what exactly did you tell him?" I was making a superhuman effort to keep my voice level when all I wanted to do was scream at her.

Completely oblivious, Luna rattled on. "I know you told me not to, but I just couldn't face lying to him anymore. I had to give him some explanation and now I don't know if he'll ever want to see me again." She grabbed some tissues and blew her nose.

Count to ten or twenty or one hundred Nui!

"Are you effing kidding me?" I spat out through clenched teeth. "You told Channon about the switch even though we both agreed you wouldn't? How dare you? You're so bloody selfish." I felt like hitting the roof, but in our house the walls were thin, and I didn't want Khun Yaa to hear us, especially me swearing.

"I am so, so sorry, Nui. I had to do something, and I trust Channon. He's the coolest guy, really." Luna looked at me pleading, as if her 'woe is me' expression would prompt my forgiveness. *As if!*

"Yeah? So what are you really sorry about, Luna? That you told him, or that you don't know if he'll want to see you again? Or how about that you broke your promise to me? Grow up Luna! You're always the victim, aren't you? Things always happen to you that leave you with no choice, right? You are the most pathetic person I know." I knew my tirade wasn't helping, but I was livid and fed-up with her selfish behaviour.

Luna jerked back. "Is that what you think? That's the meanest thing anyone has ever said to me."

We glared at each other. *Nui, careful, you still need Luna if you want to get back into your own body.* Big IF aside, my stomach clenched, but I ignored my own warning.

"See, you're doing it again. It's always about you, isn't it? Can't you snap out of it for once and even remotely consider my side? He probably didn't even believe you, did he? And how am I supposed to treat him after we switch back?

Remember, he's Krit's friend too." Another thought occurred to me. "You do want to switch back, don't you?"

"Of course I do." Luna sounded indignant. "Do you? After all, you're the one who's so desperate to leave Thailand."

"That's just great. Here we go again. You know Luna, you're the one who's messed things up left, right and centre. I have played by our rules and all you had to do was lie low, but no, you had to go and get involved with a guy the minute you were in my body. Why don't you tell me how you plan to get out of this?"

"This would never have happened if you hadn't suggested the swap in the first place." Luna sounded petulant and anything but remorseful.

"That's old news and may I remind you this couldn't have happened if you hadn't willingly gone along, so stop blaming me for your mess-ups!" I knew fighting wouldn't get us anywhere, but I couldn't stop myself. "And by the way, how do you expect Channon to react? He must be mad as hell at you. I know you like to think he's your knight in shining armour, but do you really expect him to just say, 'Sure Nui, I believe you're Luna. Let's continue as though nothing has changed'? He's not that stupid."

"Leave Channon out of this! This is between you and me," Luna snapped back. "I know I messed up, and no, I don't know yet how to fix it, but this is not helping either."

"How can I leave Channon out? You brought him into this. What do you expect him to do? His only option is to walk away from you. Don't you get that? How can he ever trust you again?" I felt like shaking some sense into her. Sometimes, I really didn't get her Pollyanna attitude.

Luna turned as pale as my Thai skin would allow. "Do you really think so?" The tears flowed again.

For crying out loud! Nui, what happened to your negoti-ating skills? You're not helping the situation by beating Luna up. Yeah, but when will she learn that there are consequences to her actions? She is so damn irresponsible.

The room was quiet except for Luna's sniffles. Joey sat between us, ears raised and alerted by the palpable tension. I petted his head to calm myself down and exhaled loudly.

"Forget it. It is what it is. Let's deal with it."

"Really?" Luna looked up with a small pathetic smile and wiped her eyes. "Thank you Nui, and for what it's worth, I really am sorry. I didn't expect it to go this way."

"Yeah, right. How could you not? But Channon will do whatever he wants to do." I rolled my shoulders. Luna kept dabbing at her tears, but maybe she had finally got an inkling that reality could not always match her daydreams.

20

LUNA

Nui's reaction was far worse than I had expected. I knew she had every right to be angry, but I wasn't sure how I could cope with both Channon *and* Nui being mad at me. I felt lost.

"I think we should switch back right now, Nui," I suggested tentatively. "We know how to do it. Ajaarn said we only have to agree and believe we can do it. We don't need him for that."

Nui frowned, her lips a thin line.

"Nii laaw-len chai mai? No way. You messed up, you fix it." She was adamant. "Plus, we agreed to wait until your mom is back."

"But don't you see it would solve all our problems if we switched now?"

"You mean it would solve *your* problems, or rather, you wouldn't have to handle it. No go, Luna."

If Nui didn't agree, I wouldn't be able to complete the switch. *Or would I? Ajaarn had said no one could force you, but he also hadn't known a switch was possible to begin with.* Where had this thought come from?

"You could tell Channon it was just a bad joke, couldn't you?" Nui suggested, but then contradicted herself. "Nah, that doesn't work. I don't want to have to deal with Channon after we switch back."

I was only half listening. *What if I try it and see what happens?*

Nui punched my arm harder than necessary. "Are you listening Luna?"

"Ouch! Yeah, I'm listening. Fine, we'll wait until Mom is back. Let's not talk about it anymore." I'd have to think about the feasibility later in more detail. For now, the practical side of things demanded my attention.

"So, what happened in school today? Any homework? Any test dates yet?" I asked Nui.

"No, no tests yet, but I think that's coming up in a day or so. I'll email you the assignments, but I missed your Thai class, so you need to ask Nat about it."

"Ok thanks. You have swim class tomorrow after lunch. Will you be ok with that?"

Nui cringed. "I haven't been in the water since Bali. Maybe I'll try out the pool at your house later to see if I can do it. I'm so not looking forward to it."

I figured she'd be ok as she'd be using my body and I was a strong swimmer.

"You'll be fine. And when you're done, we have to leave right away to meet Toey and Dearn at four, remember?"

"Geez, maybe we should just cancel. This is all getting too much." Nui squeezed her eyes shut. "And now we have to deal with Yumi too."

"They are your friends. You really want to cancel?" I

wouldn't have minded since I really didn't know them, anyway.

Nui shook her head. "Nah, we better meet, otherwise they'll think we're avoiding them. I gotta go. There's so much to do." Nui stood and looked down at me. The muscles in her jaw were clenched as if she was grinding her teeth. She started to say something, but then shook her head as if any comment would be futile.

"I'll see you tomorrow." She turned to open the door. "And try not to mess up anything else in the meantime."

I rolled my eyes at her back.

21

NUI

I GLIMPSED KHUN BPOO WATCHING TV IN THE LIVING ROOM as I walked down the corridor and wai'ed briefly. Khun Yaa pressed a small food parcel into my hands and escorted me to the door. Luna held Joey by his collar as he whined and strained to follow me out. I almost felt jealous seeing Luna and Khun Yaa standing side by side, but my to-do list was already dominating my thoughts again. I was still angry with Luna, but right now I didn't have time to think about her messed up romantic life.

Fortunately, I didn't see Yumi on the train this time. Back at the apartment, I knocked on Luke's door to make sure he'd got home ok. No answer. I detoured to the kitchen.

"Pi' Bo, have you seen Luke?" I asked in Thai.

She nodded. "He's gone to the pool." She looked at her watch. "You want to eat at seven, chai mai kha? Khun Mark is not coming."

"Chai kha. Thank you, Pi' Bo. I'll get Luke."

We had about one hour before dinner. Plenty of time to

get the swimming part over with. I changed into a swimsuit, grabbed a towel, and headed to the pool terrace.

Luke was trying different twists, jumping off the one-meter springboard into the deep end. He waved as he came up for air. "Did you see that? I almost did a full somersault," he beamed. "And I managed two forward loops. Want to see?"

I smiled at his eagerness. "Sure, show me." A couple sat on lounge chairs at the far end, not paying attention to us. Otherwise, the terrace was empty.

I dropped the towel onto a chair and dipped my toes over the infinity edge into the water. It was chilly compared to the surrounding air. Luke raced around and hopped back up on the board. Even if it was only his sister, he was probably grateful to have an audience. He made diving look so easy, even if he finished the jump with a big splash. He waggled his head like a dolphin, grinning from ear to ear. I gave him a double thumbs up.

"Aren't you coming in?" Luke shouted.

I hesitated. Moment of truth. Did I dare? *Come on Nui, you can do it,* I tried to reason with myself. *Luna can swim in my body, so why shouldn't I be able to swim in hers?*

Luke eyed me curiously, treading water. "Are you afraid because of what happened in Bali, Luna?"

Wow, pretty perceptive for a twelve-year-old, even if he didn't know the entire story.

"I'm not really sure, to be honest."

"Don't worry, I'm here and can get you if you're nervous," Luke reassured me, all serious now.

This is ridiculous! My kid 'brother' offering to save me?! *Kind of sweet, though. Come on Nui, don't be such a baby.*

I sat down, put my legs into the water and almost yelped at the cold temperature. Better get this over with quickly. Holding my breath, I pushed off. Water gushed over my head and blocked my ears. My eyes were wide open, but the background was fuzzy, like blurred glass. I could just about see the blue tiles at the bottom and the fading sunshine shimmering on top. Luke was kicking towards me, his face distorted by the water. Too embarrassed to be shown up by Luna's brother, I finally moved my arms and legs and I easily shot back up to the surface to gulp some air. My legs automatically started treading water, my arms spread wide for balance. I turned twice to see how this worked and didn't even have to think about it. Dipping under the surface once more and bobbing back up was so easy. This was amazing. I felt completely at ease, like a mermaid. I snorted at the idea.

"You ok?" Luke was watching me from a short distance away. I nodded, spitting out water and grinning.

"See, it's just like riding a bike." He laughed. "Come on, I'll race you to the other end. Winner gets to pick dessert." He twisted around and set off.

Luna's muscle memory had fully kicked in and I easily fell into a smooth crawl, closing in on Luke. I could have beaten him, but let him win as a thank you for being so supportive. It felt absolutely liberating cutting through the water. How ridiculous that I had been so afraid.

We raced two more lengths before I called a halt. It was fully dark now and the terrace lights had come on. Despite all the food at Khun Yaa's, I had worked up an appetite again. Luke accepted Khun Yaa's care package as his prize, so in the end, we both won.

LUNA

KHUN YAA HELD ON TO MY ARM AS SHE CLOSED THE DOOR behind Nui.

"Come with me, Nui. I want to know what's wrong with you. You've been acting strange these last two weeks." She pulled the kitchen door shut us to give us some privacy. "Sit down. Do you want a cup of ginger tea?"

I declined, nervous of what was coming next.

"Tell me, what is bothering you?" Khun Yaa pulled up a chair next to me and waited.

I gulped, not sure what she wanted me to say.

"Well?" Khun Yaa prompted.

"I don't know what to tell you."

"Does it have something to do with Channon?"

"Hmm, sort of, but that's not really the issue."

"Then what *is* the issue?" She insisted. "For two weeks now, you behave like your mind is somewhere else, your dog is acting up, you forget things, and now you are crying and having some kind of problem with Channon. Did you fight with Luna too? Do you want me to go on? Something is not right, Nui. Are you sick? Do you need to see a doctor?" She looked more puzzled and concerned than angry. I swallowed hard. I didn't want to cry again in front of Khun Yaa.

I wish I could tell her, but Nui's tantrum over Channon would be minor compared to telling her grandma about the switch. It just wasn't possible.

"I'm so sorry, Khun Yaa. I know I've been a bit off." I watched my hands curl around a soggy tissue instead of looking at her.

"Is school too much for you? Do you want to go back to your old school?"

"What? No! Absolutely not." I shouted much too loudly and shook my head. "Sorry, but no, it's not school, school is fine." The last thing Nui and I needed was to be separated at school.

Khun Yaa's eyes narrowed. "Are you pregnant?"

My mouth dropped open, the question catching me completely off guard. It also provided the much needed shock to snap me out of my funk. I started laughing.

"No Khun Yaa, I'm definitely not pregnant. Don't worry!"

Though her question had sounded more pragmatic than judgmental, her shoulders dropped in relief.

"Seriously, Khun Yaa, it's something I need to handle myself. I promise I'll figure it out."

"Make sure you do. You know what will happen if your grades slip. Maybe you shouldn't see Channon for a while if he's distracting you."

I was about to object, but then paused. I'd be off the hook if the family forbade me to see him. It would be an easy way out. *Come on Luna, don't be such a coward. You got yourself into this mess, so you have to handle it somehow.*

"It's not Channon's fault, Khun Yaa, seriously. And I still have to do my volunteer shifts anyway, so I can't really avoid him at the shelter."

She shook her head. "Whatever it is, Nui, sort it out. We'll keep it between us for now, but if you keep going like this, I will speak with your parents." It sounded like a threat.

"I promise, Khun Yaa. Thank you." I got up and hugged her. "I'll take Joey for a quick walk and then get started on homework." At the door, I turned around. "I'm not really hungry, so I'll skip dinner, ok?"

I knew she thought food was the answer to everything, but I needed to get control of my emotions before facing the family again. Khun Yaa frowned but shooed me out the door, apparently satisfied she had put me on notice.

After taking Joey to the park, I went back to the boys' room and took a moment to just sit and breathe. Instead of having a peaceful day off, I'd had three super tough conversations, and I wasn't sure which was the worst. I had really boxed myself into a corner. If I told Channon the whole thing was a joke, I'd never get the chance to know him in my own body. Nui, on the other hand, would probably never trust me again after I broke my promise to her. And now, on top of that, with Khun Yaa watching me, I'd have to be even more careful about letting my emotions show too clearly.

I didn't want to think about any of it, so instead I tackled the homework and notes Nui had emailed. In the back of my mind, though, I was still mulling over the idea of initiating a one-sided switch. Would I be able to push my way into my body and force Nui back into hers? We'd said we would wait until Mom got back, but if I could make it happen before then, I wouldn't have to deal with all this stuff anymore. *Only one way to find out, Luna.*

I pushed the papers aside and sat back on Krit's bed.

Headphones on, I pulled up Ajaarn Anurak's last recorded session. He said because we'd assumed his voice was more powerful, we had an easier time letting go and achieving an out-of-body state. If that was true, I could do this on my own too, right? I told myself I only wanted to test how far I could go to reach Nui. I pressed play.

The familiar surge of energy ran from my head to my toes and back again in rhythmic cycles. For the first time that day, I was completely at ease. Wave after wave of what felt like electrical tremors pulsed through me in harmony with Ajaarn's sing-song mantras. With the next surge, I suddenly felt myself looking down at Nui's body. Her eyes were closed, but my mind felt completely alert. I concentrated on isolating Nui's vibration out of the translucent web of spirit threads that had appeared around me. I had connected with her before and I was sure I could do it again. Ajaarn said that each soul identified with a particular body in this world, so I only needed to locate my body, and there I would find Nui's spirit.

Normal space and time rules don't apply in astral travel and I instantly shifted to our dining room at home. Nui and Luke were just getting up from the table. I sensed Nui's spirit thread and nudged against it.

23

NUI

THE GLASS AND PLATE SLIPPED FROM MY HANDS AND BROKE into a thousand pieces on the marble floor. My body spasmed, my legs turned into jello, and I collapsed on top of the shards, puncturing bare legs and arms. At the same time, my head felt as though something had gripped it in a vice, with someone slowly tightening the screws. Only a few more turns and my head would burst open under the pressure.

My eyes squeezed shut, my back arched in a rigid curve. The pain was excruciating. A knife thrust into my brain. My heart was racing and sweat was breaking out of every pore. I was close to passing out, a cottony fog buffering all perception.

"Argh!" I croaked through gritted teeth, not having enough breath left to scream.

"Luna! What's wrong? What's happening?" Luke's voice sounded far away and fuzzy.

"I don't know. It hurts!" I barely squeezed out.

"Khun Bo, Khun Bo! Help!" Luke screamed. "Luna! I'm gonna call Dad."

I couldn't open my eyes but heard shards being swished aside and then I felt a warm, calloused hand on my forehead. My skin was on fire.

"Nong Luna, pen arai?" Khun Bo asked in Thai. Like Luke, she sounded terrified.

"Mai roo!" I hissed.

"Is she having a seizure?" Luke's panicked voice boomed in my head. "Khun Bo, I don't know the number for the ambulance. Can you call quickly?"

Just then, the pain left as quickly as it had come. I cautiously inhaled, finally managing a full breath in and out. My muscles released one by one. I squinted through half-closed lids—the hallway light was still too bright for my addled brain. Khun Bo and Luke were hovering above me, anxiously watching my face.

"Are you ok Luna? What was that? I called Dad. He's on his way."

The whole thing couldn't have lasted for more than a minute or two, but I felt completely drained and weak, as if something had attacked my brain and short-circuited my nerves. Did Luna have a history of seizures that she never mentioned?

I wanted to get up, but Khun Bo put her hand on my shoulder.

"You stay. I clean glass first."

"Yikes Luna, you got cuts everywhere. Wait, I'll get some Band-Aids." Luke rushed off, eager to be doing something. While they were both gone, I took a moment to catch my breath, relieved the episode was over.

Khun Bo and Luke returned, busying themselves by clearing the broken glass and plate, dabbing at some cuts with antiseptic wipes, and applying an assortment of plasters. My legs and arms looked like an amateur patch-up job on a broken porcelain bowl. Thankfully, none of the cuts seemed deep enough to require stitches.

Once they had finished, they helped me up and into my room. I just wanted to crawl into bed, but knew I didn't have that luxury just yet. I still had too much to do.

"Let me rest for a bit. I'm fine now, really. I hope you didn't call an ambulance, Khun Bo. Can I please have a glass of water?" She nodded, relieved, and went to the kitchen.

"You sure you're ok? That was really scary. You looked awful." Luke still hadn't recovered his usual bravado. It must have been even worse for him, watching and not being able to help.

"Thanks Luke. I really feel much better now. Let's just wait for Dad to come home. I'm gonna take a quick nap for now."

"I'll get your phone and you call me if you need anything, ok?"

I smiled at him. Even if he was annoying sometimes, he really cared. First at the pool and now this. "Thanks Luke. You've been really great." He dismissed the compliment with a shrug and left to get my phone.

After Khun Bo dropped off the water, I closed my eyes and tried to breathe and relax. The sweat was cooling off quickly, with the A/C going at full speed. I shivered and pulled the throw over me. A few minutes later, I heard the front door open, and seconds later, a knock on my door. Luna's dad didn't wait for my 'come in' but rushed in with worry lines etched on his face. He sat on the side of the bed and brushed my hair away from my face. Luke peeked into the room.

"What happened sweetheart? Luke sounded really upset." He looked me up and down. "You feel better now?"

"I'm fine Dad. Honestly, I don't know what it was. It came out of the blue, then went away just as quickly. Strange."

"I have Khun Pak waiting downstairs. I think we should go to Bumrungrad to get you checked out." It had been terribly painful, so perhaps that was a good idea. But I felt fine now, so unless there was a repeat episode, I didn't think it would be necessary.

"Actually, Dad, I think I'm ok now. Don't worry. Maybe it was just…" I stopped mid-sentence as a thought occurred to me. I had been so busy dealing with the immediate impact that I hadn't had time to think properly. *What if it's related to our switch? I have to ask Luna if she felt something similar.*

"Just… what?" Khun Mark asked.

"I'm not sure. Maybe I ate too much after swimming or something," I said, pulling a stupid explanation out of thin air.

"After swimming?" Luna's dad looked unconvinced. "You always eat after swimming. That makes no sense. I'd rather have you checked out. We can leave right now."

My phone pinged and lit up with a message from Luna. 'Nui, you ok?'

Luna's dad look down just then and frowned. "Why is Nui calling you Nui?"

Oops! Talk about bad timing. Think Nui!

"It's just a silly game we're playing. She thinks I'm becoming more Thai by the minute." I shrugged, pretending it wasn't a big deal, and turned the phone over. *But why is she asking me if I'm ok? She must have felt something, too.*

Khun Mark raised his eyebrows, then shook his head as if teenagers were some kind of other species.

"Dad, seriously, I'm fine. I think it was just a one-off. Let me do my homework and if I feel worse I'll call you, ok? I'm sorry to drag you home early."

"I was just finishing up, anyway." He looked me over again, then feeling reassured, kissed my forehead and backed off. As he left the room, he pulled Luke with him in a one-arm hug.

I exhaled. I had lost too much time already with this episode and needed to get started on my 'PinkElephant' blog while I still had the chance. But first, I had to call Luna.

24

LUNA

OUCH, THAT HURT! CONNECTING WITH NUI'S SPIRIT uninvited felt like a slap in the face, catapulting me back into my current body. I slumped over, breathing hard. The recording with Ajaarn's meditation session was still running. I tapped stop and tugged the headphones off. Staring into space, I rubbed my arms, disgusted with myself. *Shit, did I just seriously try to force my way back into my body without Nui's consent? You are insane, Luna.* Hugging a pillow to my chest I tried to figure out what I should do. If I felt such pain instigating the push, how much worse would it have been for Nui? I needed to know that she was ok, and that I hadn't injured my own body. Looking at the papers strewn around the bed, I picked up her notes on the media studies class. This gave me the pretext I needed to message her.

'Hey, can you send me the article for your media studies so I can prepare myself?'

The class was her favourite, so I expected her to reply

quickly. The screen remained dark. *Shit, I really hope she's alright. I never should have done that.*

I tried to do some homework but found myself doodling on a piece of paper while keeping an eye on the phone. Twenty minutes later she still hadn't responded. I picked up the phone again. 'Nui, you ok?'

Another ten minutes went by and finally the screen lit up with Nui's FaceTime request.

I hesitated to answer, afraid she might see the guilt in my face but I had to confirm that she was ok. Nui looked anaemic, her eyes slightly glassy as if she had a fever.

"Hey. What's up? Did you get my messages?" *I was such a hypocrite.*

"Luna, I think I just had a seizure."

No, no, no!

"You what? No way. I don't get seizures."

Shit, Luna, what did you do?

"It really hurt," Nui said.

I was glad I hadn't eaten dinner. I felt like throwing up.

"We had just finished dinner and then I got this spasm. It felt like someone was squeezing my head. It was so bad I almost passed out. Luke even called your dad to come home early. Have you ever had anything like this before? I didn't want to ask your dad?" Nui asked.

"No, definitely not. What did you do after you left here?"

"Nothing much really, went to the pool with Luke and then we had dinner."

"Hmm, maybe it was a combination of you eating so much here and then being so nervous about swimming?" I knew that was ridiculous but I was grasping at straws.

"Actually, I was thinking, isn't it more likely it had something to do with the switch?" Nui asked.

Oh no! Don't let her go down that route. I immediately

rejected the idea. "I doubt it. Otherwise, I would have felt something too, don't you think?" I couldn't let Nui make the association or become suspicious. "It was probably just nerves and food. You're fine now, right?"

"No, seriously, if you don't have seizures and I definitely don't have them, the only explanation is the switch." Nui said. "It really felt like something was pushing against me, trying to get into my head. Do you think other spirits can do that to you?" Nui looked scared by her own suggestion. "Maybe we've opened some sort of portal or something?"

My mouth dropped open. That idea had never occurred to me.

"Seriously? That's pretty far-fetched. Remember, Ajaarn said no-one can force you." I dismissed her suggestion instantly, then hesitated. What if? Now she'd got me thinking. Was that indeed a possibility? *No way! You know it was you who did this, not some ghost.*

"I think you just need some sleep, Nui. I'll see you tomorrow."

"Hmm, I guess. I'd better get back to my homework. I sent you the article, by the way. And remember, Yumi is going to be there tomorrow."

"Yeah, I know. I'll meet you at the gate and we can walk in together. Night Nui, glad you're feeling better."

"Night Luna."

I signed off and threw my phone on the bed.

2 5

NUI

Why did I have the niggling feeling that Luna was holding something back—again? She had been awfully quick to dismiss my suggestion the seizure could have been related to the switch, and her explanation was as lame as mine had been with her dad. It seemed perfectly logical to me that there could be some kind of connection, and the idea of a portal, while scary, wasn't so absurd, either. I'd have to think more about that later.

I was still a bit wobbly, but I thought as long as I simply sat at my desk, I would manage. Khun Yaa always recommended fresh ginger tea for any ailments, and that sounded like a great remedy right now. I detoured to the kitchen. Khun Bo was happy to brew a cup for me. She was probably relieved she wouldn't have to deal with a serious medical incident now that Khun Mark was home.

Back at my desk, it was time to get serious and complete the set-up for pinkelephant. After we switch back, I could run the blog from home with no-one being any the wiser. I decided to use a template that wouldn't require much tweaking and would be quick to set up. Unfortunately, I had to give Luna's credit card details for hosting the site and the mailing list service provider. I hoped Luna's dad wouldn't ask me about it, but I had to use a card that matched the registration. Besides, Luna had my debit card, and I couldn't remember the number off the top of my head. I found a simple, stylized image of a pink elephant that would work nicely as the background. Now for the content. While I was waiting to get into the more meaty stuff about Thai politics with Mom Luang, I thought I'd start with some general essays about Thai vs expat culture, now that I had a viewpoint on both.

When I looked up to check the time, it was past nine-thirty. I realized I still had homework to do, or at the least the reading part for Luna's English class.

Reluctantly, I put the laptop into sleep mode and grabbed Steinbeck's 'The Pearl.' Twenty minutes later, my head jerked upright at a knock on my door. I'd nodded off.

"Come in."

Khun Mark poked his head around the door. "How are you feeling honey? Any more pain?"

"Nah Dad, I'm fine. Just finishing up some reading, then I'll call it a night." I waved the book at him as proof, though I couldn't even recall the first two pages.

"By the way, I forgot to mention earlier; Jake Wilson called this afternoon. Did you know they moved here?"

"Jake who?"

"You know, Yumi's dad from Shanghai."

"Oh yeah, Yumi showed up at school today out of the blue. I didn't know they were coming."

"So, you're no longer in touch with her? I thought you were such good friends back then?"

"Dad! That was over three years ago. We were just kids then." I shook my head.

"Ah yes, of course, and you're so adult now." Khun Mark deadpanned. "Anyway, apparently Yumi told her dad she saw you, so Jake called to invite us to the Embassy tomorrow night for a little reception they're having to introduce Jake to local Americans. He asked if you wanted to come as Yumi will be there too."

Drat! This girl is a real pain. Is she stalking me?

"Um, let me talk to her at school tomorrow, ok, Dad? I'm meeting some other friends at four, so it might get tight. What time does it start?"

"At six. Just text me so I can let Jake know. It won't be for long, but I need to attend for work and you should come. It'll be nice to catch up with Jake and I'm sure he'd like to see you too."

"Ok Dad. I'll try to make it. By the way, here's my note for Mom Luang. Can you pass it on to him?" I needed some ammunition for my blog, and I was still hoping I could get some insights from Mom Luang.

"Sure, but don't push it. He'll be there briefly at the staff party on Saturday, but I don't want you to bother him, understood?" Khun Mark sounded exasperated with the subject.

"Don't worry Dad. I won't. I'm gonna turn in now. I'm exhausted. Goodnight."

I didn't have to fake the yawn.

"Night honey. See you in the morning."

Luna's dad had reminded me I still hadn't given Yumi my phone number. I guess there was no way around it now, so I quickly texted it to her. Ten seconds later, a tsunami of WhatsApp messages flooded my phone.

'Finally! Are you coming tomorrow night?'

'What class do you have in the morning?'

'Shall we have lunch together?'

Geez, this was going to be so awkward.

I simply texted back, 'I'll see you tomorrow morning. I'm going to bed. Night.' Then I switched off notifications.

26

LUNA

I SLEPT BETTER THAN EXPECTED, BUT AS SOON AS I OPENED my eyes, I started fretting about the day ahead. I hadn't finished all my homework but hoped I would get a pass because of the sick day. Mentally, I ticked off items on my schedule, reminding myself of potential landmines.

- Avoid Channon at Pi' Ohm's
- Don't give Khun Yaa a reason to talk with the parents
- Mediate between Nui and Yumi
- Meet Toey and Dearn
- Volunteering?
- and minor little things like school and studying

I was tempted to plead sickness, but I forced myself to get up and dash into the bathroom. Luckily, Channon hadn't shown up by the time Joey and I left the park. I wasn't mentally prepared yet to see him, or more to the point, I was afraid of his reaction to my confession the day before. To appease Khun Yaa, I ate a whole bowl of congee without being asked, but skipped the fish sauce and other condiments, then I made my bed, offered to start a load of laundry, fed Joey, then rushed off to meet Nui before class.

I was waiting by the gates when Yumi arrived. She was hard to miss in her outfit: short black and white plaid skirt, black t-shirt with fishnet sleeves underneath, knee-high black tights, chunky platform shoes, Cleopatra-style black hair worn straight with a heavy fringe, and a black tattoo neck choker. Wow! BIS was pretty lenient on dress codes, but Yumi was pushing the boundaries. The younger kids in their uniforms were gawking at her with admiration and shock. She hadn't changed a bit, though in Shanghai she could only dress up like this after school and did it mostly to annoy her mom, who was super conservative. Yumi bounced through the courtyard in her usual style, soaking up the attention like a Hollywood diva. Just as she walked into the building, I felt a tap on my shoulder.

"Did you see her?" Nui asked.

"Hahaha, you could hardly miss her in that outfit," I laughed.

"She's weird! Please don't let me get stuck with her by myself," Nui begged.

"She's fine, don't worry. Just let her talk. When I knew her, she was actually quite shy but didn't like to admit it, so I think this is her way of overcompensating."

"Shy? Her? Could have fooled me." Nui said. "Let me show you how shy she is." She pulled out her phone and scrolled through what must have been at least twenty messages from Yumi from last night and this morning. "I haven't even read all of them yet." She shuddered.

"Don't forget, she thinks you're her best friend from Shanghai, so of course she would text you."

"Yeah, one message, but twenty? And then her dad called your dad last night and invited him to a reception at the American Embassy. Your dad said I should go too because Yumi will be there. What do I do?"

"If it's a reception, you don't have to worry. There'll be lots of other people around. But yeah, you need to go if Dad asked you, especially since Mom is not here."

"Hmm, if you say so. Ok, let's go in, shall we?" Nui hooked her arm through mine and we started walking to the main building. Only then did I notice several angry looking cuts and at least four plasters on her arm.

"Nui! What the heck happened? Did you fall into a cactus?" Some scrapes looked quite red. "Damn it. Is that going to leave scars?"

"Ha, hilarious. Not! This happened last night when I had the seizure, or whatever it was. I dropped a glass and a plate and then fell on top of the pieces. You should see my legs. I mean your legs. Not too pretty, I'm afraid. Sorry." She pointed at the long linen trousers she was wearing.

"Are you serious? I had no idea. You didn't say anything about injuries last night."

Nui waved me off. "It's superficial. But you know, Luna, I was thinking about the seizure. I still believe it has something to do with the switch. I mean, you said you've never had an episode like it, and neither have I. So why would it happen now? Should I go to the hospital for a check-up?"

Dammit.

"Nah, I honestly don't think that's necessary. It probably was just a one-off. Let's forget about it unless something else happens. Don't worry so much."

Nui stopped walking and pulled me back to look at her.

"Me, worrying? Seriously? You're the one who's always worried about everything." Unexpectedly, she started laughing. "Khun Luna, you so Thai, mai pen rai, na kha?"

With that, she pushed open the door to our classroom.

I blew out a breath. *I really hate that phrase, but if it got Nui off the subject, I'd take it. Crisis averted. For now.*

27

NUI

A CLUSTER OF CLASSMATES HAD GATHERED AROUND A DESK at the back of the room. I couldn't see what had gotten everyone's attention, but I could hear giggling and suppressed snorting. Suddenly, a familiar voice raised over the clamour.

"No, really, that's what happened. You should have seen the size of…" The rest was lost in more laughter.

"Ahem, ladies and gentlemen, seats please!" Mr Adams, our math teacher, had entered the room.

The group looked up and drifted, still sniggering, back to their own desks, revealing the source of the entertainment: Yumi. Naturally.

As soon as she saw me, she jumped up and windmilled her arms to get my attention. "Luna, over here! I saved you a seat."

"That's ok Yumi, I have a seat right here." I waved at her and sat down next to Luna. Yumi looked crestfallen, but quickly picked up her phone and started typing. Sure enough, my phone pinged.

'What's your next class? I'm in English Lit. Shall we
have lunch together?'

"Ms. Wilson, is that correct?" Mr Adams called from the
front. "You're new here, so I assume you're not yet familiar
with our rules. Please turn off your phone and put it in your
bag. Unless you want me to confiscate it right now?"

Yumi rolled her eyes, but did as she was asked. I had
already turned mine off to avoid more messages.

"Shit Luna, she'll be in English Lit and you won't be
there." I whispered out of the side of my mouth. Luna was
clamping her lips to keep from laughing. At least someone
was having fun!

"Relax. What can she do? You'll get used to her," Luna
whispered back.

"Ladies, anything important you want to share with the
class?" Mr Adams called from the front, looking pointedly at
us and sounding slightly annoyed. "If I could get everyone's
attention please, so we can start?"

The rest of the class was uneventful except for a test date
announced for the following Monday. I wasn't too worried
about that since Luna and I were pretty equal in math.

As soon as the bell rang, Yumi popped up and ran over,
hooking her arm through mine. "Are you in English Lit too?
Shall we go?"

I seriously didn't know how she breathed and talked at
the same time. Turning to Luna, I made introductions. "Yumi
this is my friend Nui, Nui this is Yumi, an old friend from
Shanghai. She just started here."

Luna smiled at her warmly. "Hi Yumi, nice to meet you.
Welcome to BIS. When did you arrive?"

Yumi perfunctorily nodded at Luna, but instead of
answering, tugged me towards the door. I made a face at
Luna.

During English Lit, Yumi repeatedly whispered questions until Miss Monroe became fed up and moved her to another desk. I didn't think I'd ever been more grateful to a teacher.

For the next two hours, Yumi thankfully had theatre class, while Luna and I were back together in 'Social Bases of Behaviour'. We were late walking into the cafeteria.

Yumi jumped up on her seat and hollered across the room, "Luna, over here. I saved you a seat."

"Argh, she is too much. Luna, help!" I groaned. Yumi's exuberance was exhausting.

Luna giggled, finding my entrapment quite amusing, which annoyed me even more. Maybe she was glad I had to deal with Yumi instead of her, even though they had claimed to be friends in the past.

"Come on, let's join her and I'll try to intervene." Luna dragged me over to Yumi's table.

"Hi Yumi. How are you finding BIS? Everything ok?" Luna asked politely.

Yumi turned to me, and with a slight head twist at Luna, said, "Zen Yang Cai Ke Yi Rang Ta Xiao Shi? Wo Xiang Dan Du He Ni Liao Liao?" I stared at her, open-mouthed. What she'd just said sounded Chinese.

Luna straightened up and without missing a beat responded in a very firm voice, "Ni Hen Wu Li, Ni Ying Gai Geng Jing Sheng, Ni Bu Hui Zhi Dao Shui Zai Shuo Tong Yi Ge Yu Yan."

Yumi's head snapped back and for the first time since she'd shown up, she was speechless.

The two girls stared at each other, daring the other to blink first.

Yumi broke first, nodded, then bowed her head slightly and said to Luna in English, "You're right. I apologize, that *was* rude of me. I'm very sorry." She sounded like she meant it, too.

Luna waved the apology aside. "Ok, let's start again. Can we sit down?"

"Sure." Yumi moved aside to make space at the table.

I didn't know what had just happened, but I figured Luna would fill me in later. At least Yumi seemed a bit more subdued now.

"So, how was your morning, Yumi?" I asked. "And tell me, when did you arrive in Bangkok? It was such a surprise when you showed up yesterday."

"Ah, it's a boring story, really. Parents, divorce, one kid goes with mom, one with dad, end of story." The words made it sound like it wasn't a big deal, but she avoided eye contact delivering what sounded like a well-rehearsed story. Clearly, it meant more to her than she let on.

"How often do you go to Japan to see your mom?" Luna asked.

"I haven't yet. Dad worries Mom won't let me come back if I do." Yumi looked down at her hands wrapped around a bottle of water in a white-knuckled grip. "Can we talk about something else, please? Luna, you're coming to the reception tonight, aren't you? Please do. I don't want to be alone with all those boring adults."

I momentarily felt sorry for her and said, "Sure, I'll come. I might be a few minutes late. Nui and I are meeting some friends beforehand."

"Can I come?"

I looked at Luna and raised my eyebrows in question.

Luna shrugged. "Sure, why not? What's one more?"

Suddenly, I felt like giggling. This was going to be one messy meeting. Toey and Dearn assuming Luna was me, and now Yumi assuming I was Luna. What could possibly go wrong?

28

LUNA

Nui's hair was still wet from her swimming class by the time we left school. She was grinning, so I assumed she had managed to not embarrass herself or me. The plasters were off and the cuts looked less red. We made sure Luke was on the school van home, then we had to rush to get to Thong Lo on time. Yumi fell into step with us walking to the station, so there was no time for Nui and me to catch up on anything privately.

As usual, Yumi kept up the non-stop string of questions and observations, but at least now both Nui and I could take turns in responding when she paused long enough to wait for an answer. She didn't have an assigned buddy yet and said she didn't need one now that I—meaning Nui, in my body— was here and could show her around.

Walking into The Coffee Club on soi four, I spotted Toey and Dearn already seated at the back. The table in front of them looked like the dessert buffet at Dad's hotel, filled with chocolate coloured frappes, brownies, and cheesecake. Even being in Nui's body, I could not bring myself to indulge like that. Years of watching my weight were simply too ingrained in me, especially in Asia, where I felt like a giant among the skinny local girls. Mom always said I was slim and toned, but I guess my head didn't quite believe it. But, perhaps a little treat was ok today since I wouldn't be putting pounds onto my own frame. A neat side benefit of the switch. The day had just become a little brighter.

"Hi Nui, sabai di mai?" Toey stood up, smiling.

"Hi Toey, how are you?" I deliberately answered in English. Nui said both Toey and Dearn spoke it reasonably well and I wanted to include Yumi in the conversation.

"I'd like you to meet Luna and this is Yumi, Luna's friend who just moved here from Shanghai." After the introductions, Nui, Yumi and I went to the counter to order. I ended up with a passionfruit-mango smoothie and a double espresso, a sort of semi-indulgence for me. Nui began ordering what looked like a massive slice of Black Forest cake when I aimed a well-placed elbow into her side with a slight headshake. She rolled her eyes but went for the lesser evil of Thai Iced Tea and a blueberry muffin.

"You pay!" I ordered Nui in Thai. After all, it was my money. Nui rolled her eyes again, but shrugged and did as I asked. Yumi was too busy chatting with the barista to notice the interplay.

Back at the table there was a slightly awkward moment, with no-one sure who to talk to. Yumi, of course, was the one to kick off.

Turning to me, she said, "How come you speak Mandarin so fluently, Nui? You really took me by surprise." Bang! Just like that, she unwittingly tossed a live grenade into the room.

Toey and Dearn started laughing. "Nui doesn't speak Chinese. Where did you get that idea, Yumi?" Toey asked in between giggles. Apparently, it was inconceivable for them that Nui would speak another language besides English and Thai.

"Yes, she does!" Yumi frowned but insisted. "And she hardly has any accent, either. Where did you learn it, Nui?" Addressing Nui, she added, "You heard it too, Luna, didn't you? And I know you speak Mandarin." She sat back with an expression that said 'so there', as if she had proven her point.

I looked at Nui for help. She shrugged, but ignored Yumi's question and instead turned to her Thai friends.

"So Toey, you and Nui have been friends since first grade?"

Thankfully, Toey focused on Nui, but Yumi was still looking at me, waiting. Why was she so insistent? Normally, she didn't even pause for any response.

"I just picked up a few phrases here and there, Yumi." I mumbled.

"That was more than just a few phrases, Nui. And pretty flawless too," she said.

"Why does it matter? It's not such a big deal. See, Luna speaks Thai too." I should have just kept my mouth shut earlier, though she deserved the telling-off for being so rude.

Nui was chatting with Toey and Dearn in Thai. If the girls were surprised by 'Luna's' fluency, they didn't question it, but seemed relieved to converse in their own language. I didn't know how Nui managed to keep her story straight and not give away the fact she knew the girls better than they were aware of.

Yumi's eyes narrowed suspiciously. "Ok, this is weird. Didn't you say this is the first time Luna is meeting your friends? And she's learned fluent Thai in just a few months? That's pretty amazing. I didn't think Thai was that easy."

"Why are you so surprised, Yumi? You speak French,

Japanese, Mandarin and English too, after all." I was hoping this would get her off the topic, but it backfired.

"How do you know I speak French?" Yumi hissed.

Yikes! I had opened that trap myself.

"Never mind, Luna must have mentioned it. Can we talk about something else, please?" I tried to brush it off and picked up my smoothie.

Slurping the drink, I noticed Nui, Toey and Dearn were looking over my shoulder towards the entrance. I was about to turn when Dearn jumped up with a big smile and waved.

"Hi Channon!"

29

NUI

I IMMEDIATELY LOOKED AT LUNA. SHE HAD FROZEN WITH THE smoothie suspended mid-air. The colour drained from my face. I hated when I looked like that, all sickly grey. Her arm started shaking, and she barely managed to put the glass back down on the table, spilling some slush in the process. Her eyes locked onto mine like a racoon caught in the headlights, and she hunched over as if she was trying to make herself small and invisible.

"Hi everyone." Channon's smooth voice always sounded like he was smiling at a private joke. "This is a pleasant surprise. Luna, Toey, Dearn. Good to see you all."

Am I imagining it, or is he looking at me longer than is necessary? Maybe he's checking out Luna's body to see what his potential girlfriend would look like. Yikes. It was creepy to be sized up by a guy I had no interest in, but since Luna had told him about the switch, it wasn't entirely inconceivable. Stop it, Nui, you're just being paranoid.

Yumi jumped up and stuck out her hand. "Hi, I'm Yumi. I'm Luna's friend and just moved here. Who are you?"

Channon grinned and shook her hand.

"I'm Channon, Nui's friend."

Luna still hadn't turned around. Channon put his hand on her shoulder and I saw her flinch. I almost flinched in sympathy. This was like Channon going on a double date on his own. Touching me, but speaking with Luna. How much more convoluted could this get?

Luna turned slowly and mumbled, "Hi Channon, how are you?"

"I'm good, thanks. Can I talk to you for a second? I have Chone outside."

Luna gulped, but nodded and slowly pushed herself up. She banged into two chairs as she followed Channon outside.

"Who was that?" Yumi immediately started her inquisition. "He's gorgeous. Is he Nui's boyfriend? How come you all know him? And who's Chone?"

"We met him through Nui a few weeks ago," Toey explained. "He works at the pet hospital down the road." Turning to me, she added, "But Nui didn't seem too happy to see him this time. What's happened?"

"Um, it's complicated," I said. Three pairs of eyes focused on me in anticipation of juicy gossip.

"What's complicated? Come on, Luna, give!" Yumi said.

"Well, they work together at the hospital and Channon is friends with Nui's brother" I said.

"So, what's the problem?" Yumi asked. "There's something else going on, isn't there?"

"They've become quite close over the last few weeks and Channon adopted a husky, Chone, for Nui." I hoped this would be enough. Of course, such a simple explanation didn't satisfy Yumi.

"Hmm, that's pretty generous of him, assuming she wanted a dog, but it still doesn't explain why it's complicated, Luna. So, are they or are they not dating? Or is he gay?" She asked, straight-faced. Toey and Dearn followed our conversation intently, their heads moving back and forth like spectators at a ping-pong match, waiting for the set-point.

"Why are you asking me? If you really want to know just ask her, ok? I'm here to meet Toey and Dearn and I thought you wanted to meet some new people too, Yumi." That was as far as I could go. I didn't want to add fuel to the gossip mill, or have Toey and Dearn expect me to have had a boyfriend when Luna and I switched back, no matter how the situation between her and Channon panned out.

Yumi rolled her eyes. My statement wasn't sufficient for her, but tough luck. I deliberately shifted the conversation to find out what Toey and Dearn had been up to and tried to include Yumi as much as possible. It was actually a blessing to have her there, as I had to be careful not to reveal accidentally how much I knew about my Thai friends. It also distracted me from trying to see what was going on with Luna and Channon outside.

30

LUNA

MY STOMACH WAS CHURNING AND MY LEGS WERE WOBBLY AS I followed Channon onto the little deck in front of the shop. Chone was wagging his tail in double time as he recognized me. I was grateful to focus on him instead of Channon.

"Chone! How is my beautiful boy?" I knelt down and hugged him tight, burrowing my head in his grey fur. He had grown so big already and kept shaking his entire body, and me with him. I sat down on the deck to pet him, trying to keep my face away from his affectionate licks.

"Calm down Chone! Yes, yes, I know you're excited and I'm happy to see you, too." He finally stretched out next to me, still wagging his tail.

Channon pulled up a chair to sit opposite. I kept my eyes on Chone.

"So, Nui, I was thinking about our conversation yesterday," Channon began.

I didn't want to look at him, afraid I would start bawling if he decided to dump me.

"How did you know we were here?" I mumbled.

"I didn't. Sheer coincidence. I wanted a coffee for the drive home."

"Oh!" *Of all the times and places…*

"Nui, can you please look at me?"

I lifted my head but focused on his nose instead of his eyes.

"Nui?" Channon sounded slightly nervous himself.

Fine! I took a deep breath and looked up into his gorgeous eyes. "So, have you decided I'm completely nuts and you don't want to hang out anymore?" Pre-empting his verdict seemed easier than having him say it out loud.

Channon sat back. "Why do you say that? You know I like you. I admit, I'm confused about what you told me, but…" He paused and raked his hands through his hair. Was he looking for the kindest way to let me down? "Ok, here's the deal. I honestly can't believe that this switch between you and Luna really happened. I mean, it's just too out there for me." He raised his hand as I was about to interrupt him again.

"Wait, let me finish. You asked if I liked you as Nui or Luna, and I told you I can't make that distinction, as I only know you as Nui, remember?"

I nodded like one of Dad's weird bobbleheads that a friend gave him as a joke and dad insisted on taking everywhere. I was losing it. *Focus, Luna!*

"So, I was thinking, if the switch really happened, wouldn't it make sense then for you to just switch back and there would be no more confusion?"

His eyes were warm as always, his expression sincere.

I felt lightheaded, unaware I had been holding my breath. I gasped for air. This was definitely not what I had expected. Just a simple and straightforward solution.

"You mean…? Are you serious? But, I thought you were

angry with me because I lied to you." *Stop arguing against yourself, Luna!*

"I definitely don't like to be lied to or misled, but since I'm not convinced you actually did a mind swap..." he paused and cleared his throat. "But you said you did, and if that's the case, it should be easy enough for you to reverse it and you would still be you, wouldn't you? Just in a different package, so to speak." His eyebrows furrowed, as if he couldn't quite believe his own argument.

"Yeah, it would be me, but I'm a farang." *Luna, stop stacking obstacles in your own path.* "I mean, would that be an issue for you?"

"No idea. I've never dated a foreigner," Channon shrugged. "So, the issue has never come up." He stood up. "But you know, if you actually did a mind-swap, then I guess anything is possible, right?" He winked. "I have to get Chone home. Think about it and let me know what you decide." He picked up Chone's lead and then added, almost as an afterthought, "I think the biggest challenge would be to convince me I'm still talking to the same person. Not sure how you would do that."

He bent down to touch my shoulder, tugged on Chone's lead, and walked down the steps to the street. "See you tomorrow."

I stayed on the floor, too shocked to get up right away. *Did that really just happen? That was way too easy.* I frowned, not quite believing Channon would let me off the hook so readily. *And did he say he wanted to date me? Me? No matter what I looked like?* My heart went into freefall and I felt my face split into a huge grin. All I had to do was to get Nui to agree to switch tonight. And if she didn't, then I would make her.

31

NUI

EITHER LUNA'S DOUBLE ESPRESSO HAD KICKED IN OR Channon must have said something nice to her. She was beaming, looking a lot happier than she did just ten minutes ago.

"You look like Gollum when he got his Precious back, Nui!" Yumi definitely had a knack for the theatrical. I almost snorted out my Thai tea, but she had a point.

"Haha, hilarious, Yumi," Luna replied, rolling her eyes, but the smile stayed.

I raised an eyebrow, and she mouthed back 'later'.

"So, are you dating this guy, Nui?" Yumi pressed. "Why didn't he come back inside? And if you're not dating him, I wouldn't mind. He's gorgeous!" Yumi feigned a shiver.

"Yumi! Cut it out, ok? It's none of your business," Luna half-heartedly scolded her, but I could tell she was too cheerful to be bothered.

"Hey Yumi, look at the time. We better get going. Dad said the reception starts at six, right?" I intervened, though I was dying to hear what had happened between Luna and Channon.

Yumi sighed. "I hate those events, but Dad would kill me if I missed it. Can I come with you and wait while you change, then we go to the embassy together? We live on the compound, so I'll be ready in five."

I shook my head. "We'll be a few minutes late. Dad said to meet him at the hotel at six. So, you better go straight home and get ready. I'll see you there." Besides, I wanted to call Luna without Yumi overhearing us.

Luna's phone pinged just as we were standing up. Her smile turned into a frown and then alarm. She jumped up flapping her hands.

"Damn. I completely forgot my rabies shots. Mae is waiting at Samitivej. Shit, shit, shit!" Luna muttered in panic.

Toey and Dearn looked at her wide-eyed. They didn't know about the dogfight and they definitely weren't used to hearing me swear like that. I felt like using a few choice words myself since it was my body getting the shots.

"A wolf, Gollum, and now rabies? You are seriously weird, Nui!" Yumi shook her head, either in wonder or envy. "And I've only known you for a few hours. Can't wait to see what's next."

I burst into a full belly laugh, my eyes streaming with tears. The girl was growing on me. I wondered what she would say if she knew about the mind swap?

32

LUNA

I HADN'T FINISHED MY SMOOTHIE, BUT THERE WAS NO TIME. It would take me at least twenty minutes to get to the hospital, even by moto-taxi. Mae sounded pissed off already, and this time it would be justified. I grabbed my bag, waved at the girls, and dashed out. There was a moto-taxi stand right in front of the café, and thankfully, in the last two weeks, I had become a pro at riding side-saddle on the back.

Mae was pacing the emergency lobby with short staccato steps that radiated annoyance when I walked up to her.

"I'm so sorry Mae. I was with Dearn and Toey and we forgot the time." I grovelled and wai'ed.

"Seriously, Nui. Where is your head these days? I had to leave the shop and you can't even be bothered to remember? This has got to stop. You've become really scattered these last weeks. If you can't take care of your responsibilities, then…"

"Mae, I'm really, really sorry. It won't happen again," I

interrupted. I didn't want her to get any ideas about curfews or stricter rules.

I could tell it didn't mollify her, but luckily we were in a public space, and I figured she wouldn't make a scene. Hopefully, by the time we got home, she would have calmed down again. She shook her head and grabbed my arm. "Come on, we're late, and I have to get back to the shop."

The doctor checked the puncture wounds and confirmed there was no infection, so I just had to use the bandage for a few more days to keep any dirt out. The shot itself wasn't a big deal, or I hardly felt it because I was replaying the conversation with Channon in my head.

After Mae had paid the bill, we jumped in a cab and she dropped me at home before continuing on to the store.

"We'll talk about this later!" Her statement sounded foreboding.

As usual, Khun Yaa was working at the counter, grinding something in her stone mortar. It had a fresh tangy smell, and I was looking forward to dinner, suddenly starving. Duen had a book open in front of her at the kitchen table, but was more interested in chatting with her grandmother.

"Did you get your shot, Nui?" Khun Yaa asked.

"Yes, done, and no infection. All good."

"Is that why you're smiling?"

I hadn't realized I was still grinning.

"It was nice to see Toey and Dearn."

"If you missed them so much, maybe you should go to their school?" Khun Yaa raised an eyebrow.

"No, no! I mean, it was nice to see them, but we can still meet even if we don't go to the same school." Why did she keep suggesting I switch schools? Nui fought really hard to get into BIS. I knew I should at least make sure she stayed.

"She's probably smiling because she saw her boyfriend, right Nui?" Duen piped up.

"What boyfriend?" I rolled my eyes and tilted my head towards Khun Yaa, hoping Duen would get the message this wasn't a subject to be discussed in front of her.

"You have more than one?" Duen laughed out loud. "I mean Chaaaannnon. Did you kiss him already?" Little sisters were a pain.

"Mind your own business! Channon is not my boyfriend. We're just friends."

Instead of letting it go, Duen launched into an old playground song, smacking her lips.

> "Nui and Channon
> Sitting in a tree
> K-I-S-S…

"Stop it!" Khun Yaa didn't understand English so I didn't have to worry about that, but how did Duen know this silly rhyme in the first place. My protest only egged her on.

> "K-I-S-S-I-N-G!
> First comes love
> Then comes marriage
> Then comes baby
> In a baby carriage!"

Khun Yaa was watching us from the stove, amused, if not puzzled. I had to laugh despite myself. "Are you done now?" I swatted Duen lightly on the shoulder, then looked at the clock above the table.

"I'm gonna get started on some homework, Khun Yaa. Or do you need help?"

"Go, go, we eat in half an hour."

Perfect, just enough time to call Nui. I went to the boys' room to avoid Duen barging in on our talk.

33

NUI

LUNA CALLED JUST AS THE TAXI PULLED INTO THE HOTEL driveway. It had been a mad dash to get home, shower, change into a dress, check on Luke, then rush to meet Luna's dad. I had five minutes before we were to leave for the embassy. I stayed near the big entrance doors to keep an eye out for Khun Mark.

"Hey Luna, everything go ok at the hospital?"

"Yeah, no problem, but your mom was furious that I forgot. Hope she's in a better mood later. "

"Just grovel a bit and she'll come around."

"Will do."

"Phew, what a crazy day today, Luna! What was that all about at lunchtime? What did Yumi say to you or, I guess, to me?"

Luna laughed. "Ha! She wanted to get rid of me so she could talk to you alone. It was quite rude, actually. Guess she didn't expect me to understand," Luna replied, sounding gleeful.

"I suppose she deserved that, but you know, Luna, we need to be more careful. I mean, I don't think anyone would ever suspect a switch, but if we mess up now, it will become too difficult to explain when we've switched back."

"Yeah, I know, but I keep forgetting Yumi doesn't know me as you."

"I hear you. I had a hard time remembering that with Toey and Dearn, too. Which reminds me, what happened between you and Channon?"

"Channon was amazing!" Luna sighed. "He said he's never dated a farang, but he has no issues with it. He said we should just reverse the switch, then see where it leads. Oh my God, Nui, he was so great. So, all we have to do is switch back tonight."

I froze. "He what? Wait a minute. You mean Channon just accepted that you and I did a mind swap? You've got to be kidding me!" There was no way anyone could just roll with something like this.

"Yeah, isn't that amazing? I don't think he fully believed it, and I totally expected him to say I was crazy, but now…" Luna trailed off, probably picturing herself walking with Channon into the sunset.

"Luna, are you nuts? That's not normal! I can't believe he would just say that."

Seriously, was this guy for real?

"I told you he's a great guy, Nui, and that just shows you." Luna's way of interpreting things was mind-boggling.

"No Luna, it actually shows he doesn't really care one way or another! You can't tell me you would just accept that if the roles were reversed, would you?"

"He said I would need to prove somehow that I'm me when I'm back in my body, but I don't think it'll be that difficult really, as you hardly talked to him. So, can we switch back tonight?"

I started pacing back and forth on the marble floor, my heels clicking loudly matching my irritation with Luna.

"No, we cannot just switch tonight, Luna. We made a deal, remember?" There she goes again, off in her own fairy-land, not even remotely considering my side. "And besides, why does everything revolve around Channon now? Yesterday, you wanted to switch back to avoid him and today you want to swap so he'll get to know you as Luna. The whole point of the switch was about experiencing each other's family life, not about dating some random guy."

There was silence on the other end.

"It's not about Channon and he's not some random guy. He's Krit's friend too, don't forget. Mom's back tomorrow anyway, so what difference does it make?"

"Exactly. In any case, I can't meet up tonight as I have to go to the reception now with your dad."

"Well, it's not like we need to be in the same room to make the switch." Luna snapped, clearly offended I hadn't caved in immediately.

"Excuse me? What do you mean, we don't have to be together? Of course we do!"

"That's not the only way," Luna replied, sourly.

I was about to snap back, but paused mid-breath and stopped in my tracks. A shiver ran down my back as a flash of dread hit me. The seizure! I nearly dropped the phone, as if Luna had kicked me. *No way. No way!*

I barely squeezed out the words through my gritted teeth, "What exactly does that mean, Luna? Are you saying you've tried before?" My thoughts were racing. *Come on, Nui, this can't be true. She wouldn't go this far. She heard Ajaarn say how dangerous it is to force a swap. But why would she make a comment like that?*

I heard Luna inhale sharply. "No, of course not. Don't be silly, Nui. I gotta go. Khun Yaa is calling. I'll talk to you later. Have fun with Yumi." Her shaky voice did not convince me in the least.

"Luna, wait!" Too late, she had clicked off.

"Who is this Luna, honey?" I jerked around as Khun Mark walked up to me. I had been too focused on the conversation to notice.

"Or were you talking to yourself?" he winked.

"What? Nah, there's a new girl at school and we happen to have the same name." Lame, but I couldn't think of anything else to say. I was nearly shaking with shock. Thankfully, he didn't question it at any further.

"Come on then. We're running late." Luna's dad took my arm as we walked out of the lobby to the waiting car. I could barely stand the thought of facing a group of strangers and having to deal with perky Yumi right now. But when would I get another chance to attend a reception at the American Embassy? Conversations with Yumi were very one-sided anyway, and maybe she would distract me for a while. I was sure I'd be up all night worrying about Luna attempting another switch.

34

LUNA

Stupid, stupid, stupid! I slapped my forehead and groaned. How could I have been so careless? Even though I hadn't outright admitted the one-sided mind push, if Nui made the connection between her 'seizure' and my comment would she dig in and refuse to switch in retaliation? She had already suggested a link between the two events. Argh, why couldn't I have waited another day or two until Mom was home? I had messed up big time.

Duen poked her head around the door, interrupting my fretting.

"Come on Nui, dinner's ready."

The family had gathered around the kitchen table waiting for Khun Yaa to put the last bowls of food on the table. Though it smelled delicious, my appetite had vanished.

"Sit down Nui, we want to talk to you," Mae began after she had filled her plate with steamed rice and red beef curry.

Darn. So she hadn't forgotten her earlier threat.

I dutifully sat and waited.

Paa said, "A few weeks ago, the mall management approached us and offered to expand our shop into the one next door. We've talked it over and we're thinking of converting the second shop into a Thai cooking school. We've hired an architect to look at what's doable in that space. If we go ahead, it'll require some investment." He paused for a moment to eat some curry. I stopped eating all together and waited, surprised. This had nothing to do with me forgetting the hospital appointment.

Mae picked up the thread. "If we go ahead, we need to find the money for the conversion and we don't want to take out another loan. So, we've been thinking. Your school costs a lot of money, and lately it doesn't seem you're taking it seriously enough to justify the expense."

I felt the blood drain from my head. *Please don't say it.*

"But…" I stammered, helplessly.

Mae raised her fork to stop my protest.

"We haven't gotten the last details and cost yet, but we wanted you to be aware."

I swallowed, although my mouth had gone completely dry.

"But… but that's not fair. Why do I have to pay the price for the stupid shop?"

"Nui!" Paa angrily slapped his hand on the table, making us all jump. "That stupid shop is paying for your tuition in the first place. You better remember that!"

"Sorry Paa, I didn't mean it that way." I carefully put my fork and spoon down on my plate. "I know that the school is expensive, but it'll give me so many more opportunities later on. Wasn't that what you wanted for me, too?"

"We understand that, Nui, and that's why we worked it out so you could go. But you seem to have forgotten our agreement." Mae raised an eyebrow.

"What agreement?" I wished I could take the words back as soon as I said them.

Mae shook her head. "See, this is what I mean. Lately, you seem to be more interested in hanging out with Channon, going to the pet hospital, playing with dogs and meeting your friends. We will not continue to pay for that."

"But…" I started, but didn't know how to continue. While I did all those things, I hadn't expected Nui's parents making an issue of it.

"Besides…" Mae continued, "Your brothers and sister all went to local schools, so it's not really fair that we pay only for you to go to BIS."

"But did they even want to go? I mean, I never heard Duen mention she's interested."

"I don't want to go because I'll become a cook like Grandma," Duen piped up. "And for that, I don't need a diploma from some fancy school."

Khun Yaa smiled at her, indulgently.

"Fine, so it's no big deal to you anyway, is it?" I countered.

"Of course it is, if it means they can't build the cooking school that I might take over one day." She gave me a pointed look, challenging me to question her statement. *Backstabber. For goodness' sake, you're only thirteen. How can you think this far ahead?* I was speechless. I never thought much about money and hadn't realized that Nui's family had to be so cautious with it.

"Anyway, we expect to get the plans back next week, then we'll look at it again." Mae continued. "In the meantime, I want to see some genuine commitment from you to your studies, and more attention to the family and your duties. It's unacceptable that you forget things like the hospital appointment today. It's bad enough that you have to have the shots. The least you could do is remember them. Is that clear?"

"Yes Mae, of course." I even wai'ed to her to show my seriousness.

Nui is going to freak out. This will jeopardize all her dreams for the future and she'll blame it on me. I can't tell her, otherwise she won't want to switch back, especially if her alternative is to go to the States with my family.

35

NUI

THE DRIVER HAD TO DROP US AT THE EMBASSY GATE FOR safety reasons. Years ago, we had been able to look into the beautiful gardens from the street, but with increased terrorist threats, they built a wall around the grounds, only allowing official vehicles inside. After the security scan, we slowly followed a few other people through the estate towards a group of low-rise buildings. A little pond with aerators bubbled to the left, and spotlights made the droplets sparkle. A few jasmine trees along the path smelled delicious. Once we reached the Embassy building, I'd almost forgotten I was in the middle of downtown Bangkok.

A doorman welcomed us inside and directed us to a lounge where at least fifty adults in suits and cocktail dresses were already standing in groups, chatting, while servers passed through with trays of canapes and drinks. Instrumental jazz played softly in the background. A photographer was roaming, taking staged photos of different clusters of people while his assistant recorded the names. The pictures would probably appear in *The Bangkok Post* or *The Nation* in the next few days. It looked surprisingly pre-arranged for what I thought was supposed to be an informal gathering, and everyone seemed to know what was expected of them except me. Khun Mark stopped to scan the room like a general surveying his battlefield. I was waiting beside him to see what would happen next.

"Finally." A hand grabbed my arm. Yumi.

"Hi Mr Taylor, how are you? Nice to see you again. Were you surprised when my dad called?"

"Hello Yumi. Lovely to see you, too. Yes, it was quite a surprise, but it's nice to have some old friends in town again. Where's your dad?" Khun Mark smiled at Yumi.

"He's making his rounds. He'll probably be here in a minute. Can I grab Luna for a moment, please?"

"I want to say hi to your dad first, Yumi," I said. It would be best to make the introduction with Khun Mark beside me, just in case Mr Wilson referred to Luna's history with the family.

"Come on then, I'll take you."

Following Yumi, I got a look at her outfit. Gone was the goth costume. Instead, she was wearing a fitted, knee-length black dress with gauzy long sleeves and a few sparkling sequins. Her hair was in a low ponytail, with no purple streaks in sight. Small silver earrings with pearl drops, strappy high heels and a fuchsia coloured stole completed the outfit. Even her lipstick matched the shawl. If she hadn't approached me, I wouldn't have recognized her. The transformation was extraordinary.

"Yumi, you look fabulous! So different from this morning."

"You mean this old dress? It's my uniform. Dad always insists I wear something 'proper' when I attend his functions." She waved off the compliment. "I wish I could shake it up a bit, but no, it's always the same-same—same kind of reception, same kind of dress, same kind of people. Same boooooring!" She whispered.

I cringed self-consciously at Yumi's casual remark. I had little time to get ready after we left the café, but I wouldn't have known how to dress differently anyway. Luna had an enormous selection of dresses, but they weren't really my style or colours. Her clothes were all much more loose fitting than mine, so I had picked a sleeveless navy chiffon dress with a tiny tulip pattern and added a thin silver belt to give it a bit of shape. Together with mid-heel sandals and a pearl necklace, I had felt pretty sophisticated until I saw Yumi's cool elegance. I rarely got a chance to dress up and didn't have the practise.

Before I could comment, Yumi spoke again, "Hey Dad, Mr Taylor and Luna want to say hello." She tugged at the jacket of a tall dark-haired gentleman who paused in mid-conversation and turned around with a slight frown.

"Yumi, don't do that, it's not polite." He turned again to apologize to the couple he had been talking to, then offered a broad smile and handshake to Luna's dad.

"Mark, it's so good to see you again. And you, Luna! Wow, you've become quite the young lady. How are you both?"

"Welcome to Bangkok, Jake! It was such a wonderful surprise to hear from you. Susan sends her regards. How do you like it here so far?"

"Thanks Mark. I guess you of all people know what it's like starting a new job in a new city. A whirlwind as usual, and I haven't really been able to catch my breath yet. We must have dinner soon to catch up." Mr Wilson turned to me.

"I'm so glad Yumi and you are going to the same school again, Luna. That'll make things easier for her."

Yumi rolled her eyes. "Dad! It's not like this is the first time we moved. Can Luna and I go now?" She tugged my arm again before I could say anything, steering me out of the room towards the terrace outside, grabbing sodas on the way out.

"This is so annoying, always the same chit-chat. Nice to see you. No, so nice to see *you*. Don't they ever get bored with that?" She shuddered.

I grinned. The dress was simply a disguise—it was definitely still Yumi inside.

We dropped into wicker chairs facing the pond. Thankfully, some citronella coils had been lit to keep the bugs away.

"So, why did Nui need to get rabies shots? That girl is so weird." Yumi said, beginning another interrogation.

"She rescued a puppy and got bitten herself. But she said everything's fine."

"So, is she your best friend now?"

I looked at Yumi, and from her expression I could tell she hoped I would say no.

"Sure, Nui and I are close, but that doesn't mean I'm not your friend, too. After all, we have history, right?" I wasn't sure how I really felt about Luna right now, but Yumi didn't need to know that. My comment perked her up.

"Right! So what are we gonna do this weekend? Can you show me around?" She waved her arms around before grabbing her soda. "What do we do first? What's your favourite part of Bangkok? Want to go to a movie?"

I wasn't paying attention as my eyes had locked onto Yumi's arm. Her sleeve had slipped back and as she grabbed her soda, the spotlights above shone down onto multiple faded scar lines on the inside of her arm. Yumi caught me staring and hastily pulled down both sleeves, a series of emotions rippling across her face. Shame, embarrassment, guilt, defensiveness. A little of each.

"Yumi?" I started.

She put up a hand like a traffic cop. "No, don't say anything. I don't want to talk about it." She didn't pretend I had imagined what I saw.

I swallowed and looked away. Did the scars mean Yumi had harmed herself? I had heard of people cutting themselves as some kind of self-therapy, but didn't know more than that. Things must have been pretty bad for her to have gone that far. I was shocked and felt sorry for her, but I didn't feel it was my place to probe.

"Sure, I can take you around and show you some places. But tomorrow is out—Mom is coming home. And tomorrow evening, Dad has his staff party and we have to attend."

"What about Sunday? Can we do something then?" Yumi was persistent, if not desperate.

"Can I text you tomorrow? I want to see how Mom is first. She'll be jetlagged. I want to keep it open in case she needs me for something, ok?"

Yumi pouted a bit, disappointed, but then nodded in understanding.

"Sure, let me know."

For the next twenty minutes, Yumi and I did our own version of mindless chit-chat. Nothing serious, just gossip about school and suggestions of places to show her in Bangkok. I tried to ask a bit more about her family, but Yumi was quick to move off that topic.

"Listen, how would you feel if you had to choose between your dad and your mom? No matter what you do, you'll end up feeling guilty and it's not fair of them to put you in that position. So, can we please not talk about it?"

"I'm so sorry Yumi. That must have been a terrible decision to make. I can't imagine what I would do."

"I guess in the end you can only do what you feel is best for yourself, even if it upsets some people. I'm ok with it now." She shrugged. "Took me a while but I really am ok now." She nodded, either to reassure me or herself.

I wasn't sure I believed her completely, but in the back of my mind I realized Luna and I were going through a similar divorce process right now. The big difference was our case involved a complete family on both sides, and they were ignorant of what was going on.

My stomach lurched as I remembered my earlier conversation with Luna. I stood up.

"I better get going, Yumi. I still have some work to do. But listen, call me if you need anything, ok? Otherwise, I'll see you maybe Sunday, or Monday in school, then we'll make some plans, alright?"

Yumi looked disappointed, but stood up.

"Sure! I'll walk you out. And Luna, please don't mention this to anyone, ok? It's my business to deal with." She tugged her arm into mine and together we walked back inside to look for our dads.

36

LUNA

EVERY TIME I TOOK ONE STEP FORWARD, I ENDED UP TAKING two steps back. First, Channon put me on cloud nine, then Mae pulled me back to planet earth, and then I tripped over my stupid blunder with Nui.

"Wouldn't it be nice if life could just move forward in one direction?" I asked Joey as we trudged through the neighbourhood. "Why does everything have to be so complicated?"

Joey looked up at me but offered no comment. I had used him as my excuse to escape the loaded atmosphere at home.

"You know Joey, here's the thing. If I go back to being 'me', then Channon may or may not want to date me. There's no guarantee either way. So, wouldn't it be better if I stayed as Nui? But what happens if Mom and Dad decide to move back to the States? I can't just let them go while I stay here, can I? But if we swap back, and then we move, I'll lose Channon and Chone, anyway. So what would you do?"

Another thought nagged at me. Although I hadn't answered Nui's question of whether I would have reacted like

Channon had if our roles were reversed, suspicion had crept in about the ease with which Channon had accepted the switch. Did that mean he didn't care one way or another what I looked like? Was that being disloyal to him, or did Nui have a point? I suppose I could take it as a compliment that he wasn't swayed by looks, but did I honestly believe that?

"What do you think, Joey? Is it normal to just say, *sure, whatever body you come in, I'll date you?*"

Joey still didn't reply, but kept sniffing every lamp post as if there was something vastly different about them since our walk earlier that day.

"Yeah, right, I thought so! There's no good answer, is there?"

I shrugged, then felt silly and quickly glanced around to make sure no one was listening to my monologue. A few people were rushing by, but no one paid me any attention. We had reached our park and Joey scampered off under the trees to do his business.

"And what about Nui? I know she wants to study abroad, but would she really leave her own family? She's definitely more ambitious than me, and if her parents end up taking her out of BIS…" I mumbled to myself. I wasn't getting anywhere with these questions, and I had no-one to ask for advice. Waiting for Joey, I picked up my phone to check messages. Nothing.

Yumi's face flashed in my mind. She too had had to decide between a traditional family life in Japan and the free expat life with her dad. How did she come up with the right solution? Maybe I could just ask her some general questions about it?

I sent a quick text to Nui to ask for Yumi's number.

37

NUI

KHUN PAK DROVE US HOME. I WAS EXHAUSTED AND mindlessly watched the traffic moving alongside us. This day had been one giant disaster. First, discovering Luna's likely violation, then finding out about Yumi's shocking secret. If I was completely honest, I was no better myself. *A month ago, your biggest concern was to be home in time for dinner, and now you're actually considering a move to the US and setting up the blog behind Luna's back.* Were we all completely messed up?

Traffic had stopped at the top of the little hill on Witthayu before it dropped to Petchaburi. There were hundreds of cars in front of us, red brake lights glowing while the traffic light at the T-section had just begun its countdown from two hundred seconds. We'd be waiting for a while.

"Dad, when did you first decide to go abroad?" I asked Khun Mark.

Luna's dad looked up from his phone in surprise. "Why do you ask, honey?"

"I'm just curious. Was there something in particular that made you decide to leave home? Did you feel guilty about leaving Grandma and Grandpa?"

"What's going on, Luna? Why do you want to know?" Khun Mark turned fully towards me, his phone forgotten.

"I was talking to Yumi, and she mentioned it was really hard to decide to go with her dad or stay with her mom and she felt guilty either way." I wasn't going to share the rest of what I had found out that night.

Luna's dad looked over my shoulder into the distance, contemplating my question. "Ah yes, I can imagine it must have been tough. For me, it was different. I think the hardest part was when I left home for the first time to go to college and then hotel school. I was really homesick for the first few months, but then it became kind of liberating, if you know what I mean?"

I nodded, though I hadn't really experienced that yet. While I wasn't living at home right then, at least I could see my family if I wanted to.

"After that, it was much easier to move abroad, and I was lucky that your uncle and aunt stayed in England, so I knew Mom and Dad had family around if they needed them. That has always been a tremendous relief."

"Yes, I can understand that."

"But do I still feel guilty sometimes? Sure I do, but mostly, I'm worried that if there's an actual emergency with your grandparents, I may not be able to get home fast enough, depending on where we're living. That's really tough to think about sometimes," he admitted.

"Hmm, I never thought of that." I knew, of course, that I wouldn't see my family much if I were to study abroad, but it would be completely different if I went as Luna. Then, there would be no valid reason to go home, even if there was a genuine emergency. Given Khun Yaa's heart condition, was I really prepared to do that?

"But Luna, you know these decisions have to be made, and only you can know what suits you best. Your Mom and I can try to guide you and help you choose, but ultimately it comes down to what you're comfortable with, no?" He smiled. "Besides, like you said, you've seen enough of the world already that you may want to stick close to home base in future, anyway." He winked.

I turned to look out the window. He was right. It was my decision to make, only in this case it involved his own daughter, too. Traffic just started rolling again.

"Thanks Dad. I'll think about it."

38

LUNA

Instead of just texting Yumi's number, Nui FaceTimed me. I was reluctant to answer, afraid she would ask about the seizure again, but I knew I would have to face her eventually.

"Hey Nui, how was the reception? Did you meet Yumi's dad? What did you do to my hair?" It looked like she had tried to twist it into some kind of updo, but it looked slightly messy. Or maybe it was intentional, sort of casual chic. Not bad. Nui blushed, quickly pulled some pins from her head and shrugged.

"Never mind. Yeah, I met him, although I didn't get to talk to him. Yumi wanted to escape from the party. She looked amazing, all dressed up. You wouldn't have recognized her." Nui looked impressed. "So, why do you need Yumi's number?"

"Why? Is it a secret?" Her question surprised me.

"No, of course not. I'll text it to you. It's just…" Nui hesitated.

"Just what? What happened?" Now I was intrigued.

"I can't really talk about it, but I think I've misjudged Yumi a bit. There's a lot more going on with her than she lets on. I think she's a bit fragile."

"Yumi, fragile?" I almost laughed at the very idea. "Not the Yumi I know."

"But you haven't talked to her in three years, so you wouldn't really know, would you?"

"Why are you being so cryptic, Nui? What's happened? Is she ok?"

"Listen, I can't say anything else. I promised her. Just be nice when you talk to her, okay?"

Now I felt put out. "Of course I'm nice to her, and remember, she was my friend first."

Nui shook her head, strangely subdued. "That's not the point, Luna. Let's just leave it at that."

Weird, but I decided not to pry any further. "Fine, I just wanted to ask her a question."

"I think she's really lonely. Maybe you could meet her tomorrow. I can't. Your mom's landing around eleven, so by the time she gets home it'll probably be noon or one o'clock, then your dad's staff party is at six."

"Let me talk to Yumi and see what she's up to. I'm not sure if I can meet her tomorrow either. Your mom was really upset with me about the hospital earlier, so I should see if I have to stick around here." I didn't want to tell Nui about the threat to her future at BIS. I needed to make sure she didn't reconsider returning to our own families for the sake of her education.

Although I was dying to bring up our switch back again, I was afraid it would only prompt Nui to ask about the seizure. *When Mom's home, she will no longer have a reason to stall, so I can wait another day.* Nui saved me from bringing up either subject.

"Luna, I better go. I want to finish up some things. I'll call you tomorrow when your mom is back, ok?" Nui said.

"Sure, don't forget to text me Yumi's number. Night," I said, then hung up.

What an odd conversation. It felt as if we were both tiptoeing around each other. Nui's strange mood had rubbed off on me. Or more likely, it was my guilt at having withheld information from her once again. These days, I barely recognized myself. I'd never thought of myself as being mean, but lying to Nui—or omitting facts from her twice—revealed a side of me I didn't want to examine too closely. Before I could slide any further down that slippery road of thought, I texted Yumi to find out what she was up to.

39

NUI

AFTER I HUNG UP, I SAT FOR A FEW MINUTES STARING AT MY laptop, pondering what to do next. Luna stayed quiet about the switch this time. Most likely, she didn't want to explain her earlier comment. I still didn't know what to make of her suggestion that we didn't have to be in the same room to swap. How would she know? The only explanation I could think of was she had tried it, and possibly caused my seizure. Would she make another attempt, even though she had agreed to wait? Now that I'd had more time to think about it, I doubted she would, especially having heard how excruciatingly painful the spasm was. If she had any sense at all, she wouldn't dare jeopardise her own body that way. But, if she tried again, there was nothing I could do except push back, and we would find out who had the stronger will. At least I was forewarned now.

I needed to concentrate on the blog and be ready to run it regardless of where I ended up next week. I wouldn't be able to hold Luna off after her mom was back without breaking our deal myself.

My hands hovered over the keyboard as another thought popped into my head. If Luna had an out-of-body experience and tried to push me out of the way, was it possible that I could do the same and find out if she was lying to me?

My heart skipped a beat, then pumped really fast at the audacity of the idea. Could I really dare to try it given the risk involved? If I did, at least I would know if I had falsely accused Luna or not. I felt queasy, but got up anyway to change out of the dress into a t-shirt and shorts. I locked the door and sat on the bed, leaning back against the headboard. Headphones on, I pressed start on Ajaarn's recorded meditation.

Breathing deeply calmed down my racing heart and I felt myself fully relax into the familiar pattern. Little pinpricks of electrical impulses ran along my spine. This was my signal that I had fully connected to the energy stream Ajaarn had talked about. I knew I was smiling and could feel the momentum building. I deepened my breathing until the full surge lifted me so I was looking at myself in Luna's body, sitting on the bed. In this state, I felt at once euphoric and calm, completely content. Like before, I sensed, rather than saw, the tendrils of my connection to other spirits, all of us securely tethered to the lifeline of pure energy. And although Luna wasn't with me, I was conscious of her essence. All I had to do was follow that link to my own body.

Two sharp knocks on the door made me jump and broke my concentration. I groaned, reluctantly returning to the ordinary world.

"Luna, are you there? Can I talk to you?" Luke shouted.

Frustrated, I stopped the recording.

"What do you want? I'm working." I snapped, not yet ready to get up and let him in.

"I need to ask you something. Can I come in?" Damn him. He was just like Tum, interrupting me when it was most inconvenient. But Luke's request to speak was unusual enough that I got up and unlocked the door.

"What is it?" I asked ungraciously, letting him walk in.

"Why are you being so cranky? I just wanted to ask if you think we should get Mom a welcome home present for tomorrow? You know, she must be pretty tired and worried, so I thought maybe we should do something nice?" Luke looked at me expectantly. My anger evaporated. *OMG, that is so sweet of him.*

"Wow, Luke! That is such a great idea. Why didn't I think of that?" I smiled to let him know I forgave his interruption. "What did you have in mind?"

"You know how Mom always likes her massages? How about we have that massage lady come here tomorrow afternoon and we pay her?"

"Seriously, Luke. I'm impressed. That's a fantastic idea. Do you know which massage lady she likes?"

Luke shrugged, his lips pursed. "I thought you'd know. You've used her too."

"Really? Never mind. I know who we can book. Let me call her and see if she's free tomorrow. Maybe around two o'clock? I'll book it for two hours and Mom can decide afterwards if she wants to go to the party or not."

Luke nodded. "And I can walk over to Terminal 21 tomorrow morning and get a card for Mom." The shopping mall was only two streets away, but I preferred not to have him walk by himself. He was only twelve and hadn't been in Bangkok that long.

"I'll come with you. Maybe we'll see something else to get, ok?"

"Sure, if you want to. I'm gonna tell Dad. Can you book the massage?"

"I'll do it now. Thanks Luke. Glad you asked." I held up my hand in a high-five. Luke slapped it with a slightly embarrassed grin and an eye roll.

Maybe Luke's interruption was perfectly timed, after all, to stop me from doing something crazy. I shook my head, then sat down to call Khun Ravi, my favourite massage therapist.

40

LUNA

Yumi was quick to respond to my text.

'What's up? Got your shot?'

'Yes, all good. Do U want to meet for coffee at Central Embassy tomorrow? @Phloen Chit.

'Why? What's Phloen Chit?'

'Skytrain station. I want to ask for your advice on something.'

This time, the text took a full minute to arrive.

'Advice on what?' She included three questioning emojis.

'Easier to ask in person.'

'Did you speak with Luna?'

Why was everyone acting so weird this evening? First, Nui was cagey, and now Yumi too. What in the world did they talk about?

'Just to get your number. Why? Everything ok?'

'Never mind. Sure, I can meet U. What time?'

'I'll text U tomorrow am. I need to check with my parents, but three-ish, ok?'

This would be after lunch and then I could still do a volunteer shift at the pet hospital afterwards. Or, if Mae and Paa didn't need me, I'd go before lunch.

'Sure. Txt me. Cya.'

It was the shortest conversation with Yumi ever. Something had clearly happened that evening between Nui and Yumi, and I wanted to know what. Did they talk about me? And why did Nui call Yumi fragile? I couldn't fathom why, but I was curious to find out what was going on. But more importantly, I hoped Yumi could help shed some light on my predicament, even if I couldn't tell her the whole story. I realized that in some odd way Yumi had both Nui's and my situation rolled into one. She too had to figure out whether to settle for a traditional life or continue as an expat. Both options had been open to her. At the very least, maybe she could tell me how she decided which path to follow.

And with Mom coming back tomorrow, Nui had no more excuses to delay our switch back. Things were looking up again at last.

41

NUI

I REALIZED I DIDN'T HAVE KHUN RAVI'S NUMBER ON LUNA'S phone. I thought I better check who Luna's mom normally used.

'Hey, who's your mom's massage lady?'

The text came back promptly.

'K Yee from Healthland on Asok or anyone else there.'

'What kind of massage?'

'Why?'

'Luke wants to book one for her tomorrow.'

'Ah, Aromatherapy, 2 hrs, 2K Baht.'

'K. Can you send me # for K Ravi from my phone?'

'0816192662'

'Txs'

That price was a rip-off, probably because it came through the spa directly. I knew Khun Ravi only charged half that for the same amount of time. The phone was ringing. A hand touched my shoulder and I jumped and dropped the phone.

"Sorry Luna, I thought you heard me come in." Khun Mark apologized.

"Sorry,Dad, give me a sec." I grabbed the phone off the floor.

"What's up Dad? Did Luke tell you about the massage for Mom?"

"Yes, he did. Great idea." Khun Mark walked over to the ottoman and sat down. He rubbed his face and clasped his hands before looking at me.

"Luna, I've been meaning to talk to you. Is everything alright? You've been acting a bit strange these last weeks."

"What do you mean?"

"There were a few things; I heard you speak Thai with Khun Bo like a native, out of the blue. How could you possibly have learned this so quickly? Then you started eating meat again, and suddenly you are interested in politics and the hotel business, stuff you never wanted to deal with. It's almost like you're a different person. What's going on? Everything okay at school?"

"I'm not sure what you mean, Dad. There's nothing going on. Everything is ok." I hadn't realized he had been watching this closely, or that I had inadvertently given so much away.

Khun Mark shook his head.

"But what worries me most is the seizure. You never had anything like that before. Have you been feeling alright after your accident in Bali? I think maybe we should have gone for a full check-up after all. I'll schedule it for next week."

"But Dad, I feel completely fine. Really! There's no reason to worry." Health issues were the least of my problems. "Seriously, Dad, it's just that the last two weeks have been kind of weird with Mom being away, but she's back tomorrow, so it's all good. And please don't worry her. She has enough on her plate with Aunt Jane and all that stuff, ok?"

Luna's dad stared at me for a long moment, obviously not sure whether or not to believe me. I could see he was torn between insisting on the check-up and letting it slide, at least for now. I needed to distract him more.

"Besides, you weren't really around that much before, because you were working so hard."

I didn't mean to suggest it was his fault, but I didn't want to have to make up some kind of explanation for why I was behaving differently.

Luna's dad jerked back as if I had slapped him. He cleared his throat multiple times.

"I am so sorry you feel that way, Luna. I suppose I should have paid a bit more attention, but you know how it is when I start a new job."

Shit. Now I felt terrible.

"No Dad, I didn't say that to make you upset. I'm sorry. It's just that I've been so busy with the temple and school, and then Mom went away. I just think we were all a bit overwhelmed."

"I promise I'll try to do better. But you know you can talk to me anytime, right?"

"I know, Dad. And I will, don't worry."

He hesitated for a moment, then relented.

"Fine, but I think I'll still book the check-up."

I shrugged. By next week, that would be Luna's problem, not mine.

"Dad, it's really unnecessary, but whatever. Are you going to pick up Mom tomorrow?"

"Yes, Khun Pak is driving me. I'll text you when we're in the car on the way back."

"Thanks Dad. Luke and I will go to Terminal 21

tomorrow morning to get something for Mom, but we'll be back by noon latest. Do you want us to wait for you for lunch?"

"Grab something there if you're hungry. Mom will probably want to take a nap first, and I have to go to the hotel for the staff party."

"Ok Dad, we'll figure it out."

He sighed, then got up and kissed me on the top of my head.

"Night honey. Don't work too late."

I exhaled slowly. *Gotta be more careful, Nui*. I glanced at my watch. It was already nine o'clock, but I still had some work to do.

42

LUNA

CRAMPS PULLED ME OUT OF A DEEP SLEEP. I MENTALLY WENT through the list of food I ate the day before but couldn't remember anything that would have caused an upset. Another wave hit me and I finally made the connection—Nui's period. Eww, yuk, gross! Logically, it shouldn't be different to taking a shower in Nui's body, but somehow this felt much more intimate and a more direct invasion of privacy.

I jumped out of bed and dashed into the bathroom. Frantically searching through the cabinet under the sink for tampons, I only found a pack of thick pads. *You have got to be kidding me.* Could this get any worse? *Don't think Luna, just handle it like you've handled everything else.*

I quickly showered and dressed. Resigned, I stripped the bed, then hassled Duen to get up too, so I could put all the sheets together in the washing machine to run a full load. There was no fabric softener to make the sheets smell nicer, so I just added an extra scoop of detergent, hoping I got the programme right. After yesterday's warning, I was on my best behaviour and ate breakfast with the family, even though my insides were hurting. My periods were never that painful, and I didn't envy Nui having to go through this every month. To add insult to injury, I realized I would have to deal with the same thing again next week in my own body. Mae and Paa declined my offer to help at the shop and even Khun Yaa didn't need a hand with her big weekly shop at Klong Toei market, as Khun Bpoo would drive her. Duen smirked at my all too obvious attempts to be the dutiful daughter, but I didn't care. Having nothing else to do, I figured I'd go to the pet hospital to see Chone.

My favourite husky was running around with the other dogs. I wasn't officially scheduled for a shift, so just pitched in with whatever needed doing. I didn't see Channon until almost lunchtime. Our conversation the day before had gone well, but I wasn't sure how to talk to him now that he knew I was really Luna in Nui's body. We sat down on a bench in the shade with Chone at our feet. I bent down to scratch between his ears, but honestly more to avoid looking at Channon.

"Did you get your second shot yesterday, Nui?" Channon asked. *God, why did everyone remember this but me?*

"I forgot, but yes, all done now. Next one is on Wednesday. Just in case, can you remind me again?"

"Will do. Do you want to come back to Mom's house later? I have the afternoon and tomorrow off, so Chone won't be here." He knew that spending extra time with Chone was always an enticement for me. He made it sound as if that was the only reason he invited me, which I thought was weird. Or was I overreacting after Nui had accused Channon of being wishy-washy? *Arghh, this whole thing is doing my head in.*

Unfortunately, I had to limit my time with Channon anyway if I didn't want to give Nui's parents more ammunition to withdraw her from school. Besides, I still wanted to see Yumi to ask her for advice.

"I wish I could, but I promised to meet Yumi for coffee. You met her yesterday. She just arrived from Shanghai and doesn't know anyone here, so I offered to help her a bit."

"That's nice of you." Channon smiled, but then grew serious. "So, did you think about what I said yesterday?"

And there it was.

"Erm, yes I did. Can I ask you something?" I didn't wait for his response, but ploughed on. "How come you're so easy about this whole thing? I mean, me being Luna in Nui's body? Don't you think it's kind of crazy?"

Channon grinned. "To be honest, I still don't really believe it, but if you say so…" He shrugged. His casual attitude kind of pissed me off.

"So, you're saying it doesn't matter to you one way or another who you're with?" I wasn't sure why I was deliberately antagonising him. I was ready to shoot Nui for putting the doubts into my head.

Channon frowned. "Listen, what *do* you want me to believe? When you first told me the story and I said 'no way', you argued it was true. So then I say, 'Ok, I'm willing to go along' and you now question that too. So what is it? I'm not the one with identity issues. I think it's time you decide what you want or who you are. You can't have it both ways." His voice had grown progressively louder, and he stood up. He almost looked angry. I had never seen him like that. Ouch! That hurt. Even more so because I knew he was right. This was all my fault.

"I'm so sorry Channon. I know I sound like a madwoman. But it's such a crazy situation. I don't know if I'm coming or going. Maybe I shouldn't have said anything to you at all?" I shrugged helplessly.

Channon looked down at me, frustrated or annoyed I couldn't tell.

"You know what? I guess you better figure that out yourself first. Maybe we should forget the whole thing while you think about it. I can't keep up with who you are or who you're supposed to be."

He bent down to pet Chone's head, then stood up. "Does Krit know?"

"No, of course not. He wasn't even here when this all happened. You can't say anything to him, promise?"

"I already said I won't. It's too crazy anyway and no-one would believe it." He scratched his head, hair poking up in all directions.

"Anyway, I gotta go back to work. Let me know what you decide."

I felt numb, staring after his retreating figure. Chone was dancing around Channon's feet as he walked to the clinic entrance, then ran back to sit next to me. I absently scratched his neck.

"I messed that one up in record time, didn't I, Chone?"

NUI

A FEW OF THE EARLIER GRADUATES AT BIS HAD SET UP A private Facebook group for current and former students. They only invited students from grade ten and up to join. Both Luna and I had signed up, but neither of us was very active on it. The group was pretty strict about what they allowed on the page and vetted any posts. Usually, subjects related directly to BIS, but students could post interesting articles, activities and events outside of BIS too if it added value to others. This all meant I had to start with something mellow or general with my blog, but once people had signed up, I wouldn't depend on the BIS page anymore and could update subscribers directly with more provocative subjects.

Pinkelephant.co.th
Question everything

Whose life is it, anyway?

Have you ever wondered why there are so many rules in our lives? Who makes them? Or more importantly, why?

Rules, standards, guidelines, and laws govern every aspect of our lives. First, our parents tell us what we can and cannot do and what they expect of us. Next it's the school and teachers. Then the job and your bosses. Religious leaders, judges, politicians, police—the list is never ending. And above all, the government, elected or not. Who gets to decide what we should and shouldn't do?

Don't get me wrong, I fully understand there needs to be some basic understanding between people in order to live with each other and share this planet. I get that we all need to agree to drive on one side of the road to avoid collisions, and that we can't take another's life or possessions. But for the majority of rules, who gets to decide what's right or wrong? Countries around the world can't even agree on the basic stuff like the drinking, voting or driving age, gun control and drug use, or yes, even which side of the road to drive on.

Most rules were established decades, if not centuries, ago and left in place without adjustments for our modern day life. Instead, new laws are layered on top of the old ones. Even when we're adults, they still expect us to abide by 'acceptable social norms', that are defined by whom? This covers everything from whom we should or shouldn't marry, how many kids are acceptable, how to dress, and so on.

And have you also noticed that people who make the rules are also often the ones who are benefitting from them? They may package it nicely to sell it to us and claim it's for our own good, but how hypocritical is this when the very people who create the rules are often the ones who break them, mostly without consequences? I'm sure I don't have to point out that bribery and corruption runs rampant in many countries, mostly benefitting those who are in charge of the rules.

I am not suggesting a revolution or anarchy by any means. I am all for peaceful co-existence, but I ask you to consider how much power you're willing to give away every single day by following random rules? And even worse that you then claim them as your lame excuse for why you can't have or do certain things. How much longer are we all willing to tolerate this victim mentality? Isn't it time to question more and accept less at face value or because 'it has always been so'?

Sign up and share your thoughts on pinkelephant.co.th

P.S. All opinions are welcome. Bullying or aggression is not, and offenders will be blocked immediately. Play nice!

Not bad for a first post and I figured it would set the basic tone. I needed at least one other topic before I could publish it. If I paired a social commentary with a more philo-sophical slant, at least at the beginning, it would strike the right balance and encourage people to sign up. A quick glance at my watch told me I still had an hour before I had to get Luke to go to the mall. Just as I pondered the next subject, there was a knock on the door and Khun Mark poked his head in.

"Hi honey. What are you doing?"

"Just working on some stuff." I pulled up the screensaver. "Are you leaving now?"

"Yes, the flight should be on time and if immigration lines aren't too bad, we should be back by twelve-thirty or so. I'll text you from the car, ok?"

"Sure Dad. Luke and I are going to the mall in a bit, but we'll be back in time."

"See you shortly."

Spirals

I had an epiphany the other day. It all started normal enough. I was talking to a friend, and she told me how she felt unfairly treated for some minor infraction, something completely inconsequential in the greater scheme of things. I nodded sympathetically, though the subject seemed trivial enough. She then listed point after point of what went wrong that day, piling on evidence that the world was out to get her. How she missed a train by a second, how her phone went on the blink, how she spilled some drink over her dress and so on. At one point, I started chiming in and comparing what happened to her to some episodes that happened to me, and off we went, commiserating about the world at large. But then, for some reason, I stopped, looked at her and said, 'You know what? Why are we playing these mind games? Nothing really major happened, but now we both feel bad and cranky.' Luckily, my friend took a minute to think about it and we both immediately felt the mood shift. 'You're right,' she said. 'Why are we doing this?' Which brings me to my epiphany...

The alarm on my phone pinged. I had lost track of time and Luke and I had to get going if we wanted to be back in time for Luna's mom's return.

44

LUNA

KHUN YAA WAS STILL AT THE STOVE WHEN I CAME HOME, BUT she had already set the table for lunch.

"Need any help, Khun Yaa?" I washed my hands at the sink.

She turned around and put her hands on her hips. "What did you do this morning? The washing machine was overflowing with bubbles. I had to redo the load." *Oops. Guess that extra scoop wasn't such a good idea after all.*

"Really? I just did a normal cupful." *God, when had lying become so easy for me?*

Khun Yaa shook her head and shushed me out. "Check that it's done now and hang up the sheets. They'll be dry by the time we've eaten and you can make the beds after lunch."

Damn! I shouldn't have offered to help so readily.

I went to the back porch to check the washer. It had stopped alright. But where the heck do I hang the sheets? A caddy with clothes pegs sat next to the washer. I looked around the backyard and, for the first time, actually noticed the lines that were stretched across. Feeling rather clever, I put the load into a laundry basket and positioned it under the lines so I wouldn't drag the sheets through the grassy patch. My arms were hurting and sweat ran down my back by the time I got four sheets and pillowcases up, stretched out, and pegged into place. In this heat, they'd be bone-dry in no time.

I briefly wondered how the family did this during the raining season when they couldn't use the lines. Not that it really concerned me, as I wouldn't be here anymore when the rains started. I felt quite accomplished that I now managed to handle my chores without a problem, except maybe for that little extra foam. Before going back to the kitchen, I sent a quick text to Yumi to confirm our three o'clock meeting at Central Embassy.

The parents and Duen arrived a few minutes later. I didn't know she had gone with Mae and Paa to the shop. *Probably to check out her future cooking school,* I thought, slightly irritated. Not that I begrudged her the shop, but I considered it unfair that Nui might have to pay for it. But if I was really honest, I was just annoyed with everything right now. Channon being ambiguous or angry with me, the parents putting pressure on me, Mom coming home and me not being there, and then Nui and Yumi's weird behaviour. Everything seemed off. I tried to shake off the gloom long enough to take part in the conversation.

"I'm meeting a new classmate this afternoon for coffee."

"Is she another one of your school buddies? I thought the programme was over." Khun Yaa said. "Do you want to bring her here?"

"No, she's not officially my buddy. She only arrived a couple of days ago, but Luna actually knew her in Shanghai, so I offered to help her a bit."

"Why isn't Luna helping her friend?" Mae asked, a touch critical. "Will this take up much of your time again?"

"Luna's mom is coming home today, so she doesn't have time. Don't worry, it's not an official assignment, just for today." I tried to appease her, though she was getting on my nerves, even trying to control whom I could meet.

With a sharp pang, I realized that the stable family environment I had wished for came with a lot more demands and restrictions than I had expected. I wasn't so sure anymore that this was much better than the nomadic life I had led up to this point. I glanced around the table. It was nice to have someone like Khun Yaa look after me. She was the only one who cared enough to ask if she could help with anything, and as far as I knew, she hadn't even told the parents about our conversation the other day. Mae and Paa were a different story. They were much stricter and demanded a lot more of me than my own parents. And Nui's mom seemed to only have two modes of talk—disapproval and criticism. Was she like that with Nui all the time, or just because I had messed up a few things? Maybe I was oversensitive but, contrary to my mom, I had never heard her say anything positive to me. The only time she approved of anything I did was when she signed the volunteering application. Plus, I missed Mom's hugs. With sudden clarity, I realized it was time to go home. I would have to take my chances that Channon would still want to see me when I was back in my body. I blew out a big breath and felt much lighter at finally having made a decision. Now it was just a matter of holding Nui to our deal to switch after Mom's return.

45

NUI

"Luna, we have to go!" Luke called as he knocked on the door.

"Coming." I quickly grabbed my backpack and made sure my wallet was inside. Terminal 21 predominately sold mid-range fashion, but it had a decent food court that was likely to be packed. We could take a peek, and if it wasn't too busy, Luke and I could get a bite there. On Saturday, the shoppers were mostly teenagers browsing in Jaspal, SuperDry, Quicksilver and the like. An AsiaBooks store on the ground floor had a selection of cards but nothing for 'Welcome Home'. Luke and I agreed on a plain card with colourful Thai paper umbrellas. We would write our own messages inside.

"Want to grab some food?" I asked.

"I forgot. Khun Bo said she'll make Som Tam and stir-fry for Mom and there'll be enough for us."

"Sounds good. Is there something else you want to look at?" I didn't think the mall offered much of a selection to fit Khun Susan's style.

Luke shrugged. "Nah, let's just go."

Five minutes later, we were waiting for the pedestrian light at Asok on the way home. With six lanes of traffic, even I didn't dare cross against the light. I glanced at Luke. Though we argued occasionally, he really was quite considerate and kind, not like Tum, even though they were the same age. Not only had he helped me after the Bali incident and the seizure, but he'd also thought of the welcome home present for his mom.

"This was a great idea Luke."

"I'm just glad Mom is home. I missed her," Luke said.

His admission gave me a small jolt, as I hadn't really thought much about my family in the last few days. I had been too focused on Luna's behaviour, Yumi and the blog. What did it say about me that I could forget my family so easily? *It's just one or two more days, Nui. Don't sweat it.*

"You know, Luke, I was wondering how do *you* feel about us moving so much and maybe even going back to the States? Doesn't that bother you at all?"

Luke looked up at me with raised eyebrows but then frowned, as if he was contemplating the question for the first time. Maybe he was.

"Not really."

"Seriously, doesn't it bother you to leave your friends behind every time we move?" Luna had said that having to start fresh every time was her biggest gripe.

Luke shrugged. "So I'll make new friends. It's not like my friends here or in Shanghai or Hong Kong aren't all moving around themselves. I think it's easier to leave than stay behind."

"Hmm, I suppose." I didn't really have a comeback to that; I could see his point. And like Luke, I didn't really understand Luna's resistance to exploring the world.

We had just arrived in the apartment when Khun Mark texted to say they were in the car on their way home. Enough time to finish and read my posts one more time and officially publish them. At least the blog was one thing I could take with me, even if I had to give up my fantasy of studying abroad. The thought was depressing, but I didn't know if or how I could hold off Luna much longer.

LUNA

MAKING BEDS WAS HARD WORK! I FINALLY UNDERSTOOD WHY Dad always said we should appreciate the hotel housekeepers more. I wouldn't be able to do this kind of work day after day, and I only had to make two twin beds. My effort would definitely not meet Dad's hotel standards. The sheets were stiff as boards and hard to tuck in, not soft like our own sheets at home. At least I didn't have to cover those huge duvets they used in the hotels. For a second, I contemplated folding the rest of the laundry, but I felt I had done my bit for the day. Besides, I had to leave to meet Yumi.

I had asked her to come to Siwilai café on the fifth floor. It was a nice casual space, and they had a little outside terrace, too. Not the best coffee in the world, but decent enough. I was already sipping my latte by the time Yumi sauntered in. Strutted was probably a better word for it. I grinned at the way everyone's heads swivelled to follow her progress. Her outfit was a study in contrast. Dressy grey pin-striped short shorts, almost totally covered by a white long-sleeved shirt over which she wore a matching pin-striped masculine vest with a fire-engine red loosely knotted tie. Her hair was in a severe low bun this time and she was wearing red plastic sunglasses with dark grey lenses and some rhinestones on the earpieces. Black, chunky combat boots rounded out the look. I almost snorted out my coffee. Yumi looked around and spotted me, waving like a Queen as she made her way over. The light caught the shiny anchor cufflinks on her sleeves.

"Hi Yumi. Great outfit. What do you call that style?" I couldn't help myself, still grinning.

"It's called *me*," Yumi stated, matter-of-fact.

"Good for you. Want to grab a coffee or some food?"

"In a minute." Yumi sat down at our little bistro table. "So, why did you want to meet?"

Huh? This didn't sound like the Yumi I knew. Normally, she would have launched into some epic story about what happened to her on the way over, or fired off a million questions. I suppose she was hesitant with me as she didn't know Nui at all, and given our confrontation at lunch the previous day, we hadn't gotten off to the best start.

"I think I might have figured it out already, but if you don't mind, I wanted to ask you a personal question," I said.

Yumi jerked back and crossed her arms in front of her chest defensively. She frowned at me, almost angry, or at least apprehensive. "What did Luna say to you?" Her tone was clipped.

"Huh? Nothing. I haven't talked to her at all. I just asked for your number. Why, what's wrong?" My question had touched a nerve, but I couldn't figure out why or how.

"Never mind. So what did you want to ask?" Yumi waved her hand, dismissing my question.

"You mentioned your parents got divorced, and that you

had to decide which parent to follow. I was wondering how you made that decision? Reason I'm asking is I have a big decision to make too. I think I know what I want, but I want to look at it from all sides."

"Why? Are your parents getting a divorce?" Yumi asked.

"No, nothing like that. It's more personal." I definitely wouldn't tell Yumi about the switch. My experience with Channon had taught me it was a mistake to share such a crazy story. Though if it came to it, she probably would be easier to convince.

Yumi sat quietly looking my way, but not really at me, rather through me. Then she stood up.

"I'm gonna get a coffee. Wait."

I watched as she walked up to the counter, scanning the menu above the coffee machines. Chatting with the cute baristo, she seemed to loosen up again, with lots of gesticulating and laughing. Only Yumi could make a simple order a big, drawn out production. When she finally returned, she carried a tray with a tall glass of granola and yoghurt topped with goji berries, dragon fruit and banana slices, plus a cappuccino liberally dusted with cinnamon.

"I didn't have lunch." She announced as she sat down and began eating.

I waited. I wasn't used to this quiet version of Yumi and it freaked me out a bit. She had seemed her usual self in class and even at the café yesterday, but now she appeared to be a completely different person, minus the dress style, of course. Something had definitely happened to make her so edgy with me. Again, I wondered if it had anything to do with Nui and the reception.

"So, you want to know how I decided?" Yumi asked, licking a spoon full of milk foam and then wielded the spoon like a pen. "I made lists, lots and lots of lists, pros and cons of going with Mom or Dad. I tried to imagine what it would be like for Mom if I went with Dad and vice versa. And then I thought about what life would be like in Japan or Bangkok, what schools I would go to etcetera. But then…" She paused dramatically. "Then I threw away all the lists!" She dropped the spoon, raised her arms and snapped her fingers as if she was throwing confetti in the air.

I sat dumbfounded. "So, then what?" This wasn't helping at all.

"I realized that all my lists were about what people expected of me, or how they'd tried to pressure me or bribe me or guilt me, and none of it was about what I wanted. So, I decided to just listen to my gut instinct, and the decision became a lot easier to make, and here I am." I almost expected her to take a bow.

"Wow. I had no idea it was so difficult. I'm sorry Yumi."

She picked up her cup. "It wasn't. It was actually easy once I understood I had to live my own life." She took a sip. "The thing is, I know my parents meant well, but I realized that somehow this whole quibble about Thailand or Japan was less about me but more about validating their decision so they could feel better about the divorce. At least that's how I see it, even though I don't think they realized it. But you know what? It's not my job to make them happy. That's up to them. It's my job to make myself happy. It's really liberating once you reach that point. And if things don't turn out the way I want them to, I'll take responsibility for that too, and I won't blame anyone but myself. Simple as that."

I was flabbergasted. This was the longest, most self-confident speech I had ever heard from Yumi or anyone else. Who would have thought she was such a philosopher?

"Wow Yumi, I'm seriously impressed. That makes total sense. Did you figure this all out by yourself?"

"Eventually yes, but I talked to our school psychologist, and she put me on the right track." Yumi admitted freely. "I could have saved myself a lot of time and grief if I had gone to her earlier."

"I get it, but…"

Yumi held up her hand to stop me. "I know what you're going to say."

"You do?"

"Probably something like, 'But Yumi, how can you say it's your choice when you still depend on them, which probably means you have to do to what they want, no?'" It sounded like she had heard it all before and she probably had. I nodded. She had pegged me right.

Yumi continued. "Sure, I still depend on them for money and stuff right now, but the point is, I only had to change my attitude to make me feel better. In two years, I'll be eighteen and can do what I want, and in the meantime, I refuse to be miserable anymore. And that's something I can decide for myself."

"Ok, but then why Bangkok? Why did you decide on Thailand instead of Japan?"

Yumi put her coffee down and blew out a breath.

"My mom is very conservative and my grandparents are even more so. That's why they insisted on her coming back. Look at me, do I look conservative?" She raised her eyebrows, wiggled her head and the sunglasses plopped from her head onto her nose with perfect timing.

I burst out laughing. "No, you're definitely not conservative." This was more like the Yumi I remembered and had fun with in Shanghai.

"Besides, we had moved a few times already and I kinda like the idea of life on the go. It's such a big world out there, and with Dad I get to experience more than I ever would with

Mom. And if I really wanted to, I could always go back to Japan. It's still there."

"Geez Yumi, looks like you got it all mapped out. That's awesome. Do you also already know what you want to study as well?"

"Either something with languages or fashion. Maybe become a translator at the UN or something to do with styling, not designing."

I kept staring at her, my mouth open in astonishment. Yumi had her act together way more than anyone I knew, myself included.

"Wow, this is really amazing! I'm super impressed. Thanks for this. I guess I have to work it out myself." I switched gears. "Do you want me to show you around Bangkok for a while? You probably haven't seen much of it yet, have you?"

Yumi looked at me suspiciously. "Why are you being so nice to me, Nui?"

I shrugged. "I know how Luna felt at the beginning, so I thought I'd offer. But never mind if you don't want to."

Yumi studied me with the same concentration on her face as when we learned to draw Hanzi in Shanghai.

"Actually, I need to get some new outfits. Do you know a good place to get some stuff? Nothing mainstream like this." She pursed her lips in disdain, pointing at the mall outside the café.

I grinned. "I know just the place. Come on, let's go."

47

NUI

Pinkelephant.co.th
Question Everything

Spirals

Which brings me to my epiphany. If you're looking for negative things to complain about, you're bound to find them. Likewise, if you look for positive things to appreciate, you will also find them. So either way, you can set yourself up for an upward or downward spiral. How does that work?

I'm sure psychologists could give you some fancy answers or send you to therapy for years. Don't believe me? Try it yourself. Someone tells you about being in an accident and most people will respond by drawing comparisons to their own lives or someone they know: Let me tell you when this happened to me. Just got dumped by your boyfriend or girlfriend? Yeah, I know how you feel, been there, done that.

And then try the same experiment the opposite way. Smile at a person for no particular reason and I promise you the majority will smile back and it will lift their mood. Hold the door for someone rushing to catch the train and you've made their day. Talk to the cashier instead of just grabbing your stuff and you'll both feel more connected.

Will this work every single time? Who cares? All that matters is you have a wonderful moment that will make you feel better. And once you start this upward trend, it might just spiral you all the way up. Try it and let me know what happens.

Sign up and share your thoughts on pinkelephant.co.th

P.S. All opinions are welcome. Bullying or aggression is not, and offenders will be blocked immediately. Play nice!

I READ THROUGH BOTH POSTS ONE MORE TIME AND HIT publish. If I could get some juicy political insights from Mom Luang later at the party, I would have a second set of posts ready.

I signed into my Facebook account and copied the blog link to the BIS alumni page with a brief comment. 'Hi all, just came across this new blog. I thought it had some fascinating viewpoints and might interest you.'

I exhaled and rotated my shoulders. *That's done. Let's see where it leads.* Unfortunately, most of my Thai friends didn't read English content so there was no point in sending it to them.

I heard voices in the hall outside my room. Luna's parents had returned. Perfect timing. I poked my head out and there was Khun Susan, hugging Luke, a tired but relieved smile on her face. She saw me and gestured me over. I walked right into her arms and strangely enough; it felt nice. Khun Susan had that kind of warm-hearted vibe.

"Hi sweetheart, I missed you so much." She kissed my temple. "How are you, honey? Everything ok? It's so good to be home."

"I'm good, Mom. How are you? How was the flight? Are you tired? It's good to have you back."

Luna's dad came out of their bedroom, where he must have dropped the bags. He bent to kiss Khun Susan right in front of us, which made me cringe a bit. I had never seen my parents kissing or displaying any kind of overt affection in public. I guess we were not a touchy-feely kind of family. The only people who hugged were Grandma or Krit and, of course, my younger cousins, Eve and Jenny. It was kind of sad to miss out on the comfort of a gentle touch.

"Honey, I gotta go to work, but I'll see you at the hotel later if you're up for it. The kids have made some plans for you." He winked at Luke and me, then grabbed his briefcase and walked out.

"Let me freshen up, then you can tell me your plans." Luna's mom smiled.

"Khun Bo made lunch for us, Mom," Luke said.

"Great, I need five minutes."

Luke and I went to the dining room. Khun Bo had set the table and, as promised, there were bowls of Som Tam, steamed rice and vegetable tofu stir-fry.

Khun Susan joined us a few minutes later. She had pulled her hair into a ponytail and changed into linen shorts.

"What have you two been up to? Did everything go alright the last two weeks? How was Bali?" She asked as she filled her plate. "Ah, I missed Thai food."

"Everything went fine, Mom. Bali was great, but we were only there for four days. School's ok too, nothing major really. How's Aunt Jane and the family?" I asked.

"As good as can be expected, I suppose. Jane is pretty strong, but the chemo is difficult and the kids are still too young to understand what's going on. Uncle Tom's mother is helping right now, but I'm not sure how long she can stay.' Her expression had clouded over. "We'll have to see how it goes. I might have to go back for a little while, but we don't have to talk about that right now. So what is the surprise Dad mentioned?" she asked, deliberately changing the subject.

"It was Luke's idea." He deserved the credit.

"Okay, now I'm curious."

"I thought you might be tired after your trip, so Luna and I booked a two-hour massage for you here. The massage lady is coming at two thirty. And Dad said Khun Pak is picking us up at five thirty. Is that ok for you?" Luke laid out his plan.

Luna's mom looked from Luke to me with a big smile and then wiped her eyes.

"That is absolutely perfect. The best welcome home present. Exactly what I need! Thank you so much." She stood up to kiss Luke and then me on the top of our heads.

"And Khun Bo made mango with sticky rice for you."

"Ahh Luke, this is great. I might have to leave more often," Khun Susan added with a wink. "Thank you both. And thank you for being such troopers. I'm really proud of you."

If she kept talking like that, I would start crying. I don't think I ever heard Mae praise me this much or openly acknowledge that I did something right. At home it was always more about 'do this', 'do that' or 'why you haven't done this?' Ok, that probably wasn't entirely fair to Mae as I knew how hard she and Paa worked to support us all. But a little appreciation once in a while would have been nice. *How could Luna resent this life?*

48

LUNA

PLATINUM FASHION MALL, JUST BEHIND PARAGON, WAS A maze of over one thousand shops spread over four floors. It reminded me of Chatuchak weekend market, except for light air-conditioning. I would have never ventured here without Nui to guide me through first. The range of clothing was mind-boggling. The shops were crammed together, some no larger than closets, offering everything from children's costumes to jeans, sundresses to evening gowns, belts, shoes, wigs, hats, cosmetics and everything wearable in between. Most of it was off-brand, a testing ground for new fashion entrepreneurs. Pricing was low and you could haggle it down even further if you bought two or more items at the same shop. Nui had me practise my bargaining skills at these shops.

Yumi stood in front of me on the escalator up, her mouth open as she turned around to take it all in. She almost tumbled off the step as we reached the top floor.

"I must have died and gone to heaven," she murmured.

I grinned. I knew this would be just her kind of scene.

"They have a really fast turnover, so you gotta decide immediately if you want something or it'll be gone the next time you come looking for it."

"Even better. More stuff to look at next time." She hummed with satisfaction.

"Right, so we'll work our way downstairs, ok? I only have about an hour, but they're open late if you want to stay longer."

"Cool." Yumi cracked her knuckles.

I had to hand it to her. She was quick in scanning shelves and racks, and if something didn't strike her immediately, she moved right on. I wished I had the same skill of eyeballing clothes to judge their fit or look.

"Don't you want to try them on?" I asked. "How will you know if they fit?"

"Too much hassle." Yumi raised her forearms to show the long sleeves and cufflinks.

"Aren't you too warm in long sleeves, anyway? You must be melting." Even in my t-shirt and shorts, I was boiling. Yumi shrugged noncommittally and resumed her hunt.

The clothes weren't my style at all. Everything was tailored for much smaller Asian girls, and even though I could have fitted into them in Nui's body, the colours, snug designs and embellishments didn't appeal to me, and I definitely wasn't interested in wasting money on stuff I couldn't wear after tomorrow. I was content to just trail after Yumi as she expertly navigated the place as if she'd been here many times before. The pieces she bought were random, and I was curious to see how she would combine them according to her 'me' style. I only jumped in a few times to help her barter.

Yumi carried a handful of bags as we took the escalator to the first floor. She had been fairly quiet, busy combing through the stores and chatting with the shop clerks. I startled when she suddenly asked me a direct question.

"So, Nui, what's the deal with you and Channon?" She didn't look at me, but kept her eyes roaming for the next shopping target.

"Erm, he's a friend." I kept my tone casual.

"That's it? He looked more than just a friend yesterday. At least from the way you reacted to him." Yumi turned and raised an eyebrow in question.

"It's complicated," I hedged.

"What's complicated? Why is everyone saying it's complicated? Luna said the same thing."

"Did you and Luna talk about us?" I felt slightly put out, but couldn't really blame Nui. When Yumi dug her heels in on a subject, it was hard to resist.

"Of course! I asked her when you went outside with Channon, but she didn't tell us anything, only that 'it's complicated,'" Yumi said.

"Then let's leave it at that, ok?"

"I think you guys look cute together, but if you don't want him, I'll be happy to take him off your hands." Yumi wiggled her eyebrows.

Ouch! With the way things were going between Channon and me, there was a good chance there would be no us in the future. Besides, if Yumi thought Nui and Channon looked good together, what would she say if I started dating him as Luna?

"Just leave it alone, ok, Yumi?" I replied, more sharply than necessary.

"Touchy! Trouble in paradise? Is that why you posted the blog?" Yumi asked.

Geez, I was getting whiplash trying to keep up with Yumi.

"What blog? What are you talking about? I didn't post anything."

"Yeah, you did. Don't tell me you forgot already. It was up on the BIS Facebook page. I read it on the train." She unlocked her phone, hit a few buttons, then turned the screen around to show me.

"Here! You said the subjects resonated with you. I liked the *Spiral* one and the *Whose life is it anyway* was pretty good too."

For a moment, I was confused, but then it cleared. *Damn it, Nui, you could at least have told me you were going to post something under your name.*

"Oh that! Yeah, I thought it was interesting." I had to look it up as soon as possible to find out what Yumi was referring to.

"I liked the name 'Pinkelephant'. I'm gonna sign up for it. Whoever wrote it made some good points. How did you find it?" Yumi asked.

"Not sure. I was just browsing." Time to get off the subject. "Hey Yumi, are you almost done, or do you want to hang around here? There's a waffle place on the ground floor too, in case you're hungry. I have to go."

Yumi looked at her bags, then at her phone to check the time.

"Nah, I better go. I can come back another time."

We walked back to Siam station. The plaza and train platform were heaving with afternoon shoppers.

"Do you want to take the train or walk? The skywalk takes you straight back to Chidlom or Ploenchit. How do you get into the Embassy?"

"Doesn't matter, I can go in from Rajadamri or Wireless. I'm having dinner with Dad later. He's in his getting-to-know phase again, which means it's gonna be another boring evening with some local expats." Yumi yawned extravagantly to show the tediousness of it all.

I grinned. "So you're the hostess?" I teased her. "I'm sure it's not so bad. And don't forget, you're an expat too. Where are you going?"

"No idea. Dad's secretary booked it. But it's so boring to pretend you're interested in how those guys ended up in Bangkok. No wonder Mom hated it." She rolled her eyes.

"I'm sure it won't be that bad. This is your stop, Yumi. Thanks again for your advice. Enjoy dinner. See you on Monday."

Yumi smiled as she left. "Thanks Nui, this was fun. See you around." She waved and swirled around, almost skipping along the platform, swinging her bags.

I felt more optimistic than I had all week. It was really nice having Yumi around again and I was ashamed to have deliberately fallen out of touch with her. I promised myself I'd do better in future. On top of that, her advice had put things into perspective. If she could ignore everyone else's opinion, maybe I could too? She made it sound easy, but I knew it would take time to tune in to that mindset. But if a simple attitude change had let her deal with her complicated family life, it was definitely worth a try.

I smiled. I would be home again tomorrow, and life would be very different. *Bring it on!*

49

NUI

After lunch, Khun Susan went to unpack and take a shower. I wanted to check on the blog post and write the next one that I hoped to pair with information I'd glean from Mom Luang at the party. Luna's dad said to not bother Mom Luang, but if I got the opportunity to talk with him, I wanted to be ready. I memorized the questions I wanted to ask.

The Facebook page showed that over one hundred and fifty people had already seen and liked the post. *What in the world are they all doing online on a Saturday afternoon?* There were a few comments, mainly positive.

'Interesting viewpoints.''

'Couldn't agree more.'

'So what does she suggest we do? We can't just ignore the rules.'

I went to the blog site and couldn't believe my eyes at the number of click-throughs and subscribers. Wow! *At this rate, I'll be an influencer soon.* I was giddy with excitement, but then realized I would have to work hard to keep the blog interesting and updated. *Good training Nui for when you become a Pulitzer prize-winning journalist.*

<hr>

Khun Ravi was right on time, a rolled-up Thai mattress hanging on a strap from her shoulder. I met her in the hallway.

"Sawasdee kha Khun Ravi. Sabai di mai kha? I'm Luna, Nui's friend. Thank you for coming," I greeted her in Thai.

"Nice to meet you. You speak Thai very well, Nong Luna. Where did you learn?"

I ignored her question as Luna's mom walked into the hallway.

"Mom, do you know what oil you want? I like the lemongrass."

Luke joined us and his mom asked him to take Khun Ravi to her bedroom.

"Why didn't you get Khun Yee from Healthland?" Khun Susan whispered, as we followed.

"Nui recommended Khun Ravi and I've had a massage with her before. She's excellent. You'll like her."

"Hmm, ok."

It suddenly occurred to me I should forewarn Khun Ravi to use proper towel draping with Luna's mom. I wasn't sure how squeamish she would be about being touched on her butt or breasts. I'd never given it much thought. A massage was a massage and that meant kneading all muscles—there was nothing sexual about it.

Khun Ravi nodded and asked for two extra towels. She said she was used to farangs and aware of their modesty needs. I was glad that neither Luke nor Khun Susan spoke enough Thai to understand the exchange. It would have been seriously awkward.

"Enjoy your massage, Mom. I'm gonna go swimming. See you soon," Luke said, disappeared into his room.

I paid Khun Ravi out of Luna's stash, which was dipping seriously low with both of us using the funds. Luna could never exist on my own meagre allowance, but I could hardly blame her for using her own money. I needed to get more cash on her debit card. Luna said her dad transferred money into her account each month and I needed to check how much money was still there after I paid for the mailing list hosting. I also needed to come up with an explanation of where that money had gone in case Luna noticed. If all else failed, I would have to plead ignorance, or maybe pretend someone had cloned the card.

50

LUNA

Nui promised to let me know when Mom got home, but I hadn't heard anything. After stopping at a drugstore to buy some tampons, I texted her on my walk home from the train station.

'Hey. Is Mom home? All ok? I want to see her.'

'She got back a few hours ago. All good. We're going to the staff party soon.'

I was waiting for more, but the phone stayed silent. *What the hell?* I had a right to know what was going on with my mother. I stepped under the awning of Krungsri Bank near soi four to FaceTime Nui. It was never a good idea to be distracted when navigating the uneven sidewalks in Bangkok, and I certainly didn't want to risk another hospital drama.

Nui was sitting at my desk, but I could only see half of my face. She must have propped up the phone against something. I heard her typing.

"Hey. So what did Mom say? How did it go? How's Aunt Jane?"

"Hey. She said she's as well as can be expected but the chemo is tough on her."

"Oh, poor Aunt Jane. How are the kids?"

"We didn't really talk much about that. Your mom was tired, and she's having a massage now." Nui kept typing away.

"What are you doing?"

Finally, she looked up. "What does it look like? I'm writing." She shook her head and turned back to the keyboard. I ignored the sarcasm, even if it was uncalled for.

"So, I'll come over tomorrow afternoon and we switch back then, right?"

That finally got her attention. She frowned at me.

"Geez Luna, can you at least give me twenty-four hours? What is your rush all of a sudden?"

"What do you mean, rush? We made a deal, remember?"

"Ah, so now you remember? What about when you ran off to tell Channon about the switch, when we'd agreed to keep it between us?"

"That's ancient history." I waved her comment aside, although she had a point.

"So you're saying I have to keep our agreement, but that doesn't apply to you? Nice one, Luna," Nui almost sneered. I didn't like how pinched my lips looked when I expressed disgust.

"What's that supposed to mean? Wait a minute, are you saying you don't want to switch? You can't do that!"

"No, that's not what I'm saying. Chill. All I meant is I never got to spend any time with your mom while you had all the fun with Channon. Speaking of, what's going on there?"

"That's between him and me, ok?!" I didn't feel I needed to tell Nui about my last weird conversation with Channon.

"Yup, still all about you, isn't it?" Nui looked irritated.

Join the club. If we kept this up, we would definitely have a problem with the mind swap, as we had to be on the same higher vibrational level. Or maybe it was best to air any issues before our next attempt.

"By the way, when you post something under your name, you could at least have forewarned me. Yumi asked me about it and I didn't know."

"What? So now I have to report when and what I post too? Seriously Luna, get a grip." Nui was frowning, but seemed distracted and continued to type at the same time.

"I'm just saying it was awkward. I had to pretend I found it cool, without knowing what it was about."

"Just read it and you'll see. Maybe you'll even learn something from it." Nui was being really snarky.

"Having a bad day, dear Nui?" I asked in a super sweet voice. Two could play that game. Nui glared at me for a moment.

"Whatever! You're such a baby, Luna. How was Yumi?"

"What is it with you and Yumi? You both are acting really weird since last night. She said you guys talked about me?"

"See, it's again about you. And for the record, we did not talk about you. You didn't even come up in our conversation last night. She and the girls asked about you and Channon at the cafe yesterday, but I kept quiet. Leave her alone."

"Leave her alone? She's my friend, remember?" I snapped at Nui. A sharp whistle nearby made me jump. One of the ever present security guards was stopping traffic so a car could turn into the driveway. It was enough diversion to stop me, but Nui wasn't done yet.

"A friend who hasn't been in touch for three years and has no clue what's going on with her. Great friend you are! Seriously, Luna, I gotta go. I have to get ready for the staff party."

"So I'm gonna come over tomorrow afternoon, and then we'll swap back, right?"

"Fine, whatever. Bye."

What the hell was wrong with Nui? Gone was the laid-back girl from when we first met. I far preferred that version to the aggressive Nui, and it was exhausting that every single conversation ended up in a fight these days. *You didn't warn her about the potential BIS withdrawal, Luna, or that you tried to force her from your body.* I knew I hadn't been upfront about some things, but I figured Nui was better off not knowing. *Who are you trying to convince here, Luna?*

I pulled up the BIS Facebook page to see what all the fuss was about.

51

NUI

I ROLLED MY NECK. LUNA'S CALL HAD INTERRUPTED MY train of thought, but it reminded me to check the post. Wow! The views on the BIS page were way over two hundred, and sign-ups on the blog were already over one hundred. There were also over twenty messages. I briefly scanned them. Most were complimentary, one or two critical, and some were suggestions for future posts. If this pace continued, I would have some serious work to do. I didn't have time to reply; I wanted to finish another post before Khun Susan's massage was over and we had to leave.

Same, same, but different.

What are your thoughts on money? On which side of the seesaw do you sit? And by that, I literally mean the money scale. Are you flying high and don't have to think about it because it's readily available, or are you sitting on the lower end of the saw and have to worry how it's going to affect your

*education, the friends you make and experiences you can
have, and so on? Does money determine a person's worthi-
ness? Why can a bored rich kid get a great education and do
nothing with it when a brilliant but poor peer can't get a foot
up the ladder? Shouldn't everyone have a fair chance at life?
And please don't say 'That's just the way it is', or 'what do
you want me to do about it?'. If we all just sit back and...*

I stopped and reread the paragraph critically. It didn't
work. Not only was the writing clunky, but it was obviously
written by someone who had no money and envied rich
people, which wasn't what I wanted to convey, even if it was
true. I wanted Pinkelephant to be thought-provoking, not a
site for jealous rantings. I deleted the entire post and started
again on another subject that had been bugging me for ages.

Traditions: Sentimentality or stagnation?

*Did you know the phrase 'The only constant in life is change'
was coined by a Greek philosopher roughly 500 years BC?
And yet, here we are, over 2000 years later, and people are
still clinging to traditions as if their lives depend on them.
Why? Do traditions give us a sense of security, or do they
simply block inevitable change and progress? Do they serve a
purpose?*

*I often think of traditions as 'Groundhog Day', reliving the
same memories over and over again. Why, for instance, do
people eat the same food for holidays, whether it's American
Thanksgiving Turkey or Kao Chae during Songkran? Seems
absurd to me. Tastes change, so why does the food remain the
same just because it's a particular date on the calendar?*

*By the same token, why does it take forever to change
outdated political systems established centuries ago? When
information is available with a swipe or click, why aren't
more people taking an interest in what is happening to their
country? Is it complacency? Fear of change? Feelings of
disempowerment? What would it take to shake up the
status quo?*

Did I dare post this? Though the post simply asked what motivated people, I was wary of it being misconstrued as a call for action. Our strict laws allowed anyone to file a complaint against the author—local or foreign—if they perceived the writing to challenge the monarchy, and while my post didn't address royalty, I didn't want anyone to misconstrue it on purpose. I knew my self-made smokescreen wasn't strong enough to withstand in-depth scrutiny. If the writing offended anyone, there could be serious conse-quences. Full-on police investigations and prison time had resulted from what many would perceive as innocent state-ments. I'd have to think more before committing myself. I hit save and headed for the shower to get ready for the party.

52

LUNA

JOEY WAS THE ONLY ONE HOME WHEN I WALKED IN.

"Hi Joey, want to go for a walk?" I scratched his head and his tail flipped back and forth like a metronome. "Just give me a second. Where is everyone?" He tilted his head like he expected me to know, then followed me down the hall, his nails clicking on the tiles. A big laundry basket sat on my bed —a silent exhibit of disapproval. There was a note tucked under a towel.

'Grandma said that after you finished the laundry, come to Auntie Varaporn. Mae and Paa will go there from the shop.' I smirked at the smiley face Duen had drawn next to the instructions.

Nobody had said anything about visiting Khun Varaporn earlier and I didn't feel like joining them. I could really use an evening on my own after being surrounded by so many people over the past weeks. It was the first time I had the house to myself. The only hitch was there would be no food, and I didn't dare poke around in Khun Yaa's kitchen. She probably planned all provisions just so, and would notice if I messed up her supplies. *Hang on a second. I'm supposed to be a family member. Doesn't that mean I can raid the fridge when I'm hungry?* Logically, I knew I was right, but I couldn't bring myself to invade Khun Yaa's domain, and I didn't feel like cleaning up afterwards, anyway. I could get a sandwich or salad at Starbucks or 7/11 while taking Joey for his walk. Besides, I missed having some plain western food for a change. I crumpled the note and threw it in the trash. Then, grabbing some treats for Joey and a few trash bags, I walked out again.

Half an hour later, I was sitting on my bed eating a mozzarella, tomato, and pesto sandwich that was dry as a bone. I washed it down with Diet Coke. The laundry basket sat on the floor next to Joey, who was watching my every move. He'd probably never seen anyone eating in bed. I tossed him a piece of the stale bread.

"Fabulous dinner, huh Joey?" I was looking forward to eating again what I wanted, when I wanted it. While I was chewing, I scrolled through the blog Nui had posted on the BIS site. There were only two entries so far, but I could see why they would appeal to Nui. It was just up her alley to question authorities, rules and regulations. She was going to get herself into trouble with this kind of stuff one day. At least this was someone else's writing and not her own. I signed up for the mailing list out of curiosity.

My phone dinged.

'Where are you? We're waiting?' It was Duen.

Shoot. What did I miss?

'I'm not feeling so good. I think I'll stay home.'

The phone rang. I wanted to ignore it, but since I had just texted her, Duen knew I was home.

"Pi' Nui? We want to go swimming with you." Jenny's

sweet voice came through with a little whine. "We already ate the cake, but Mae said we have to wait for you. When are you coming?"

Yikes! Was today Jenny's birthday? I felt bad about letting the little girl down. *Suck it up Luna. It's the last night, anyway.*

"Ok, ok, I'm on my way." I hung up and sighed. So much for a quiet evening at home. I never caught a break in this family and I missed having my own free time. I eyed the unfinished laundry and shrugged. *There's only so much I can do.*

Thirty minutes later, I walked out onto the pool terrace at Khun Varaporn's condo building. Strings of lanterns lit up a gazebo on the far side, where roughly twenty people stood around a table piled high with food and drinks. A barbeque sat off to the side, still smoking, but most people seemed to have eaten and were just drinking now.

Jenny and Eve were hopping from foot to foot by the pool in their bathing suits, either eager to jump in or just fascinated with the shimmer of the underwater lights. They saw me first and raced towards me.

"Pi' Nui, Pi' Nui. Can we go swimming now?"

I bent down to hug them, glad I had made the trek after all.

"Hi girls. So, whose birthday is it? Yours Jenny, or yours Eve?" I hadn't brought a present, but would ask Nui to get them something next time she visited.

"Nooo, it's Papa's." They chorused, jumping up and down. "Can we go? Can we go?"

"Let me just say happy birthday to your dad and then we jump in, alright? Can you grab some towels, please? Put them on the other side, ok?" The girls dashed off, and I walked over to the adults. Right on cue, Mae frowned at me, annoyed I'd shown up so late. I pretended not to notice.

"Sorry I'm late, Uncle Karl. Happy birthday." I wai'ed to him, almost certain Nui wasn't close enough to him to hug him.

"Thank you Nui. Don't worry. Glad you're here now. The girls are really excited to go swimming with you. They said they had so much fun with you the last time. Are you ok with that or do you want to eat something first?"

"No, thank you. I'm not hungry. I'll just take them."

"I thought you didn't like swimming, Nui," Duen said, rather patronizingly.

"It's fun with the girls and it's none of your business, anyway."

"Nui!" Mae said sharply.

"You're weird." Duen shrugged and turned away to grab a slice of Guava, dipping it into a bowl of sugar-chilli mix.

I figured I'd spend an hour with the girls. They were the only reason I was there, anyway. As a bonus, being in the pool meant I could avoid Mae. I had become hypersensitive to her criticism and took any opportunity to escape the constant scrutiny. I don't know why I thought it would be fun to live in a traditional family if it was always like this.

The girls were jumping up and down at the shallow end of the pool. For the next half hour, I ignored the adults and had fun teaching the kids how to float and do leg kicks. They were pretty good at the breaststroke already and I wanted to make sure they became confident and not mortally afraid of the water like Nui. Another twenty minutes of *Marco Polo* play had us all giggling and snorting water. I finally dragged them out of the pool and wrapped them up in their towels before shuffling back to the gazebo. Their nanny was waiting to take them to bed.

"Thank you Nui, for doing that. Have a piece of cake," Khun Varaporn said.

"That's ok. Thank you. Give me a minute to dry off and dress."

Though I had wrapped the towel high under my arms, I could sense from the sidelong glances that Khun Yaa and Mae weren't happy with me standing around half-dressed with other adults present. The constant silent, or not so silent, disapproval was really getting to me. If Nui had to put up with that all the time, I couldn't blame her for wanting out. I excused myself to go up to the apartment and change there. On my way back, I contemplated leaving without saying goodbye. If it had been up to me, I would have, but I knew Nui would get grief about it when she was back home. *Come on Luna, another half hour won't kill you.* As it was my last chance to take advantage of having Nui's thin body, I ate some cake after all to make up for the dry sandwich earlier. *See, always a bright side somewhere.*

I had to wait almost an hour before Khun Yaa wanted to leave. Mae, Paa and Duen were going to stay longer, but I offered to go with the grandparents. Thank God I wouldn't have to deal with all those family obligations anymore after tomorrow.

53

NUI

THE BALLROOM LOOKED FABULOUS, DECORATED extravagantly in gold and silver with streamers hanging from the ceiling, disco balls over two stages and a cage—*seriously?!*—on a raised dais in the centre of the room. Large round tables were set up for dinner, with a huge buffet running almost the entire length of the room. A DJ was playing Thai pop tunes mixed with dance music from the eighties. People were spilling in and out of the foyer, where a bar served free drinks for the staff. Some people were still in uniform and easy to recognize, but looking at others, I had to do a double take to even figure out if they were male or female. I had seen a live Kathoey show at Calypso Cabaret Riverside once, and I'd admired the gorgeous make up, dresses and bodies of the ladyboys, but I certainly hadn't expected to see them so openly displaying their status at a staff party in front of their bosses. *Good for them*. I grinned. Luke's eyes widened, and even Khun Susan looked slightly shocked. Some outfits were quite risqué, showing a lot more skin than necessary, but most simply looked gorgeous in full drag. Compared to them, I felt bland and frumpy in Luna's mint-green linen sheath dress.

Khun Mark and Mom Luang Teerawat were standing in front of a large backdrop that announced the twenty-first annual hotel staff party. Employees lined up to have their picture taken with them. The Kathoeys took extra time posing, and everyone laughed good-naturedly at their flamboyant displays. I greeted Mom Luang with a wai and waved to Khun Mark. Khun Susan wai'ed to Mom Luang too. He returned the gesture but then reached out and air-kissed her left and right. Wow! That was unusual because in our hierarchy he was higher up the social ranks than Luna's mom, but his gesture showed that he didn't stand on ceremony. They chatted about her trip, so I had to wait to speak with Mom Luang until the reception was over and the staff began to eat. Luke and I grabbed a soda, then stood around like unwanted distant cousins to watch the action. Most staff wai'ed to us as if we had a higher status than they did, which I found extremely awkward. Luna had mentioned how uncomfortable it made her to be treated like that by the staff, and I finally got it. Only a few were bold enough to stop by and say hello.

"Who are those people? Do they work here?" Luke whispered in awe, gawking at one particular ladyboy in a full, body-hugging white strapless ballgown, complete with crystal embellishments, Marilyn Monroe wig, elaborate make-up and four-inch stilettos. I couldn't imagine myself taking more than a step in those shoes, but this guy glided confidently over the slippery marble floor without a misstep.

"They are Kathoeys," I told him.

"What's that?" Luke asked.

"I guess you could say it's the third gender."

"Third gender? What does that mean?" Luke scrunched his eyes in confusion.

"You know, they don't identify as either male or female, so it's called third gender. It's quite common and totally accepted in Thailand."

"Really? How strange. You mean they work as guys here and dress up like that in the evening? Do you recognize them?"

I laughed. "Actually, no, to be honest, I don't recognize them. It's hard to tell with all the make-up and the outfits, but I'm pretty sure we both have seen them before in uniform."

Luke seemed unconvinced. "How do you know all that?"

"I read about it somewhere," I shrugged. My attention was still on Mom Luang and Luna's dad as they waited in front of the backdrop for stragglers. At this pace, he'd be leaving before I had time to speak with him.

Just then, one of the uniformed staff touched Khun Mark's arm and whispered in his ear. A second staff member walked through the foyer with a gong to announce that the buffet was open. The crowd moved at once into the ballroom and towards the food.

"Come on Luke, let's see Dad." We put our drinks down and walked towards them. Luna's dad turned and, with an open arm, invited Mom Luang to join him in the ballroom. *No!* Once they were inside, there would be no chance to speak with him. *Dammit!*

"Ok guys, what do you say we get out of here and grab dinner at Ravello?" Khun Susan said, blocking my way forward. "Dad said they'll do some speeches now, but we don't need to be there for that." *Arghh.* I felt like tearing my hair out. I had prepared those questions and now it was all wasted.

"Sorry Mom, can I just speak with Mom Luang quickly?" I really wanted to get some insights from him, although asking my questions casually, surrounded by hundreds of staff, was going to be a challenge. I glanced over my shoulder into the ballroom, where the cage was now occupied by two Kathoeys dancing provocatively.

"Yes, let's do that. I'm hungry," Luke said, immediately accepting his mom's invite.

"Come on Luna, don't bother Mom Luang right now. You can see he and Dad are busy." Khun Susan tugged my arm under hers and started moving towards the exit.

"Can we come back later and see maybe some performances?" I asked. "Dad said each department has prepared something and they've been practising for months."

"Let's see how we feel after dinner, ok? I'm still pretty tired and want to get an early night," Khun Susan said.

Reluctantly, I followed them out and into Ravello. *Damn, damn, damn!* If I couldn't get Mom Luang's comments, I'd have to come up with my own and I wasn't sure I knew enough to give my article enough credibility. At least the blog was opinion-based, not strictly factual, so I'd have some leeway.

"Luke, Dad said he wanted to take you to Zanook Wake park tomorrow if you're up for it," his mom said.

"Oh cool! I'm totally up for that." Luke wriggled in his seat with excitement.

She turned to me. "And Luna, I thought maybe you and I could do a girly afternoon and get a manicure and pedicure and maybe even a facial at Take Care. I didn't have time for that in Chicago."

I pulled myself out of my funk over the missed opportunity. A pampering afternoon did sound wonderful, except…

"That would be great. The only thing is, Nui said she wanted to come over."

"Does that have to be tomorrow? I haven't seen you in

two weeks and I want to spend some time with you. Tell Nui you'll see her on Monday, ok?"

That'll go over well. Not!

"Sure Mom. What time did you want to go?"

"If we can get the appointments, we'll go after lunch. I want to sleep in a bit tomorrow morning."

"Sure, that sounds good." I guess I would have to tell Luna her mom had made other plans for the afternoon, and we would have to postpone the switch. She couldn't really argue with that, could she? *Convenient, Nui, isn't it?*

54

LUNA

I woke up early Sunday morning, already smiling in anticipation of sleeping in my own bed that night. After a quick walk with Joey, I had breakfast with the grandparents.

"Do you want to come to the temple with us?" Khun Yaa asked as we finished.

"I am on volunteer duty this morning, Khun Yaa." Technically, I wasn't on the schedule, but I wasn't in the mood for another temple visit, and volunteering would help fill the hours until I could go home. I also needed to figure out what to do about the job if Nui refused to take it over. To make the trip from my home would eat up a lot of time, but I didn't want to flake on my promise to Channon, especially if we were going to date. A little shiver ran down my arms and back. *You'll figure it out, Luna. One step at a time.* The most important thing was the switch this afternoon. I had to focus on that.

Before I left, I finished folding the laundry. It was easy to separate the women's stuff, but I probably mixed up some of

Paa's and Khun Bpoo's stuff and they would have to sort it out themselves. Duen was still in bed, texting on her phone. I asked her to put the clothes away later, but she simply rolled her eyes and turned over, ignoring me. Whoever said sisters had a special bond didn't know the Apichart siblings, but then again, I wouldn't know as I didn't have any sisters, nor had I seen Nui and Duen interact much.

There were only two volunteers at the shelter that morning, and they were grateful for the extra pair of hands. Cleaning out the cages and the run area kept me busy. I tried to remember how it felt when we did the switch at the temple, to return to our own bodies and then back again. That would be the key to make it work this afternoon. I refused to consider anything less than success.

A bump against my legs brought me out of my reverie. Chone!

"What are you doing here, buddy?" I bent down to scratch his head and then looked up. Channon was standing by the door to the adoption centre, talking with one of the staff. I felt myself blushing. He wasn't supposed to be working that day, and if I was honest, I had hoped for a bit of reprieve while everything between us was still in flux.

Channon waved and casually walked over.

"Hey Nui. How are you? I thought you were off today."

"Guess that makes two of us. I didn't realize you were coming in. Are you working?"

"No, I just had to drop off something. I'm heading over to my friend's now."

"Ahh, ok," I said, then busied myself again petting Chone, who was circling around me.

I wasn't sure what to make of the sudden awkwardness between us. Once I was back in my body, I hoped we could fall back into our normal pattern. I would have to convince

Channon I was actually me, but I didn't think that would be a problem, especially if Chone recognized me.

"I better go," Channon said. "Nice to see you, Nui. Come Chone."

Chone was reluctant to leave until I told him to go with Channon, but he kept glancing back at me, expecting me to follow. It made me smile to see how Chone listened more to me than his actual owner. *Nice to see you, Nui?* Seriously, when had things become so messed up we now resorted to platitudes?

I left soon after to have lunch with the family. The house smelled delicious, as usual, when I walked in. Hopefully, I would still get to sample Khun Yaa's cooking in the future. It was definitely something I was going to miss.

"I'm going to Luna's this afternoon but I'll be back by six latest, ok?"

"Have you finished your studies?" Mae asked. "I thought you had tests coming up this week?"

"That's why Luna and I are meeting. We want to go over some stuff," I lied easily. Accounting for every minute of my day was getting really old.

"That's good," Mae approved. *Wow! I actually did something right, even if I was lying.*

During the rest of the meal, I just sat back and listened to the family chatting about this and that, making plans for the week. None of this would concern me anymore. Duen and I cleaned up together as she laid out her plans for becoming a chef and what she would teach in her cooking school. I let her drone on, but secretly it amazed me how far she had thought this out already. It seemed like everyone had their life under control except me. Yumi knew what she wanted to do, Nui had her ambitions, and I was just drifting along with no idea of what to make of my life. I felt inept compared to those overachievers, but promised myself it would change once I was back with my family. As Nui said, the world was my oyster, and I had lots of options to choose from. It was just a matter of narrowing down what appealed to me the most. Maybe I could look seriously into a job with animals. I enjoyed being involved with their rescue and care.

I imagined saying goodbye to the family before closing this chapter for good, but that, of course, was silly. Besides, if Nui and I remained friends after the mess we had made, I would still get to see them occasionally. I couldn't resist hugging Khun Yaa though, but I pretended it was to thank her for lunch. She seemed surprised, but smiled and hugged me back. I was looking forward to being home again, but had slightly mixed emotions. The glimpse of traditional family life, rooted in one place, had been interesting, as it made me realize how much more freedom I had at home. But, I wasn't sure if the differences were about family dynamics in general or rather based on cultural conventions. Maybe the switch happened at the right time after all, so I could appreciate what I had more.

In the end, I just grabbed my bag, scratched Joey's head, and closed the front door behind me. I took a big breath, ready to resume my rightful place in the world.

55

NUI

Same, same, but different.

The other day I read this quote (sorry, can't remember who said it): Worrying is using your imagination to create something you don't want. It got me wondering. If worrying creates something you don't want, was it possible that imagining what you do want can create that very thing? What a lovely concept. What would you wish for? More money? An exciting job? Better body? Cooler friends? Would we all wish for the same things? I don't know about you, but for me right now, education is at the top of my list. I have this dream of what I want to do, even if finances won't allow me to pursue my dream. Should I give up on it? Would you? Why does it have to be so much easier for people with financial means to pursue their dreams? Is that fair?

I FIGURED THIS WAS A BETTER APPROACH TO THE MONEY question, but I had to be careful not to give too much away about my situation. I didn't want people to realise who was behind the blog. My rumbling stomach reminded me it was past my usual breakfast time. I went to the kitchen to grab some fruit and a cup of tea.

Khun Mark was at the stove scrambling eggs, talking with Luke, who was sitting at the table slurping Honey Nut Cheerios swimming in milk. *Yuk*!

"Morning honey, do you want cereal or eggs?" Khun Mark asked.

"I'd love some eggs, please. Thanks."

"Coffee is ready."

"That's ok, I'll just make myself some tea."

"You sure?" Khun Mark asked.

"Yeah, you better have some coffee, Luna, otherwise you'll be cranky all day." Luke spoke with a full mouth, but I could tell he was just trying to needle me.

I stuck my tongue out at him, turned the kettle on, then looked into the fridge for some yoghurt or fruit. If Khun Bo were here, I would have asked her to make me a congee or Thai noodles. I could have cooked it myself, but I would have to explain how Luna had suddenly learned some domestic skills.

"How was the party last night?"

Khun Mark laughed. "It was quite a show. I thought I'd seen it all, but the staff here really know how to let their hair down. Thank goodness we had an alcohol limit, otherwise no one would work today," he grinned.

"Dad, when are we leaving for Zanook?" Luke interrupted.

"That's up to you, Luke. We could go for brunch with Mom and Luna and leave right after, or we could go when you're finished with breakfast."

"Let's go early. It'll be less crowded."

"Sure, finish up and grab your stuff. Don't forget your sunscreen. I'll see if Mom is awake." He placed a plate of eggs and toast in front of me.

"When are your appointments at the salon, Luna?"

I shrugged. "Not sure. I suppose Mom made them last night. Why?"

"I was thinking we could go to for an early dinner by the river when we're all back, but we can play it by ear."

"I still need to finish some homework, Dad, so let's see what time we're done, ok?"

"Sure." He put his own dish and coffee cup in the sink and left the kitchen.

I got up to get some Sriracha sauce for the eggs, then sat down to check the blog. Just under three hundred views and now over one hundred and sixty sign ups. Pretty good outcome for just one day, I thought. Time to get back to work.

I put the used dishes into the dishwasher and cleaned the counter before returning to my room. Still no sign of Luna's mom.

Half an hour later, there was a knock on the door and Luke yelled. "We're leaving."

"Ok, have fun," I shouted back.

I looked over the last paragraph of my previous saved post.

By the same token, why does it take forever to change outdated political systems established centuries ago? When information is available with a swipe or click, why aren't more people taking an interest in what is happening to their country? Complacency? Fear of change? Feelings of disempowerment? What would it take to shake up the status quo?

What should I do? Could someone misconstrue this as a call to abolish our monarchy and, if so, what would happen if the authorities caught it? I decided to soften it a bit, not quite daring to challenge the laws, even if it was innocent and the blog was anonymous.

Do political systems change out of natural evolution? If so, what and who prompts it, and when does the old outgrow its viability?

HMM, PRETTY VAGUE. BUT IT FELT SAFER TO LEAVE IT AT THAT. No need to risk repercussions when all I wanted to do was use the blog for my portfolio when applying to universities. *Come on, Nui, this is what you're meant to do. Reporters have to be tough, so don't chicken out now.* I hit publish on both posts and crossed my fingers in front of the screen.

I got up to take a shower and check on Luna's mom and her plans. I found her in the kitchen drinking coffee.

"Morning honey, did you sleep well?" Khun Susan smiled at me.

I nodded. "Yes, thank you. And you? Any jetlag?"

"Not too bad. So, I was thinking. Shall we go for a light brunch at About Eatery in that little strip mall on soi nineteen? We can walk from there to Take Care. Our appointment is at twelve-thirty."

"Sounds good. I'm ready to go. What did you book?"

"Mani, pedi and facial. I need it."

"Great. Let me grab my bag."

I figured I should text Luna to let her know, but I could do that after brunch. She was likely to throw a fit anyway, and I didn't need her to spoil my time with her mom.

IT WAS TEMPTING TO ORDER A BIG PLATE AS IT MIGHT BE MY last meal with Luna's mom, but I was still full from breakfast so I just nibbled on a blueberry muffin with my Thai tea.

"Since when do you drink that sweet stuff, honey?" Luna's mom wrinkled her nose as she speared her kale salad.

"Hmm, it kind of becomes addictive once you start," I grinned. "You should try it sometime."

"No thanks. I tried it once, but it's like drinking dessert." She shuddered. "So tell me, what have you been up to? Sorry we didn't get to speak much while I was away."

"Nothing special really, Mom. You know we were in Bali and then school started. By the way, did Dad tell you Yumi and her dad are here?"

"I heard. That was a pleasant surprise. I look forward to seeing them. You must be glad to have one of your old friends back. It was sad to hear about the divorce, though. How's Yumi doing with that?"

"I think the whole thing was really tough for her, but she seems better now."

"Invite her over soon. I'd love to see her again," Khun Susan suggested.

"Sure." I looked at my watch. "I think it's time we leave if we want to make our appointment."

Khun Susan signalled for the check, then hooked her arm through mine as we walked outside. It felt like something I would do with a girlfriend, not my mom. Weird, but nice.

"So, did you think more about the move back, Luna? Are you still ok with the idea?"

"Sure Mom. But you said we should go first to Songkran to check out some colleges too. That's only three months from now. Were you planning to leave earlier than that?"

"We'll see. All depends on how things go with Aunt Jane."

LUNA

Mom and Dad loved long, drawn-out Sunday luncheons, appreciating the luxury of time they didn't have during the week and, more often than not, to try out a new restaurant. Nui and I hadn't set a particular time, but while we were attending meditation classes, we usually met around three o'clock. Until then, I figured I could just do what most Thai girls did: hang out in a mall. I picked Terminal 21 as it was closest to home and I could have a coffee and read while I waited.

I found a corner spot at CPS Café on the first floor, which had some of the best coffee in all of Bangkok. Dad had an obsession with excellent coffee both in his hotels and at home, and he and I had a little ritual of finding our favourite coffee shop in each city we visited. Although I had planned to read, I ended up watching people pass by on the skywalk outside, while the past few weeks played out like a movie in my head. If I hadn't experienced everything first hand, I would have said it was a fantasy or a dream. Mind/body swap, girl meets boy and a first kiss that still set off quivers in my stomach. I had only meant to thank Channon for helping me, but he—intentionally, I hoped—had turned his head and our lips connected. I smiled at the memory. All this besides semi-adopting Chone, saving a puppy and risking rabies, and another move looming on the horizon. It would have been tough to deal with any of the issues popping up by themselves, but combined, it was almost too much to grasp for any sane person.

The weirdest part was how quickly both Nui and I had adapted to being in each other's bodies. It had felt creepy and confusing at first, then somehow, I must have accepted it as my new reality and it hadn't been so bad after that. Of course, there were still odd moments when I looked in the mirror and was surprised to see Nui's face, but my initial aversion to handling her body had faded. Now, though, I was ready to go home. Whatever I had thought traditional family life would be like, I hadn't counted on all the commitments and rules that came with it. I realized that my family and our lifestyle were actually quite nice, and I missed my parents, and even Luke. The switch back had to work. We had done it twice now, once accidentally and once deliberately, so I had to believe we could do it again this afternoon.

I texted Nui.

'I'm on my way. See you soon.'

I RANG THE DOORBELL AND WAITED, ANXIOUS TO SEE MOM again, even if she thought I was Nui. No response. I knew it was Khun Bo's day off, but where was Nui? She knew I was coming over that afternoon. I knocked in case the bell wasn't working. Still no answer.

Annoyed, I pulled out my phone.

'Where R U?' I texted Nui. Waited. Nothing.

I pressed call, but it went straight to voicemail. This made no sense. *She can't avoid me by ignoring me.* I took the elevator to the second floor to check the pool area. A few of our neighbours were relaxing in the shade, some of their kids playing in the water, but there was no sign of Nui, Mom, Dad, or Luke.

What the hell? I debated what to do. As I had no other plans for the afternoon, I could wait by the pool for a while. I wish I had brought a swimsuit, but in the absence of that, I picked a spot in the shade where I could read on my phone. I noticed a few side glances from the residents, probably wondering who I was, but no one bothered to ask. They were either too polite or assumed I had just moved in. There was a notification for new posts on Pinkelephant. I casually glanced at it, but almost sat up when I read the last sentence and the comments about it.

'Do political systems change out of natural evolution? If so, what and who prompts it, and when does the old outgrow its viability?'

Whoever wrote this was being bold, challenging the system, even if it was just framed as a question. One of the first things they told us in orientation, both at BIS and the family's 'cultural adaptation' course at the hotel, was to never, ever question the politics here. Whoever posted this was brave to stick their neck out. I admired their gumption. Some comments echoed my own sentiment.

The heat was getting to me. I had forgotten to bring any water, but I knew there was a dispenser in the gym. After getting a drink, I went back to my spot and promptly dozed off. I woke up when the sun was burning my bare legs. Disoriented, I sat up and checked my phone. Still no message from Nui. Damn it! I went back to the apartment one more time to ring the bell, only to get the same result as before.

Is this how you want to play it? I was furious with Nui. She clearly had a private agenda, but ignoring me wouldn't get her what she wanted.

NUI

"Ahh, I've been sooo looking forward to this." Khun Susan almost purred with pleasure. We were seated on the second floor in huge pedicure chairs with our feet in warm soapy water. Gentle massage ripples in the seatback and foot tank induced a comfortable drowsiness. I considered sending Luna a message, but I didn't have time as the pedicure lady put a blanket over my legs and lifted one foot out to start with a scrub. Two more therapists grabbed my hands to start the manicure. They literally fixed me in place. At least that's what I told myself, not wanting to give up the afternoon with Khun Susan and our special treat.

"Mom?"

"Hmm?" Khun Susan had her eyes closed.

"I was wondering."

"About what?"

"I'm curious. Do you enjoy being an expat?"

Luna's mom turned to me with raised eyebrows, then

looked back up at the ceiling as if she was contemplating how to answer.

"Why do you ask, honey?"

"You know, with this situation with Aunt Jane now, do you regret living abroad?"

"Do I regret it? No, of course not. Sure, it would be good to be closer to Jane, but your dad and I made that decision a long time ago."

"But don't you miss your own job? I mean, you had a career too, didn't you?"

"Sure, it wasn't easy giving that up at first, but your dad and I agreed we would go wherever his career took us, as he was on a fast track programme. I don't regret it at all. It hasn't always been easy, but don't forget I can still use my skills in different ways, like with the bazaar and volunteering. And when you're both in college, I could still go back to work. There's always a need for experienced hoteliers."

"Hmm, ok."

She glanced back at me.

"Why are you asking, sweetheart? What's on your mind? Is it the move we were talking about?"

"I'm just trying to figure out why some people choose to travel while others stick in the same place their whole life and are perfectly fine with it. Don't you find that strange? Maybe there is such a thing as a travel gene. I was reading about that the other day," I shrugged.

Khun Susan laughed. "Of course, if it's genetic, then you and Luke are predisposed."

"But isn't it strange that you and Dad both left home, and the rest of your families stayed put? So, I don't think that can be it." No-one in my family had ever said they wanted to leave Thailand, yet I could hardly wait to get out.

"You know, honey, I don't think it's anything genetic. It's

something everyone has to decide for themselves. Same as with choosing a job, or a partner, or food—anything, really. Imagine if we all wanted the same thing. What a boring world that would be." Luna's mom snuggled deeper into her chair.

"I guess." I turned away and closed my eyes, relaxing into the foot and hand massage. At least I knew what I wanted, even if it didn't fit the rest of my family's wishes. I just had to figure out how to make it happen. What would Luna do if I didn't agree to the switch back? There was no way she could prove it had happened. Who would believe her?

LUNA

Nui had lied to me. All her talk about our deal had meant nothing. Not being home or responding to my messages when we had agreed to meet proved it. *The coward! She doesn't even have the guts to tell me to my face.* I was furious and scared at the same time. What do I do now? I don't want her life anymore. I want to be me again. And I want Channon to get to know me as Luna.

I turned my back and slid down the door to sit on the floor, fantasising about how I'd get my revenge once I saw Nui. I thought about waiting right there in front of the apartment. At some point, they had to come home. But how would I explain to Mom and Dad why I was there? My emotions seesawed between rage and despair, and unbidden tears began flowing freely. It was all so unfair and entirely Nui's fault. Why had I ever agreed to her hare-brained idea of a swap? With a heavy sigh, I pushed myself up and wiped my face. There was nothing I could accomplish by sitting around, but I didn't want to go back to Nui's home just yet. On impulse, I texted Yumi.

'Hey, what R U doing? Want to hang out for a bit?'

'Sure, want to come here? Got the house to myself. I'll clear you with security.'

'Great. OMW.'

'U know where to go?'

'Yup.'

'Cya.'

On my way to the train station, my phone pinged with a WhatsApp message from Nui.

'I am so sorry, Luna. Your mom insisted on going for brunch and then to Take Care. I thought we would be back by now.'

Lame! At the very least, she could have let me know beforehand instead of wasting my time going back and forth. I put the phone in my pocket. There was nothing to say in that moment. Let her stew; she deserved it.

Stomping up the stairs to the platform, I continued planning my revenge. I could tell her I was going to sleep with Channon. Yikes! Even as a scare tactic, that felt extreme, but if that wouldn't make her want to switch back, nothing would. Especially since she had warned me against it previously. It just might work, too, since Nui didn't know that Channon and I were at odds. I felt queasy just thinking of using Channon as a threat. It was wrong, and not how I wanted to think of our relationship, however tenuous it was.

I definitely couldn't tell her about her parents' plans for the cooking school. If she knew they were thinking of withdrawing her from BIS, she would never agree to the switch. Let her find that out later. And if she left school, as luck would have it, I wouldn't have to see her again. I was too angry to contemplate staying friends with her. None of that would happen though if we didn't complete the swap. With horror, I realised Nui had the upper hand. So unfair. Unless…

I replayed my previous attempt to reach Nui's spirit thread. What if I tried to take it further? I had nothing to lose. All I had to do was push a bit more and see what happened. I felt slightly better at the idea of doing *something,* even if it was dangerous. Nui had said there were no lasting effects from her 'seizure', so maybe it wasn't so risky after all. I could always back away if necessary.

Another message pinged.

'Where R you? Ur parents now want to go for an early dinner on the river. Can we meet tomorrow after school? Sorry xoxo.'

Nice try Nui. Do you think I will trust anything you say again? She had been cagey about the timing to begin with, and I was pretty sure she was secretly planning something else altogether. How could she think I would sit by quietly and let her live my life, or even leave the country with my parents? All that negative talk about Channon was probably fake too, and I had let it influence my relationship with him. *Dammit.* I couldn't decide if I was more angry with Nui or with myself for being so gullible.

59

NUI

THE AFTERNOON HAD BEEN DIVINE, AND I FELT LIKE A NEW person. I actually fell asleep when the therapist put all kinds of lotions and potions on my skin and massaged my face. There were definite benefits to living with an affluent family. My mom and I would never indulge in a spa session at a fancy salon on a Sunday afternoon. Too expensive and there were usually too many other commitments.

While Luna's mom was paying the bill and tipping the therapists, I sent a message to Luna. Most likely, she was furious with me for not being in touch earlier or responding to her messages. I knew I should have, but I wanted to enjoy an uninterrupted afternoon instead. The message was delivered and read, but there was no response. *Fine, so she's in a funk. She'll get over it.* I didn't think it was too much to ask to have one full day with her mom after she spent over two weeks with mine.

Khun Susan and I took a taxi from Asok to the restaurant

just off Rama III on the river. It only took twenty minutes going via the toll-way across town.

"How do you know Baan Klang Naam?" I asked her. The restaurant was one of the best mom-and-pop seafood places in town. There was nothing fancy about it with its plastic chairs, waxed table cloths and cheap paper napkins. Located beside a pier jutting out into the Chayo Praya, it was one of those secrets Thais liked to keep to themselves to make sure farangs wouldn't overrun the place and consequently increase the pricing. The only drawback was the mosquitos at sunset. But the quality of the food was well worth a few bites.

"What do you mean? We've been there a few times." Khun Susan said, looking at me with surprise.

"No, I meant how do you know about it?"

"What are you talking about, Luna? You said Nui recommended it and it was one of her favourites."

Oops! It hadn't occurred to me that Luna would have taken up my recommendation. She never mentioned it.

"What's wrong with you, sweetheart? You seem a bit out of it. Are you alright?"

"I'm fine Mom."

"You sure?"

"I'm sure. I think I am not fully awake yet from the facial." I fake-yawned.

Thankfully, we had arrived at the parking lot and Luna's mom paid the cab driver. The guys were already sitting at a table on the main terrace, Luke demonstrating something waving his arms around, his dad shaking his head but laughing.

"How was the water park, honey?" Khun Susan asked Luke. "Did you have fun?"

"It was awesome. I almost did a full turn on the water ski," Luke said.

"And you girls had a good time, too?" Khun Mark asked.

"Can't you tell?" Khun Susan teased him. "Aren't we both glowing?"

"You are indeed." Khun Mark leaned over to kiss her on the cheek.

"Eww!" Luke squealed. "Stop it. You're embarrassing."

"You mean stop this?" His father leaned over and made a loud smacking sound as he kissed her again. Both parents grinned at Luke's discomfort. I thought it was really quite sweet, even if we mostly frowned upon PDAs in my family.

"How about I order some food?" I asked. The menu was in Thai and only showed pictures of dishes for the foreigners. "What does everyone want?"

"How about that amazing steamed fish we had the last time? You know, the whole fish. What was it?" Khun Susan asked.

"How about I just order for all of us?" I waved the server over.

"I want the shrimp," Luke said.

I knew the menu almost by heart and was pretty clear about Luke and Khun Mark's preferences after spending the last weeks with them. I just hoped Khun Susan didn't have any allergies. After conferring with the server in Thai about specials, I ordered a wide selection of dishes including fried rice with pineapple, pak choy, green mango salad, coconut shrimp for Luke, red snapper steamed in banana leaf, chilli crab cakes, Tom Yum Goong and rice noodles with tofu. I figured this would be enough of all of us and if not, I could still add more later. I planned to leave space for the tapioca pudding and sweet Thai crepes, which were delicious here. The server repeated the order and left.

By the time I'd finished, all three family members were staring at me.

"What?"

"Since when do you speak Thai? How in the world did you learn that so fast?" Luna's mom looked stunned. Even Luke seemed impressed.

I shrugged. "Ordering is simple once you know the basics." Dammit, I should have at least pretended to scramble a bit for words.

"But you were reading off the menu. You mean, you can read Thai too? I can't believe it. What else have I missed?"

"Yeah, and you spoke Thai too after the accident. That was weird... ouch!" Luke cried out, then bent to rub both legs. Apparently, his dad and I had kicked him at the same time.

"Accident? What accident, Luke?" His mom asked.

"Um, nothing, Mom. Not a big deal."

Khun Susan looked at each of us suspiciously.

"What are you not telling me?" Her tone was light, but I heard an underlying tinge of warning.

"It's nothing, honey. Let's just enjoy the evening and the view. Tell us more about Chicago. Did you get to see any friends at all while you were there? How about Heather and Dale?" Khun Mark asked.

The look she gave him made it clear the topic wasn't off the table yet.

60

LUNA

As promised, Yumi had added my name to the visitor list at the embassy gate. After I passed the security screening, a guard directed me to her house. The gardens were as beautiful as I remembered. I texted Yumi to say I was inside the compound, and she was waiting by the door as I arrived. She was barefoot, wearing casual denim shorts and a long-sleeved, tie-dyed t-shirt. Very understated for her, even if the tee could trigger vertigo with its psychedelic neon colours. Her toenails were bright orange, but she wasn't wearing any make-up and her hair fell straight to her shoulders.

"Hey, come in. Good timing. I was bored, but didn't want to go out." Yumi stepped back for me to enter. I kicked off my sandals at the door.

"I was at Luna's. We had planned to meet but she no-showed.'

"That's odd. She told me she couldn't plan anything. I thought her mom just got back."

"I guess, but she could at least have told me." It was stupid badmouthing 'myself' to Yumi, but I needed to let off some steam.

"Shit happens. Anyway, want to sit inside or outside?" Yumi asked.

After spending time on the pool deck, I'd had enough heat for one day.

"Let's stay inside. It's still too warm."

Instead of going to the living room, Yumi led the way to her own room. Surprisingly, it looked like a standard Thai hotel room with hardly any personal touches. A teak four-poster bed dominated the space, with a maroon silk covered bench in front of it. The walls were whitewashed instead of wood, otherwise it would have been too depressing and dark. Someone had tried to lighten it up with a bright turquoise bed runner, a light woven rug and a few jewel-coloured throw pillows. There was a bay window, two wicker lounge chairs, and a small table. French doors led to a small covered porch overlooking the gardens. The simplicity of it surprised me as much as the tidiness. Maybe Yumi wasn't allowed to change much, given that they were living on government property. Plus, she'd only been there for a few days. In a month's time, the place might look entirely different.

"You want a glass of wine or something?" Yumi asked.

"Seriously?" My parents were pretty relaxed about me having a glass occasionally, saying it was better to drink with them rather than trying to sneak alcohol behind their backs. I always assumed it was natural to them because they both worked in hospitality and wanted to introduce Luke and me to high-quality food and drinks.

Yumi shrugged. "Sure, why not? Dad's not here. Or are you one of those sticklers who follow the age rule?" If she meant that as a challenge, it didn't faze me, and after the day I'd had, a glass of wine sounded good.

"Alright, I'd love a glass. White, if you don't mind."

"Be right back."

I looked around. A desk sat next to a door leading to an en-suite bathroom. Most notable was the absence of a wardrobe, especially given Yumi's penchant for clothes. A dresser below the flat screen TV was the only furniture item designed to store stuff.

Yumi returned with a bottle in a wine cooler tucked under her arm, two glasses and a bowl of mixed nuts. She unscrewed the top and poured.

"Cheers!"

We clinked glasses and took a sip.

"Hmm, this is nice."

"Yup. From Dad's stash for when he entertains." Yumi winked at me.

"So, what have you been up to today?" I asked.

"Nothing much, really. Dad and I went to the Jim Thompson museum and got some stuff." She pointed at the pillows. "Then we had lunch at The Grove, and now Dad is playing golf with some guys. Kind of boring, really. And you?" Yumi seemed strangely subdued compared to her normal bouncy mode.

"I did a shift at the pet hospital this morning, lunch with the family and then I went to see Luna and wasted time waiting around."

"That's so weird. She told *me* she didn't have time." Yumi sounded slightly put out.

"We made our plans quite a while ago. There's something we have to work on that couldn't wait. But now, I don't know." I took a sip. "Let's talk about something else, shall we?"

Yumi shrugged. "Whatever."

"Where is all your stuff?" I asked. "This looks like a hotel room, no offense."

Yumi grinned and got up to walk towards the dresser. She cracked her fingers and wiggled them in front of her.

"Ready? Abracadabra!" She pushed a spot next to the dresser, which turned out to be an inset swing door I had completely overlooked. Yumi put her back against the door and invited me in to look. The room was the same size as her bedroom, but designed as a walk-in closet, and here the real Yumi came through bright and clear. There seemed to be hundreds of dresses and skirts in different colours, lengths and fabrics, piles of t-shirts, tops, jeans, and shorts. There were racks full of shoes, scarves held together by clips hanging from rails, a few hats on hooks and shelves, drawers and baskets overflowing with God knows what, plus a vanity table with tons of make-up paraphernalia and a good sized, brightly lit mirror. It looked like a typhoon had blasted through, but I was pretty sure Yumi knew exactly where everything was.

"Wow! This is amazing. What a fab space. I never would have guessed."

"It is cool, isn't it? But we're only here for a month or so."

"How come? You're not leaving already, are you?"

"Nah. It's just that newcomers can only stay here for a short while. Dad has a month to find us a place to live. He said he'll ask Luna's parents if they know of something," Yumi said.

"That would be fantastic. Maybe even in the same building? I know there are some two and three-bedroom condos too. And we could hang out more often."

"Huh? What has that got to do with hanging out? I mean, you don't live there, do you?"

"No, I mean maybe you, Luna and I could hang out together?" *Watch it Luna.* In my head, I was already back home.

61

NUI

KHUN SUSAN CHANGED THE SUBJECT.

"Shall we talk about Songkran? I want to look at flights and use our frequent flyer miles if possible. Luna, have you thought about the colleges you want to visit? It'll take some planning to set this up. How much time do you think you can get off work, Mark?"

"I'm hoping for the full two weeks, but at least ten days, I should think. So, I'll either join you as you leave or come later." Khun Mark asked.

"I figured we could go to Chicago for a week first, then take the other week to look at some unis and maybe visit John and Laura in San Francisco for the weekend if there's enough time."

I didn't know if John and Laura were friends or family, but I'd find out. It was so exciting to plan a trip three months out, and to places I had never been to. On top of that, we would look at my choice of universities.

Stop Nui. What are you doing? You promised Luna you'd

switch with her. You can't make plans like this.

"So honey, did you think about which places you want to apply to and what you want to study?" Luna's mom asked.

"Dad and I spoke about some hospitality schools like UNLV or Cornell. I also started looking into some journalism programs. Two of them are in Chicago, actually—Loyola and DePaul. They have great journalism schools."

"Oh? That's new." Her spoon hung suspended halfway to her mouth. "When did that come up? You never said anything about either before. Something else I missed?"

"Dad didn't tell you I might be the new Teen Concierge at the hotel? That was my idea." I was still proud of it.

"And it's a really great idea," Khun Mark said. "I forgot to tell you, I've been speaking with our HR people and they think we can make it work."

"Hahaha, that's funny. I thought you hated being a tourist, Luna, and now you want to give sightseeing tours to other teenagers? See, I told you something happened after the..." Luke didn't finish the sentence as his dad gave him a stern look.

"Ok, that's it!" Khun Susan put her fork and spoon down and looked at the three of us. "What happened? And don't tell me it was nothing."

"Seriously honey, don't worry, all is ok," Khun Mark said, twisting in his seat.

"Don't 'honey' me. Tell me right now what happened. Someone." She again glanced at each of us. Luke ducked his head, probably regretting bringing it up.

I almost grinned. I couldn't imagine my mom talking to my dad like this.

I decided to come clean and rescue Khun Mark.

"Mom, seriously, nothing much happened. When we were in Bali, we went white-water rafting and I fell off the boat and hit my head and was out for a little while. But I got checked out at the hospital and everything was fine. Just a few minor scratches and cuts. Really!"

"And none of you thought to tell me?"

"But Mom, you were in Chicago and had enough going on, and we didn't want to worry you. It was really nothing major and I'm fine."

"Yeah, but what about the seizure, Luna?" Luke asked. If looks could kill, he would have toppled over from the daggers his dad and I shot at him.

"Seizure? Oh my God! What? How? When?" Khun Susan's face went white as the words tumbled over themselves.

"Luke, seriously. Did you have to upset your mother like that?" His dad was pissed off, but I suspected it might be because he felt guilty for withholding the information.

"But, Dad..." Luke protested, but then looked away. "Sorry."

"Don't be sorry, Luke. You were absolutely right to tell me. What happened?"

"It was a fluke, Mom, really. It felt like a big body cramp, but only lasted a few seconds. And I was completely fine after and I have been since. Don't worry."

She looked at me for a long moment and finally turned to her husband. "You and I will talk later. And Luna, we're scheduling a check-up for you at Bumrungrad this week, understood?"

"Yes Mom."

We turned back to our food, but Khun Mark and I exchanged a sheepish grin. Luke aimed a half-hearted kick at me, but I let it go. He probably had been right to tell his mom. In some ways, she reminded me of Khun Yaa, who would have reacted the same and coaxed the information out of us.

62

LUNA

"LET'S HAVE SOME MORE WINE," YUMI WALKED BACK INTO the bedroom and plopped down in her seat. "So, did you make your big decision yet?"

I finished my first glass and held it out for a top up, even though I already felt a slight buzz. Maybe I should go easy on the wine, as I didn't know how Nui's smaller body would react to the alcohol. The spiked drinks on New Year's Eve weren't a good reference point, as they had been watered down with soda. It immediately made me think of Channon and how he came to my rescue that night. A delicious tingle ran down my spine at the memory of the kiss that followed.

"Nui?" Yumi asked again.

"Uh, sorry. Yes, I have. It's just a matter now of making it happen."

"Make what happen?" Yumi asked.

"I can't tell you, sorry. It's personal. But let me ask you something. Have you ever imagined living someone else's life?"

"What do you mean? Like wanting what they have?"

"Yeah, sort of, but not just what they own. I mean, more like their experience. You know, their kind of family life, maybe a boyfriend. I don't know, just different from what you have." I knew I wasn't making much sense, but I hoped Yumi would understand, somehow.

"You mean like walking in their shoes? Nah, can't say I have. Sure, I sometimes look at what someone has, and that gives me ideas for what I want, but I bet if I were in their shoes, I'd probably want what I have now. It's this grass is always greener thing, isn't it?"

"Geez Yumi, when did you get so wise? You really hit it spot on."

Yumi looked at me with an odd expression, a cross between frustration and scorn.

"And that surprises you because…?"

"I find it amazing that you seem to have everything figured out."

"And again, that surprises you because…?"

"Well, you didn't use to…" I stopped myself just in time.

"Didn't use to what? What's that supposed to mean?" Yumi's eyes narrowed. "How would you know? It's not like you know me, is it?"

"Erm, no. Sorry, didn't mean it like that."

"You know, Nui, you and Luna are acting really strange. Luna seems to have forgotten everything about me and our time in Shanghai and you talk like we've known each other for ages. What's up with that?"

My mouth fell open, but I was scrambling for a response.

"I… I don't know what you're talking about."

Yumi raised her hand to tick off her points.

"One: you speak Chinese, but your friends say you don't, and I got the feeling Luna didn't understand a word of what we said at lunch. Two: You forget about a blog you posted only an hour ago, and Luna has completely forgotten about my family and all the stuff we did in Shanghai. And three: I've only met you twice and not only are you asking for my advice, but you come to visit out of the blue to hang out, and now you make it sound like you knew me from way back when. What's going on here? It's almost like you guys switched positions."

Yikes! I hadn't seen that one coming. I tried to come up with a response, but my thoughts were sluggish from the wine. *Play it cool. Play it down.*

"Come on Yumi, don't be silly. Of course Luna remembers you. She told me quite a bit about you. How else would I know so much?"

Yumi shook her head. She didn't buy my explanation.

"And how do you explain the other things, then?"

"I don't know what you're getting at." *Don't encourage that discussion.* I looked outside the window where the garden lights had come on, casting a friendly glow over the greenery. *Lights?*

"Oh, shit… What time is it?"

"Don't change the subject. Six-thirty, why? Here, let's finish the wine." Yumi divided the rest of the bottle between our glasses.

"No way. Did we finish that bottle?" I jumped up and instantly sat back down, feeling wobbly on my feet. "Uh oh."

"What's wrong?" Yumi asked, apparently able to hold her own with the booze much better than me.

"Not feeling so good. But I gotta get home. I told the family I'd be home by six. Can I get some water please, and do you have any mints or something? I can't go like this. Mae is going to kill me." Not that I really cared anymore, but for now I still had to live by her rules until I could complete the switch back.

"Chill. Can't be that bad. I'll get you some gum and you can use the mouthwash if that helps."

I slowly pushed myself up again and took a wobbly step towards the bathroom.

Come on Luna, get it together.

My legs didn't want to follow my brain's orders, but I managed to get to the sink and splash some cold water on my face. My eyes in the mirror looked glassy. This was so not going to go over well with the family. What had I been thinking, drinking that much wine in the afternoon?

Yumi came in carrying a bottle of water that I drank down fast. She handed me another.

"Take one for the road. And here's some gum."

"Thanks Yumi, do you think your guys at the front could call me a taxi? I don't think I'll manage the train."

"Sure. Do you need some food?" It was annoying how chipper Yumi was when I felt woozy.

"Don't think I could eat anything right now."

She passed me a pack of gum. "Here. Come on, I'll walk you out."

Yumi and I slipped into our sandals at the door. She grabbed my arm to steady me as I swayed a bit and had to brace my hand against the wall.

"Damn. I'm in such big trouble."

"Come on. What are they gonna do? I'm sure they had their share of hangovers too when they weren't supposed to."

"You don't know them at all. They are soooooo strict and they've already threatened to take me out of BIS. It's all so unfair."

"I'm sure it's not that bad, Nui. Relax. Come on, let's go."

Together, we made our way to the front gates. While

Yumi asked the guard to flag down a cab, I tried to straighten up and stand still, but continued to sway from side to side. When the cab pulled up, I hugged Yumi.

"Thanks Yumi. I'll see you tomorrow. Wish me luck."

"And then we'll finish our conversation," Yumi said. She waved me off as I sank into the seat. All I wanted to do was go to sleep, but I had to prepare myself mentally for the battle ahead. More like two or three battles if I included the conversation with Nui about her no-show, and Yumi's uncomfortably accurate observations.

63

NUI

ONLY LUKE KEPT HIS APPETITE AND INSISTED ON HAVING dessert. I passed up my favourite Thai crepes, something I'd probably regret later, but my craving for them had gone. I hadn't meant to make Luna's mom mad. I tried to bring the talk back to the college selection and visit, but Khun Susan stewed over the earlier discoveries and only half-heartedly took part in the conversation. Too bad this day had to end on an uncomfortable note. Khun Mark paid the bill and ordered a taxi to take us back home. Luke kept prattling on about something, but I don't think anyone was really paying attention. Luna still hadn't replied to my messages, but Yumi had texted to tell me about Luna's visit and weird behaviour. I would call both of them later to smooth the waters.

As soon as we got home, Luke and I went straight to our rooms to avoid getting drawn into a more serious conversation with the parents. I wouldn't want to be in Khun Mark's shoes. Besides, I wanted to check on my posts and get ready for school the next day.

*Safari can't open the page "pinkelephant.co.th" because
Safari can't find the server "pinkelephant.co.th"*

What the heck? I tried Google Chrome—same result.

I double checked my typing which was correct. What was going on? I went to the Facebook alumni page to click on the link I had posted earlier—ditto. An icy shiver ran down my back and my stomach cramped at the idea of what this could mean. *Come on, Nui, don't be paranoid. Just because you were nervous about posting the political change question doesn't mean this is the reason for the inaccessibility.* Maybe not, but what could it be otherwise? A page doesn't just disappear. *You should have trusted your gut instinct and not posted it.*

I checked my phone. The Wi-Fi was working. *Maybe I should check on another computer.* My mind refused to accept the most likely reason I couldn't locate the page, and I had to try other options first. I went to Luke's room.

"Luke, can I look up something on your laptop real quick? I have a problem with mine and want to see if I can access it from yours."

He was sitting on his bed playing on his iPad and casually waved me towards his desk. Wishful thinking didn't change the fact that I couldn't access the site there either.

Damn! Something was seriously wrong. I got up to leave.

"You know, you should have told Mom about the accident and seizure." Luke said without looking at me.

"I thought it was better not to worry her."

"She always finds out. You know that."

"Whatever."

My heart wasn't into fighting with Luke. He had a point, but honestly, I had bigger concerns now than a hospital check-up. There was no way the police would have reacted this quickly. Or was there? Why would they monitor a simple blog like mine and go to the effort of blocking it? It wasn't as if it had a huge number of followers. They surely must have bigger fish to fry. As much as I tried to reassure and calm myself, the thought persisted, and I started conjuring up worst-case scenarios. What if they traced it back to me? And if so, what would they do? How could I talk myself out of this? Would I get arrested and sent to jail? Images of the notorious so-called 'Bangkok Hilton' prison started playing in my head.

Stop being such a drama queen, Nui. You're overreacting. You don't even know what happened. Maybe the servers are down.

One thing I hadn't tried was accessing the hosting service for my blog, where I was the only administrator. I could feel the tension in my shoulders, hoping I would have more luck there. The main site was accessible, but when I entered my log-in details, a new page appeared: *Access denied.*

My hands were trembling, and my heart was pounding. This couldn't be happening. What had I done? Was there any way to find out what was going on without raising more red flags? I wracked my brain trying to come up with ideas, but drew a complete blank. From reading the newspapers, I had a vague notion of what lèse majesté meant, but the reports were never very detailed. Googling the term and clicking on link after link pulled me into a rabbit hole of hell. I felt like throwing up. The severity of the verdicts was harsh and criticized by international organizations, but that didn't make a difference. Knowing there were consequences for certain actions differed completely from realising they actually applied to me.

If anyone gets caught, it'll be Luna. I cringed when the thought popped into my head. *You are such a hypocrite, Nui.*

First you talk about being a tough reporter, and now you want to put it all on Luna? And how would I do that, anyway? I'd have to switch back first. While I had been flirting with the idea of remaining in Luna's body, the prospect of a prison sentence definitely made me reconsider. Stupid, stupid, stupid! I hit my palm against my forehead in disgust.

I had been banking on the fact that, as Luna, I at least stood a better chance of not getting caught, whether or not I switched back with her. But now that the threat was real, was I willing to play this out to the end? *What if they deport Luna? In that case, you could get what you want if you remained in Luna's body, couldn't you, Nui? Stop it!*

You're just assuming right now that a) the government is behind this, b) they blocked the site and c) they know who's behind the blog. Duh, if they can shut it down, then they can definitely find out who wrote it. Shit, I was in so much trouble.

64

LUNA

My eyes wanted to close, but every time they did, I felt nauseous and dizzy. Instead, I chewed the gum, focused on the traffic in front and swallowed compulsively to keep the bile down. It had felt liberating to drink wine, but now I dreaded the reaction I would get at Nui's home, unless I could hold it together long enough to escape to bed.

Did I even have enough money with me for the cab? I hadn't planned for this ride. The meter was inching up to one hundred baht and would probably end up around one-fifty.

My wallet only held eighty.

'Hey, can you meet me outside and lend me one hundred baht for a taxi? I'm running short,' I texted Duen to ask.

'Where are you? Mae has been asking.'

'On my way back. Luna and I ran late studying.' That was the only excuse that might deflect another confrontation with Mae. The thought sobered me up a bit. I just needed to pass up dinner and go straight to bed, and think about everything else tomorrow.

The ride took longer than expected and by the time we finally stopped in front of the house, Duen was sitting on the front stoop tapping her feet. Joey was next to her. I rolled down the window and waved at her. She casually strolled over and handed me the cash. I paid the driver and got out, stumbling in the process and almost tripping over Joey. As I bent over, a wave of nausea hit me and I barely managed to turn around and throw up on the curb.

"Ewww!" Duen shrieked. "Gross!" Joey sniffed the mess, but Duen quickly grabbed his collar and pulled him away.

"Sorry." I wiped my mouth, feeling slightly better once some of the alcohol was out.

"Are you drunk?" Duen asked. Her face twitched as if she couldn't decide to be disgusted or in awe of me for breaking the rules.

"Of course not. I must have eaten something bad at Luna's," I said, turning to head inside. "Thanks for the money. I'll pay you back tomorrow, ok? And can you tell Mae and Khun Yaa that I'm going to bed? I'm not feeling so good." Looking up, I saw Khun Yaa standing on the stoop, frowning.

"What's wrong with you, Nui? Are you ill?"

"I'm fine, Khun Yaa. I think I ate something bad. I'm going to lie down, ok?"

Khun Yaa let me pass by and I walked right into the person I most wanted to avoid. Mae. I kept my head down, but one glimpse of her was enough to catch her thunderous expression.

"I'm not feeling so good. I better lie down." I almost succeeded too, until she grabbed my arm and spun me to face her.

"Have you been drinking?" Her voice was low and even more foreboding than if she had been shouting.

"Noooo." My voice was shaky, and the lie sounded unconvincing, even to me.

"Don't lie to me, Nui. Have you been drinking?" She asked again.

"I had one glass of wine, ok? No big deal, alright?" I tried not to slur.

"And Luna's parents allowed you to?"

"They weren't there."

"So, you stole alcohol from them?"

"Why are you making such a big deal of this? Did you never drink anything when you were younger?"

"Go to the kitchen right now."

"Come on Mae, I'm tired and want to go to bed." I was still swaying a bit, but the confrontation helped me to concentrate.

"Now!" Mae's voice had become louder. Khun Yaa, Duen and Joey were silent witnesses.

"Whatever! You're so mean. My mom is much nicer than you and would never make such a fuss." I was aware enough to mumble in English rather than Thai, but walked into the kitchen as told.

Paa and Khun Bpoo were still eating dinner as if they weren't part of the drama playing out. I poured a glass of water and sat in my usual spot. The other three came in slowly and sat down. Paa and Khun Bpoo looked up at the unusual silence.

"Your daughter has been drinking," Mae said to Paa.

Oh, effing fantastic. Now he's going to get on my case, too.

Silence. Paa resumed eating quietly. Maybe he was too mad to speak.

"Did you hear what I said? Your daughter has been drinking, and she just threw up on the street, embarrassing us all," Mae said again, louder this time.

"It was bound to happen," Paa said quietly. "At least she got it out of her system now and she'll be more careful in future."

My mouth dropped open and I could smell my own foul breath. *That* was the most amazing and least expected thing I had ever heard from Paa. Apparently, Mae didn't agree.

"That's all you have to say?" She practically choked on her words.

"What do you want me to say? We've all done it at one point. Remember Krit?" Paa asked.

Oh! My! God! I could hug him right now.

"Krit is a boy. This is different."

Seriously? What century does she live in?

Getting no support from her husband, Mae unleashed her full fury on me.

"Get a bucket of water and clean up the mess outside. And then go to your room. You will not see Luna again and you will come straight home from school every day."

"You can't do that." I protested. *I'm definitely going to my house tomorrow to my house to complete the switch and you can't hold me back.* After that, I didn't care what happened with Nui, though I probably would have to explain my recent missteps to her. Not something I was looking forward to.

"I can and I do. You brought this on yourself. Now deal with it," Mae said with finality.

I looked to Paa for help, but he wisely kept quiet this time. His mouth twitched slightly though, as if amused. I didn't have to look at Duen to know she'd get a kick out of this mess. Everyone was quiet.

"Fine, have it your way." I got up, having sobered up somewhat.

I left the kitchen to go to the back porch to grab a bucket. *That's it. I'm done. I'm gonna make Nui switch right now. I don't care if she agrees or not.*

It took three buckets of water to clean up the mess outside. Just smelling and seeing the puke made me retch again. I finally managed to swirl it all down the closest gutter. A few people walked by, scrunching their noses, openly showing their disgust. *God, people are so judgemental. As if they had never done anything stupid.* I couldn't be bothered to feel embarrassed.

My night-time walk with Joey became another tirade. "This is all so unfair, Joey! Mae is so mean. No wonder Nui wants to escape her." I was mumbling to myself the whole way to the park. "I gotta get out of here. It's worse than a prison." There was only one way I could think of to make it work.

After showering and brushing my teeth, I felt more human again, if still a little fuzzy around the edges. Instead of falling into my bed, I nipped into the boys' room with my phone and sat down on Krit's bed. Joey stretched out on the floor.

Am I really going to do this? Warning bells went off in my head. I took a few calming breaths. *Hell yes, I'm done with this shit.*

NUI

"Luna, come to the living room, please. We need to talk to you." Luna's mom called.

Not now. I had been staring at my laptop long enough that the screensaver had come on. The geometric patterns dissolving and reforming mirrored my thoughts, going nowhere.

"Luna!" This time Khun Mark called.

What was so important that we had to discuss it here and now? Maybe Khun Susan wanted to get my side of the story about the accident and seizure.

I got up and froze.

66

LUNA

AJAARN ANURAK'S VOICE SOUNDED PEACEFUL AND reassuring, and the recording had its usual calming effect on me. I tampered down any stray thoughts and deeply focused on my breathing until I felt the familiar tingle of electrical currents running through my veins. It was the best feeling in the world, pure joy, a state I gladly would have remained in forever. My breath slowed down even more and the energy flow increased, surging and lifting me out of my body. I felt euphoric and completely at ease, connected to the life stream. In this state, I had complete control to direct my mind where I wanted it to go. The spirit threads of other life forms appeared translucent, yet I felt an intense connection to each of them. Simply wanting to find Nui's thread pointed me in the right direction, like a cosmic radar following it home to where my body sat at my desk in my room. I hesitated for a nanosecond, then nudged against the cord.

A lightning bolt of energy hit me.

NUI

THE SPIKE OF PAIN IN MY HEAD RADIATED INTO EVERY NERVE in my body, holding me rigid, unable to move a single muscle. *Noooooo*! *Not again.* I couldn't breathe, and dark spots danced in front of my eyes. It felt as if I had been catapulted into an overhead power line and now was being scorched from the inside out. *No, not this time!* Summoning every ounce of willpower, I fought against the looming darkness. *You can do this Nui, come on, you know what to do!* And somehow I did, as if by some innate animal instinct. Deep inside, I absolutely knew I had the ability to stop the spasm.

I hung on to that thought for dear life and mentally pushed back against the surge of power that was holding me. Inch by inch, I clawed my way back to control, the dark spots receding slightly until, finally, I was able to take in a shallow breath. The pain lessened a fraction, but I didn't let up and continued to focus on the merciless jackhammer centred in my head. Nothing else mattered. I directed all my senses to the centre of the pain and, with one final massive thrust, the agony receded. My body felt boneless as I slid to the floor. *Luna?* flashed into my head before everything went dark.

68

LUNA

"WHAT ARE YOU DOING, NUI? MAE'S LOOKING FOR YOU." I heard Duen's voice, but she sounded far away. I tried to turn my head but found I couldn't do it. Instead, my eyes were locked onto the ceiling. *What just happened?* I had the vague sense that something had gone horribly wrong but couldn't remember exactly what, beyond sitting down with my meditation tape. Ajaarn was still chanting in the recording.

"Come on Nui, Mae's already pissed off. Get up." Duen's face swam into my field of vision. "What's wrong with you? You think if you play dead, Mae will leave you alone? That's not gonna happen." Duen laughed at her own joke. She tapped the phone, and the room went silent.

I felt her touch my shoulder and tried to swat her hand away, but the command didn't complete the journey from my brain to my arm. *Something isn't right.*

A shiver of fear zinged down my back.

"…"

I tried to tell Duen to back off, but I couldn't form the

words or make a sound. Duen kept looking at me, her eyes narrowed in confusion.

"What's going on? Say something." Her voice was more subdued now.

Again, I tried to form words without success.

"Nui? What's wrong?"

I looked into her eyes with approaching panic.

Duen must have realized something was off.

"Mae, Khun Yaa, can you come? There's something wrong with Nui." Duen shouted over her shoulder.

I heard footsteps, but couldn't tell who it was until Khun Yaa's face came into my field of vision.

"What's wrong Nui? Say something. Are you hurting?"

My eyes started tearing involuntarily as I looked into her face. I wanted to scream *Help,* but nothing came out of my mouth. My pulse was racing out of control and I felt sweat break out across my entire body.

"What is going on now? Get up, Nui. Stop this nonsense." Mae's gruff voice came closer.

"I don't think she can, can you Nui?" Khun Yaa said softly, more in response to Mae than asking me.

"Why ever not? What game is she playing now?" Mae was still mad at me.

I blinked at Khun Yaa, tears now streaming freely down my face.

"Something's not right. Nui, can you hear me?" Khun Yaa asked.

I blinked, hoping she'd understand.

"Can you move?"

I could only stare at her.

Mae's face joined Khun Yaa's in my field of vision.

"What is she doing?" Mae's voice was more puzzled than angry now.

"I'm not sure, but it looks like she can hear us but not speak or move," Khun Yaa said. She grabbed my hand and lifted it. I felt her fingers on mine, even if my muscles did nothing. She let go and my hand dropped straight back down, limp as a cooked noodle. I felt completely detached from myself, confused and scared. *Why is my body not responding?*

"I think we should take her to the hospital, Mae," Duen said in the background.

Khun Yaa and Mae looked at each other while still bent over me. I could see the worried exchange between them, though they didn't speak. Mae nodded and turned away.

"Call your father, Duen, and ask him to bring the car around."

I heard footsteps recede, and Duen call out to Paa.

"I'll get my purse," Khun Yaa said.

"Maybe you should stay here with Duen," Mae suggested.

"I'm coming. Go get what you need."

If I had to go to the hospital, I was glad Khun Yaa would come with us, but what I really wanted was my own mom. My body felt insubstantial, as if it didn't exist or was separated from me.

I tried to focus on one part of my body at a time. Toes, legs, belly, fingers, arms, shoulders, neck… not a single muscle was even twitching. Only my tears were proof that I was alive. I closed my eyes, too overwhelmed to contemplate what was going on. Maybe it was just a nightmare and I would wake up completely normal, or what passed for normal these days. *You tried to push Nui out of your body.* My eyes snapped open.

69

NUI

"HONEY?" KHUN SUSAN'S VOICE BROUGHT ME BACK TO reality. I was curled up on the floor, shivering and feeling nauseous. *How did I end up here?* I tried to roll over to get up but my muscles felt like jello.

"Luna, why aren't you answering?"

"I'm coming," I croaked.

The door opened. "What are you doing on the floor?" Khun Susan asked. Her voice held a tinge of amusement.

I tried to clear my throat. "I'm not really sure. I think I fainted," I whispered.

"You what?" Luna's mom rushed over and knelt next to me, worry replacing her glee. She touched my forehead and then my arms. "What's going on? You're all sweaty."

"I'm not sure, Mom. I felt this pain and then I fainted."

"You mean you had another seizure?"

She turned toward the door and yelled. "Mark! Mark, come here! Luna fainted." She sounded anxious, but in control. A few moments later, Khun Mark rushed in, followed by Luke.

"What's wrong?" He bent down. "Please tell me you didn't have another seizure. I knew we should have gone to the hospital the first time this happened."

"Honestly, I'm feeling fine now, just a bit wobbly. I'm not in pain. Let me sit up and can I have a glass of water, please?"

"I'll get it." Luke turned around and dashed out.

"Come on honey, let's get you up on the bed. Mark, go get the car, we're going to Bumrungrad," Khun Susan said, taking charge. She helped me up to sit on the side of the bed.

"Rest for a moment." She went to the bathroom and came back with a wet towel and wiped it across my face and neck, and down my arms. It felt nice to be mothered like that.

"Mom, I'm not sure if I need to go to the hospital," I tried once more, but just one look at her told me it was a futile attempt. She had made up her mind.

"We're going. Wait here. I'm going to grab my purse."

"I'll wait with her." Luke had come back and handed me a glass of ice-water. I took little sips, careful not to induce another brain freeze.

His mom came back and hooked her arm around my waist. "Can you walk?"

"Sure." The first steps were a bit wobbly, but by the time we were at the front door, I felt more in control again. Luke brought up the rear.

I hadn't been to Bumrungrad before, but apparently the family knew exactly where to go. Khun Mark dropped us at the emergency entrance and went to park the car. Khun Susan talked to the reception desk, and within fifteen minutes, I was in a treatment bay waiting for an emergency doctor. The cubicle became crowded when a doctor and nurse arrived.

Only Khun Susan was allowed to stay. She explained what had happened, and the doctor asked me a few questions about the type of pain I had experienced. They decided I should get an MRI to scan my brain and find out if there were any abnormalities. I was pretty confident they wouldn't find anything if what I suspected had happened was true.

70

LUNA

THE OVERHEAD FLUORESCENT LIGHTS WERE TOO BRIGHT AS they wheeled me on a stretcher through the hospital corridors. I closed my eyes. Between this, the bite incident and rabies treatment, I'd spent more time in this hospital in the last two weeks than my entire life previously, but never had I been as scared. By now, I had given up the hope this was simply a nightmare I could brush off as soon I woke up. No bad dream had ever been this vivid.

I recognized the doctor who had also handled my rabies shots. She must have thought me some kind of disaster magnet. I wanted to laugh at the thought just to relieve some of my fear, but I couldn't do that either.

Mae explained how they had found me while a nurse took my blood pressure and connected a pulse oxygen clip to my right forefinger. I felt the slight pressure of both devices, but it seemed muted somehow. The doctor's instructions to turn my head or curl a finger went nowhere. She lifted my hand and dropped it with the same result as Khun Yaa's test.

"Can you hear me, Nui?" She finally looked me directly in the eyes. I blinked.

"We're going to do a full body MRI to see what might have caused this. It's going to take a while, around one hour. The technician will explain to you exactly what will happen, but it's important that you stay still during the scan, so the images are clear. Do you think you can do that?" I glared at her and she seemed to realize what an absurd question that was, since my immobility was the reason I was there in the first place.

"Ahem. Right. Let's do it." She ordered the nurse to call for transport to radiology, which was on a different floor. Mae and Khun Yaa stood on either side of me, covering my hands while we waited. Their distress was shocking and unexpected, especially after our earlier confrontation.

"You'll be fine, Nui," Khun Yaa said, stroking my cheek. "We'll be right outside waiting for you when you come out, ok?" I blinked as fresh tears ran down my temples into my hair. We didn't have to wait long for two attendees to come and get me. Most of the technician's explanation went straight over my head. All I could think about was being paralysed inside a metal tube with no way out. The guy put earplugs into my ears, but they didn't sit right and didn't block out even normal conversation.

"You need to stay absolutely still, but there's a built-in microphone so you can speak if you need to, but try not to move your head. And here's the emergency buzzer you can press… Ah, sorry. Never mind." The technician caught his mistake, embarrassed.

"Don't worry, we're monitoring you the whole time." A nurse reassured me as she clipped on another oxygen meter and attached some electrodes to my chest. Under other circumstances, I might have been embarrassed, but since there was absolutely nothing I could do, I resigned myself to endure the procedure. She covered me with two blankets, hit a button to pull the MRI sleigh backwards into the metal tomb, and the clanking and buzzing started.

71

NUI

THANK GOD ONLY MY HEAD AND NECK NEEDED TO BE INSIDE the MRI machine. I wasn't claustrophobic, but being fully immersed in a metal tube was simply too creepy. It was going to be hard enough to keep my head completely immobile inside the neck brace for half an hour. They offered me a choice of earplugs or headset and I thought relaxing music would make the time pass quicker. My temperature had cooled off, but two blankets kept me from shivering from the A/C blasting away.

The music muffled the chirping and clicking of the machine enough to allow me to concentrate and think through what might have happened. I knew I had upset Luna when I wasn't home this afternoon, as agreed. Would she have been angry enough to try to force me from her body? Was that even possible? When I attempted it, Luke inter-rupted me, so I had no evidence it was doable. I only knew I had managed to consciously fight the pain. Therefore, it seemed logical that the pain had a mental rather than physical cause. I had to talk to Luna. If it really was her, she must have felt something for sure when I pushed back. I had to call her as soon as the doctors were done with me. *What will you do if you find out she was trying to force you? Where did she expect me to go? Just jump magically back into my body as she left it? Or would I have died?* The thought almost made me jerk. I didn't want to even consider that possibility. *Come on Nui, you're still here, aren't you?* In some odd way, it was reassuring to know I had been able to fight back and had the power to block the intrusion. Of course, it would be a huge violation by Luna, but could I really judge her given that I had been prepared to test the theory myself? Either way, Luna and I were at a major cross-road. I wished it hadn't come to this, but I had to accept my responsibility, as I had used flimsy excuses to stall our agreed deal.

I need facts! This emotional back and forth was getting me nowhere. *Talk to Luna and then you'll see.*

I didn't know how much time had passed, but the banging suddenly stopped and someone pulled me out of the tube.

"We're finished. Are you ok to get up? The nurse will escort you back to the doctor's office."

The family was waiting for me outside the room.

"How are you feeling, honey?"

"I'm fine, Mom. Almost took a nap," I said, trying to lighten the mood. "The doctor wants to see us again." I nodded towards the nurse who was standing by.

The parents walked either side of me with Luke tucked under his dad's arm.

Dr Anong asked us to take a seat in her office and swivelled her computer screen around so we could follow along with her explanation.

"The MRI came back clear. There are no signs of

aneurysms, or a build-up of spinal fluid in the brain, no tumours or cysts that we can see."

"So, what could it have been?" asked Khun Susan. Apparently, she took the lead for the family in all things medical.

"To be honest, we're not sure. We're running some blood tests to rule out any infections, but there are no immediate physical indicators of anything wrong. Have you been under particular stress lately, Luna?"

I wanted to laugh out loud. If only she knew.

"No, not really." My lying skills had expanded significantly over the past weeks. I could probably have beaten a lie detector test. *You might need it if the police are coming for you.* The thought was like an ice-cold shower.

"I suggest you rest at home for twenty-four hours. We'll have the lab results by tomorrow and will know more then. I recommend you check on Luna a few times during the night to make sure there are no lingering effects," Dr Anong said to the parents.

"Yes, of course," Khun Susan nodded. "Will you let us know when you have the results?"

"We'll call or email you. Try to get some sleep now." Dr Anong got up to shake hands, and a nurse handed Khun Mark the paperwork for the cashier. At least I wouldn't have to take any medicine. Small blessings.

When we got home, Khun Susan sent Luke to bed. She ordered me to take a shower and then come to the living room, as they still had something to discuss with me that couldn't wait.

Luna's parents were sipping wine when I returned. I felt much better dressed in soft yoga pants and t-shirt.

"What's up?"

"I wasn't sure we should bring it up tonight, but since you appear to be ok, we thought it best to deal with this now. I got a strange phone call from the police a few hours ago, " Khun Mark said and frowned.

"They said they've blocked a site called pinkelephant because of circumspect content, as they put it. But the strange thing is that they found the IP address and credit card for the site leading back to us. I told them it couldn't have come from here and perhaps someone had cloned the address. They said they were going to verify it, but I'm also having our IT guy from the hotel run a security check." Khun Mark paused, like he wasn't sure if he wanted to ask the next question.

My mouth was dry, and fresh sweat broke out all over my body. Inside, I was ice cold. This time, I was certain I was going to have a real stroke. My heart was hammering so hard that I could hear my pulse in my ears.

"Do you know anything about this pinkelephant, Luna?" Khun Mark asked.

Was it possible to faint on demand?

72

LUNA

Paralysed! The word looped around in my head, pulsing in time with the pounding of the machine, over and over, until it lost all meaning and simply became a string of letters. My heart rate was spiking, yet not a single muscle twitched, even if I was ready to jump out of my skin. Distantly, I knew I was approaching a full-blown panic attack. The only movement I had left was opening and closing my eyelids. I desperately wanted to keep them closed and not look at the ceiling of the metal tube surrounding me, but I felt an uncontrollable need to check that my eyes continued to work. Until now, being *buried alive* was just the plot of some horror movie. Experiencing the real-life version was a million times worse. It was hot inside the machine, and I was boiling under the blankets. If I could have moved my fingers, I would have pushed the panic button. I felt utterly helpless. A trapped animal had more control than I did.

The very worst of it was that I had no one to blame but

myself. How could I have been so cavalier as to assume a mind swap was as easy as flipping a light switch? Sure, I had been mad at Nui and the wine hadn't helped, but *this?* I just wanted to go home to my family, where I belonged. It hadn't even occurred to me that Nui would fight back. Had I really expected my will to be stronger than hers and that I could just push her aside? *Stupid, stupid, stupid.*

What would happen next? I would have bet my last cent the doctors wouldn't find anything physically wrong. I had to believe this was not a conventional paralysis, otherwise I'd go mad. It reminded me of Ajaarn's words when we did our first astral projection. *"You don't want to risk cutting yourself off from your own energy and not being able to reconnect."* Is that what had happened? Had I severed that link and was now that human vegetable I was worried about becoming after Ajaarn's warning? *Come on Luna, Ajaarn also said that there are no conclusive answers yet.* If I severed the link, logically, shouldn't I be able to reconnect it? After all, my mind was still clear. It was only my body that didn't obey me. If I had caused this with my misguided attempt to force Nui from my body, maybe there was a way to reverse it.

Mind over matter, Luna, mind over matter. I kept repeating the phrase in my head to talk myself off the cliff. It didn't work. The looming prospect of being permanently paralyzed wouldn't let go. I was crying freely now; the tears trailing down my temples. My nose became congested, making breathing more and more difficult. I tried to open my mouth to suck in air, but my jaw didn't respond. It felt as if someone was slowly squeezing my throat, blocking off the oxygen. The blankets felt like sheets of lead, crushing and suffocating me. My breath hitched and the next inhale didn't get through at all. My nose was completely blocked. Dark spots danced behind my closed eyes, alternating with white flashes. *I can't breathe. I'm gonna die, I'm so sorry, Mom and…*

A shrieking alarm penetrated my brain fog and the mechanical clanking miraculously stopped. I felt the motion of being pulled out of the machine and cool air touched my face. Someone roughly forced my jaw open and shoved some sort of device into my mouth, my lips and teeth clamping down on the plastic by default. Air! I greedily sucked in the oxygen. *Breathe, just breathe.*

A different doctor was bent over me when I slowly opened my eyes.

"Nui, can you hear me?" He had a stethoscope in his ears and I felt the cool disk pressed against my chest.

"We had to stop the MRI. It looks like you panicked. How are you feeling now?" I was too grateful to be outside the tube to be bothered by the question.

"I know it must have felt scary, but you're ok now."

If he had meant to be reassuring, he had to work on his delivery. I was far from ok but at least I was outside the metal tomb and I had air. He immediately dashed my hopes.

"I'm afraid we have to try again, but we've just given you a light sedative and we'll keep the tube in so you can breathe, ok? Let's wait a few minutes until the drug kicks in. You think you can do that?" He looked me in the eye and I stared back to show I had heard. For all I cared right now, they could have put me under full anaesthesia so I could get it over with. A nurse dried off the sweat on my forehead and then removed one blanket, pulled out the earplugs and replaced them with a headset that sat much more snugly over my ears. Piano music with birds and water sounds instantly made me feel better. I could have hugged her for her thoughtfulness.

By the time they rolled me back under, I was indifferent, either squashed by the sensory overload or simply numbed by the drug. The clanging and hissing sounded dull. I drifted off into no-man's-land.

73

NUI

"Luna! Say something." Khun Susan's words jolted me out of my stupor. "What do you know? Did you do this? What was on the site?"

For a split second, I debated blaming it on myself, the real Nui, but that would only put me in a double bind. As Luna, my chances were probably higher that I'd get out of this with a slap on the wrist.

"Erm, yeah." I started slowly, trying to feel my way through and out of the predicament. "I have been experimenting a bit with my writing and I thought a blog would be a good idea to post some general thoughts."

"How general? What are we talking about?" Khun Mark asked. "What exactly did you write? And why would the police get involved and block it?" It amazed me how cool Luna's parents were being about this. My own would have been screaming at me at this point or they would have marched me down to the police station themselves. Maybe not quite that, but I was sure they wouldn't be calmly discussing it. Perhaps I was lucky to have just had a medical emergency after all, and Luna's parents were treating me more carefully. I was not above taking full advantage of that.

"I only asked some hypothetical questions, mostly stuff about education, and how people treat each other and things we've been discussing in school, like political systems, etcetera." I hoped that linking it to school would prove it wasn't a big deal.

"What exactly did you say about politics, Luna?" Khun Mark's voice sharpened. "Is that why you've been pestering me about speaking with Mom Luang? Please don't tell me you wrote something offensive or prohibited. Tell me you weren't that careless." He almost begged me to not open that can of worms.

"I really didn't think anyone would take offense, Dad."

"Luna! What did you write? Stop beating about the bush!" Khun Susan interrupted.

I dry-swallowed. "I said: 'Do political systems change out of natural evolution? If so, what and who prompts it and when does the old outgrow its viability?'" I knew the sentence by heart, having agonized about it at length, even though I thought it was actually pretty non-descript. I was so glad I had changed the earlier version, which had been much more pointed. If this tame question could get me in trouble, it would have been much worse with a direct challenge.

Khun Mark slumped back in his seat and groaned.

"Are you out of your freaking mind? What the hell were you thinking?"

"Mark! Language." There was no real heat in Khun Susan's reprimand. But then she turned to me.

"How could you, Luna? Do you have any idea what could happen to you? Or us, for that matter. How many times have we talked about not getting publicly involved in our host country's politics? Do you realize how this could be construed?"

"But how is this any different from what we're doing in school? We're always discussing this kind of stuff in political science, and they ask us to be critical."

"There's a big difference between having discussions for learning, and actually applying it in real life. You know better than that. You're also learning how to read music, but you're not a musician, are you?"

What she said made sense, but what was the point of going to school then?

"So, you're saying what we learn in school is pointless?"

"Don't make this about education, Luna. *This* is about you potentially breaking the law of the country we're guests in."

"I didn't break any laws. I just asked a question." It was stupid to argue with Luna's parents since they were on my side. *Practise for when you need it with the police?* I hugged myself, my hands squeezed under my armpits.

"Semantics! That question could get you and us in real trouble. Why did you do it in the first place? It's not like you've ever been interested in politics before."

"I thought if I wanted to apply for colleges with journalism majors, I might need a portfolio to show that I can write." I was scrambling.

"Didn't you just say at dinner that you were interested in hospitality schools?"

"Yeah, both really." I shrugged, a bit sheepishly.

She rolled her eyes and turned away from me.

"Mark, I think you should talk to Mom Luang tomorrow. Maybe he can recommend a lawyer if we need one."

"I don't think I can involve Mom Luang in this. It's a personal matter."

"Ok, then what? We have to do something in case this goes any further. Do we need to talk to the police?" The two were talking as if I wasn't in the room.

"Why would they even pick up on something like this? It's not like my blog has a mega following." Despite my nervousness, I was curious, too. I couldn't believe they would bother to skim every little site that was available in Thailand.

"That's pretty obvious, don't you think? Because they want to nip things in the bud right away. I'm sure they have automated systems that scan for this type of content." She was right, of course. It was obvious if I had stopped to think about it.

"How long has this been going on?" Luna's dad asked.

"I only posted yesterday for the first time."

"Let's hope then that they won't see it as defamatory, and that since it has gotten no traction yet, they won't see the need for further action."

"Does that mean I get the blog back?" I asked, but even I knew that this was naïve thinking.

"Luna! Don't push your luck. Go to your room and let's hope we can sort this out as quickly as possible," Khun Susan ordered.

"I am really, really sorry. I thought it was a legitimate question and didn't realize someone could misconstrue it." Ok, that wasn't entirely true, but I owed them an apology. "I promise I'll be more careful in future."

Khun Susan sighed. "Go to bed Luna. We'll deal with it tomorrow."

I got up and walked around the table to kiss them on the cheek. "Night Mom, night Dad. I'm very sorry, and thank you. Love you."

"Love you too."

I closed the door to my room and let out a long breath.

Shit. I hadn't realized the police were so on the ball. I didn't know what was going to happen, but hoped Luna's parents would somehow get me out of this mess. This only proved what I had been afraid of. There was no way for me, as Nui, to pursue the type of reporting I wanted to do here if a simple comment like that could get me in hot water. Maybe I really was better off leaving the country. There was nothing I could do about it right now, but it was time to tackle that other big elephant in the room. Luna and the cause of my seizure.

74

LUNA

I FELT GROGGY COMING OUT OF THE MRI. THE LITTLE NAP hadn't helped, but had wrapped me in a cocoon of apathy. My brain felt too sluggish to even worry about the outcome of the test. Khun Yaa and Mae, who'd been waiting outside the radiology chamber, accompanied me back to a treatment bay in the emergency department. Paa joined them while a doctor took up the other side of my gurney.

"Right, looking at the scan I can see no indications of a stroke or tumours. We're still running blood tests for potential infections."

He turned to the parents and Khun Yaa. "As Nui doesn't have any motor function, we'll have to admit her to maintain her nutrition, breathing and hydration."

"What does that mean?" Khun Yaa asked.

"We'll have to set up infusions, and a catheter, and keep her oxygenated in case her airways become obstructed."

"But what could be the cause?" Mae asked. "Duen said

she was just listening to a meditation tape when she found Nui like this."

"I don't want to speculate without having seen the lab results. And we need to conduct a series of neurological tests, too. But the only other time I've seen such a sudden and complete paralysis of all muscles except the eyes was a case of locked-in syndrome. I came across it while I was studying in America. It seems that Nui has full consciousness and can hear us. This is very similar to what I've seen before."

And? What are you going to do about it? I wanted to scream the question.

"What does that mean, locked-in?" Mae asked. Contrary to her usual roughness, she sounded terrified.

"Again, we don't know yet if that's what this is. I don't see any abnormalities on the scan that would otherwise explain the symptoms, and there's the one variation that makes me hesitant to give a definite diagnosis; Nui can breathe on her own unless she's crying. Locked-in patients normally don't have that capacity."

Why was no one asking the most important question?

"But what can you do?" Thankfully, Khun Yaa asked it for me.

The doctor said nothing for a minute. My eyes were straining to catch the look on his face. Did he look uncertain?

"We'll wait for the test results, then I want to discuss this with a few colleagues before we talk about treatments. For now, we'll admit Nui and monitor her here. Tomorrow, we'll know more."

Khun Yaa and Mae went quiet, but I could feel the tension in the room.

"Alright. I'll stay with her," Khun Yaa said, taking charge.

"Mae, you need to go home to sleep. You have your heart to think about. I'll stay." Nui's mom said to Khun Yaa.

"How do you expect me to sleep with Nui being here? I'll stay. You go on home and look after Duen and Khun Bpoo."

Mae said nothing for a long moment, then bent over to look at me. Her eyes were shiny.

"Get some rest, Nui. I'm sure it'll all be fine. They'll find out what's wrong and make it right. I'll come back first thing in the morning." She then actually kissed my forehead and touched my shoulder, and I felt her fingers tremble. Wow! If I hadn't already been paralysed, I would have frozen at the unexpected gesture. I felt myself tearing up again seeing Nui's strong mother so helpless and upset. This situation was getting worse by the minute.

Mae straightened up, wiped her eyes and then grabbed Paa's arm to leave. Khun Yaa touched my hand and looked down at me. "We'll take good care of you, Nui. Don't worry, you'll be home in no time."

I stared into her eyes, desperately wanting to believe her. *Dear God or Buddha or whoever is up there, if you get me out of this, I promise I will never ever complain about anything again.* Exhausted, I closed my eyes.

75

NUI

It was late, but I FaceTimed Luna anyway, figuring she wouldn't be able to fake a story if she was looking straight at me. No answer. Strange. I got ready for bed and brushed my teeth before trying again. This time, Duen answered. Her eyes were red and swollen. My stomach clenched. Why did Duen answer Luna's phone and why was she so upset? Duen rarely got worked up about stuff. *Please, let Khun Yaa be ok.* I sent a quick prayer to the Buddha.

"Hey Luna," Duen said, her voice subdued between sniffles.

"Duen? What's wrong? Where's Nui?" I wanted to shake her, or hold her, or both, to make her speak up.

She started crying. My heart sank. *What's going on?* I didn't think I could handle another crisis tonight.

"Duen, what's wrong?"

"Nu… Nui is in the hospital," she hiccupped.

"Huh? Why? What happened?"

"We don't know. She couldn't move. She's paralysed. I found her on the bed. And then Mae, Paa and Khun Yaa took her to the hospital. They're not back yet."

"Oh no! What happened?" I kept repeating the same question and getting the same answers.

"I don't know. I think she was meditating, but she wasn't moving at all. Oh, Luna, it was horrible. And she looked so scared, but she couldn't say anything."

I felt like a brick had dropped squarely on my head. This couldn't be a coincidence. Was this proof of what I had suspected? Had Luna really tried to push me out of her body but got stuck when I pushed back? And now *my body* was paralysed? What the hell had she done to me? I was furious and scared at the same time. My mind was leaping around like a frog on drugs. Wait a minute; had I caused this by pushing back? Meaning, I had done this to my own body? No! If Luna hadn't tried in the first place, I wouldn't have pushed back. This was *her* fault. *But it's your body. Concentrate.*

"That sounds awful. I'm so sorry, Duen. I'm sure she'll be fine. What hospital is she in?"

"Samitivej. It happened right after dinner. Nui was late coming home, and she said she'd been drinking with you. She threw up outside and Mae was furious. She said Nui can't see you anymore."

What? Why would Luna lie about seeing me? Where did Luna go when I stood her up? I doubted that any of my friends would have served her alcohol if she had shown up. There was only one wild card I wasn't sure about—Yumi.

"I'm really sorry, but listen Duen, I'm sure Nui will be fine. Can you text me when you know something more? I'll try to come and see her tomorrow."

"Hmm, ya, ok. Thanks Luna." Duen signed off, still snif-fling. I felt sorry for her, but touched that she cared about me, even if we didn't always agree.

What was I supposed to do now? My world was imploding.

76

LUNA

FOR SOMEONE WHO HAD NEVER HAD SO MUCH AS A BROKEN arm, it was horrifying to be at the mercy of the medical staff. While I couldn't move, my nerves still felt every little pinch and prick. It was invasive and painful when they set up the catheter and infusion lines. I tried to block out whatever they were doing to my body—or rather, Nui's body—but it didn't help much. Internally, I was howling, but no sound came out. *I'm so sorry, Nui. I didn't mean for this to happen.*

By the time they finally rolled me out of the emergency area into a semi-private room, it must have been well past midnight. Khun Yaa picked the chair closest to my bed to keep hold of my hand. I could see in her face she was exhausted, and I felt even more guilty.

"Don't worry, Nui. Just rest for now. We'll figure it all out tomorrow."

If only she knew what I had done. The only person who might be able to help me was Nui, and I didn't even know how she, or my body, had reacted to my reckless attack. I really hoped she was ok, otherwise I would be truly stuck. How could I get her to visit if I couldn't ask? I closed my eyes. Maybe I could send her a telepathic message? *You're definitely losing it, Luna.* The only time that had worked was when we were both out-of-body and *willing* to communicate. *Remember where your uninvited approach got you.* I didn't dare try that again.

Khun Yaa released my hand to sit back in her chair. I wished I could tell her to at least lie down in the empty bed next to mine. I didn't want her to risk her own health on top of everything. The night passed slowly. I couldn't turn to sleep on my side like I normally did. A nurse came through at certain intervals to check my blood pressure, pulse, and other vital signs. I must have dozed off a few times, but when I did, I had nightmares of being tied up, first to an active railroad track, then to a raft just about to go over a huge waterfall. Each time, I woke myself up, my heart pounding, then each time it became harder to fall asleep again, afraid of what the next nightmare would bring.

77

NUI

YUMI! I HAD TO TALK TO YUMI. IF I'D GUESSED RIGHT AND Luna had been drinking with her, maybe she had a clue what Luna had been planning. It was almost midnight, but I wanted to at least let her know neither Luna nor I would be in class the next day.

'Hey Yumi, just fyi, Nui is in the hospital and she and I won't be in school tomorrow.'

My phone rang with a WhatsApp video call.

"Hey, Yumi, you're up late."

"Hey, what's wrong with Nui? And why won't you be in school tomorrow?" Yumi asked. She was sitting on her bed in a purple nightshirt, her hair in pigtail braids, and some kind of goo on her face. The look made me smile despite the previous hours of drama.

"I just spoke to Duen, her sister, and she said Nui is paralysed. They don't know what caused it, but she's in the hospital."

"What?! How did that happen?" Yumi sat up, her face

scrunched up, which looked peculiar with the mask she had on. "We had a glass of wine here this afternoon and she was pretty buzzed but functioning. You think that had something to do with it?"

"I have no idea. Was Nui ok when you saw her? She didn't reply to my messages at all."

"I think she was mad at you. She said you were supposed to meet and then you no-showed. What was that all about?"

"Yeah, I know, but Mom decided she wanted to spend some time with me alone, so we went for lunch and then to a salon for some treatments. That reminds me, she told me to say hello, and she'd love to see you."

"Oh, tell her I said hi. So, why aren't *you* coming to school tomorrow?"

"Nothing big really. I fainted and because it was the second time, my parents wanted me to get a check-up at the hospital. We got back late, and the doc said to rest tomorrow until they have the results from the blood tests." I was actually grateful to not be going to school while I was waiting to hear from the police. I would be useless in class.

"You mean you and Nui went to the hospital at the same time? That is so bizarre. What are the chances of that?"

"I know, weird coincidence."

"I don't really believe in coincidences, Luna. There's something going on with you two. I asked Nui the same thing this afternoon."

"What do you mean? Asked her what?" I wasn't sure I wanted to go down that road, but I was curious to find out what Yumi was getting at.

"I asked her why she seems to know me so well and you can't remember the first thing about me," Yumi said, giving me a challenging look.

"Come on Yumi, don't be silly. Of course I remember you. And Nui only knows what I told her about you."

"Oh yeah? Then tell me what you remember about my 13th birthday party. Where was it and who was there? Or just tell me when my birthday is."

Shit!

"I don't want to play games now, Yumi. I'm worried about Nui and I'm tired, too. I better go."

"It was a simple question, Luna. Are you saying you don't know or you can't remember?" Yumi was like Joey with a bone and wouldn't let go.

"I…" For the life of me, I couldn't think of anything to say. Why did this have to come up now on top of everything else?

"Yes?" Yumi asked.

"I gotta go. I need to sleep. If you want to come to the hospital with me tomorrow afternoon, text me, ok? Night." I quickly hung up and realized I was panting, almost in panic.

All things really do come in threes, don't they? First Pinkelephant and the police, then Luna paralysed in the hospital—in my body—and now Yumi suspecting the truth. How was I going to convince Yumi she was imagining things when I didn't have Luna to back me up? I threw myself face down onto the bed, screaming silently into the pillows.

78

LUNA

By the time the morning shift started, I was exhausted. Between my nightmares and the nurse's visits, I had run the gamut of emotions from utter panic, to guilt, to anger, to frustration, and back again. Khun Yaa looked drained. I wished I could tell her to go home and rest or at least get something to eat, but I was selfish enough to admit it was reassuring to have her here. The nurse said my vitals were normal while she sponged my body, changed the catheter bags and stomach tube and remade the bed. I tried to envision myself somewhere else to ignore the indignity. Normally, I loved to daydream, but this time, it didn't work. The embarrassment of having people handle my body like a mannequin was almost worse than the thought of being stuck in this state. *Get over it. It's not even your own body. But it's the body you're stuck in.* Arghh! If I could have, I would have screamed at my twisted thoughts.

Mae arrived early with Duen in tow. Duen promised to

stay with me while Mae took Khun Yaa to the coffee shop to get some food. She wiped her eyes while talking non-stop.

"Oh, Nui, this is all so horrible. Khun Bpoo and I waited until Mae and Paa came home and they said they didn't know what was wrong with you. I took Joey for his walks. He misses you, but don't worry, I'll take care of him. Luna called, by the way. She was really upset too when I told her. She said she'd been trying to reach you and will come here tomorrow, I mean today. And Mae said she'll take Khun Yaa home but then will come back. Are you hurting?" She bent over to look at me. How was I supposed to let her know I had heard, and no, I wasn't hurting right now? But then Duen solved the problem in the simplest possible way.

"How about you blink once for yes, and two times for no? Will that work?"

Blink.

Duen grinned through her tears, pleased to have come up with her system.

"Are you hurting?"

Blink, blink.

"Do you know what happened?"

Blink, blink. Lying was easy if you didn't have to say the words out loud.

"Mae said the doctors will know after some tests."

Blink.

"I'm sure you'll be home soon."

There was nothing to blink about.

"I have to go soon or I'll be late for school, but I'll come back later, ok?"

Blink.

She leaned over to hug me, carefully avoiding the lines running into my body. I hoped my eyes conveyed how much I appreciated her gesture. Duen stood up and again looked at me.

"Do you need anything?"

Blink, blink. I did, but how was I supposed to communicate that?

At least Duen had given me two vital pieces of information. Nui was ok, and I hadn't put her into a coma or something worse, which meant at least one of us was functioning. I felt hugely relieved. Better yet, she was coming here. I had to believe that together we could figure out how to unlock me. How, I didn't know, but right now I didn't even care which body I ended up in. I just wanted to be free to move.

There was a knock on the door, and Paa peered in. Khun Yaa and Mae were right behind him. Paa smiled and came over to stroke my head and cheek. Shockingly, this was only my second instance of physical contact with him, and he seemed self-conscious about the gesture. I missed my dad's hugs. Nui's family didn't normally go for public displays of affection, apart from Khun Yaa. Maybe that's why I had taken to her so quickly. But clearly Mae and Paa cared as well, even if they didn't show it often or openly. Another knock came at the door and the nurse walked in, followed by two doctors. They stood at the foot of the bed with the family gathered on one side. The new doctor briefly glanced at me over his reading glasses, then consulted the board he was holding in his hand and addressed Nui's parents.

"Good morning, I'm Dr Sunchawee. I'm in charge of the neurological department here. My colleague, Dr Chomploy here, admitted Nui last night." The family wai'ed in unison to the doctors. Only Dr Chomploy wai'ed back.

"I've had a look at Nui's chart and we also received the lab reports back. There are a few other neurological tests I want to run, but right now, it appears that Nui has a form of locked-in syndrome." I heard Mae and Khun Yaa gasp and Duen mutter under her breath.

Why isn't the doc talking to me? I found him arrogant and irritating, which gave me something to focus on other than the diagnosis he had delivered impassively.

"Does this have anything to do with the rabies shots she's been getting or the alcohol she drank yesterday?" Mae asked. "Without our permission," she added, with a pinch of defensiveness.

"Rabies?" Dr Chomploy asked. "You didn't mention that last night." He sounded indignant, as if they had deliberately left out a vital piece of information. Everyone talked over each other until Dr Sunchawee regained control.

"Excuse me! No, I don't think the rabies shots or the alcohol caused this. As for the locked-in syndrome, it's extremely rare and is associated with damage to a particular part of the brainstem. I don't want to bother you with too much detail, but basically it's caused by an interruption of the motor fibres between the brain and the muscular system…" I tuned him out. I didn't want to hear any medical reasons, but had to believe that my explanation was the correct one.

"… infarct or stroke… MRI…" No, none of this applied. I knew what caused it.

"… big difference… good news… Nui can breathe on her own, which is not normally the case with this syndrome."

See? I knew it. This isn't locked-in. So, it's up to Nui and me.

"She can also talk. I mean say yes or no, I mean, blink." Duen spoke up.

Mae shushed her, but Duen insisted.

"But she can! Ask her something and she blinks once for yes and twice for no. Try it."

"Yes, that makes sense," Dr Sunchawee confirmed.

"Locked-in patients are usually fully cognitive, so she can probably hear and understand everything. Again, that's good news too."

"So, what happens now?" Mae asked.

"We'll run some more tests, like I said, and we'll keep her under observation. We'll speak more when we have the results."

"Can you cure her?" Khun Yaa asked, her voice wobbly but determined.

Dr Sunchawee cleared his throat. "I suggest we wait until we have all the results. We should know more by this evening. There are too many unknown factors right now." *Yeah, right, you know nothing.* It felt good to contradict him, if only to myself.

"But you *can* heal her, right?" Khun Yaa asked again, more insistent. "Just tell us."

"There are rehabilitation treatments that can help recover slight voluntary movements. There are a few documented cases of spontaneous recovery, but again, you're asking me to speculate right now. First, I'd like to run the additional tests to rule out everything else. I will speak with you this evening." *Cop-out. You just don't want to admit that you can't help.*

He flipped his clipboard closed, nodded to the family, and walked out, followed by the other medical staff. Not once had he actually looked at me, which pissed me off. And he hadn't had the decency to return a wai. *Idiot*! Anger felt better than fear.

The family surrounded the bed, staring down at me. Khun Yaa brushed my hair back, her eyes shiny with tears, which almost set off my own tears again. Mae cleared her throat, but her voice was still raspy, as if she had to battle her own emotions. That, more than anything, made me realise how grim the situation was, and how much it affected everyone in the family. Nui will never forgive me for worrying them so much. *If you ever get out of this in the first place, Luna. Yes, I will.* The merry-go-round in my head continued.

"Here's what we're going to do, Nui," said Mae. "Paa will take Khun Yaa back home to get some rest and he'll open the shop afterwards. I'll stay here with you while they do the tests. Do you understand?"

Blink.

"Mae, Luna said she'd come by this afternoon to see Nui, just so you know." Duen said.

"I don't think so! If she got Nui drunk, I never want to see her again."

Shit. I needed Nui. She was the only one who could help me. I stared at Duen, silently imploring her to say something.

"But Mae, Luna is Nui's best friend. It's not fair to not let her see Nui. Besides, you can tell Luna off about the drinking yourself." *Way to go, Duen! Thanks.*

"We'll see," Mae grumbled.

Khun Yaa kissed my forehead.

"I'm sure everything will work out, Nui. I'll be back later. Try not to worry."

Paa stroked my shoulder and then ushered his mother and daughter out.

Mae settled herself in the chair by the bed and picked up her phone. At least I wouldn't have to talk to her, but could use the time to think about how to convince Nui to help me.

NUI

As soon as I got up, I checked the pinkelephant site. Still blocked. Damn. So it hadn't been a bad dream after all. What now? I fell back on the bed, moaning. Technically, I was supposed to rest today, but with everything going on, I thought it highly unlikely I'd be able to stay still. My priority was to find out what Luna's parents were going to do about the police. I also needed to tell Khun Susan that I had to go see Luna in the hospital.

On my way to the kitchen, I ran into Luke, who was leaving for school.

"Feeling better, Luna?" he asked, hiking his backpack over his shoulder. "I can't believe you had that same thing again. I'm glad Mom and Dad were here this time. See, it was good after all that I told Mom."

"I know. Thanks Luke, and yes, I'm feeling better."

"Did Mom and Dad give you a hard time about it? I heard them say they had to discuss something serious with you." He looked as if he was ready to jump into battle with me against the parents. I smiled.

"Nah, it wasn't about that; it was about something completely different. But don't worry, it'll be alright." I crossed my fingers behind my back. "You better run or you'll miss the van."

"See ya," he replied, slamming the front door behind him.

Khun Bo was bustling around the kitchen, chatting with Khun Susan, catching her up on the events of the previous two weeks. Luna's mom stood near the door with her coffee cup in hand, poised to escape as soon as Khun Bo stopped talking.

"Morning honey. How are you feeling?"

"Morning Mom. I'm totally fine. Slept well, actually."

"I noticed. I came to check on you a few times and had to shake you to wake you up."

"You did? I don't remember."

"Well, that means at least one of us got some sleep."

Oops. I instantly felt guilty. "Sorry Mom, for that, and you know, the other stuff."

"Come to my office after you've had breakfast. Dad left early to find out if we need a lawyer."

I cringed. I hoped the police might just review the site and decide it wasn't a big enough deal to justify further action. For now, all I could do was wait. "Mom, I found out last night that Nui is in the hospital. It's really serious. She's paralysed."

"What? Oh my God. What happened?"

"I don't know. When I spoke to her sister, her parents hadn't returned home from the hospital yet. But I want to visit her if you're ok with that?"

"Let's see what Dad says. We need to deal with this first."

"Yeah, ok. But I'm really worried about her." As scary as it was, I had to see the damage Luna had done to my body.

"I know, honey. You can go if nothing else comes up. Have some breakfast, then we'll call Dad to see if he has any updates."

Having Khun Bo back was great. Despite the knot in my stomach, I was looking forward to a proper Thai breakfast. Half an hour later, I went to join Luna's mom in her office and find out how big a mess I was in.

LUNA

Now I knew how it felt to be a human pincushion. Dr Sunchawee hadn't said what tests he had planned, but it involved a lot of needles to check my nerve response, which apparently was working just fine. I felt every single pin prick, even though my muscles didn't react. My eyes became tired from having to blink yes and no in response to the poking. Not being able to move had given me a strange sense of disembodiment, like I was observing myself without really being there. It was different to the out-of-body experience during meditation, which had felt blissful. I wondered if this was how test animals felt being just a specimen for researchers to use—trapped, without being able to do anything about it.

Mae came into the treatment room to observe the procedures without saying anything. My mom would have asked a million questions about why and how, but Mae was more deferential to the medical staff.

Duen hadn't said what time Nui was coming over, but school didn't let out until three, so at the earliest, she'd be at the hospital by four. A long wait. Then there was the risk of Mae not allowing her to visit because of my lie about the drinking. I hoped Mae would be gone by then.

It was almost lunchtime by the time the doctors and nurses had finished their jabbing and taken me back to my room. Not that lunch meant anything in my current state, as they pumped whatever sustenance they thought I needed into my stomach directly. I refused to look when the nurse showed Mae how she did it and how much fluid she administered. The thought alone disgusted me.

Mae hardly spoke at all the entire time she was with me, but she had a pinched look of worry on her face while she scrolled and typed on her phone. Whether the worry was about my condition, or the cost involved, or something else, I couldn't guess. I was glad when Khun Yaa and Khun Bpoo showed up to relieve her.

"I'll be back later to hear what the doctor has to say, Nui," Mae said.

"Take your time. At least one of us will be here," Khun Yaa assured her. She fussed with the bed, straightening the cover and stroking my hair, anything to keep her hands busy. Khun Bpoo sat in the chair, watching his wife bustle about. During the time I'd spent with the family, I never had much interaction with him. To me, he was almost like a stranger living in the same house. I closed my eyes, pretending to be tired. I was just about to doze off when a thought occurred to me. If Duen had spoken to Nui on my phone, did that mean she had the passcode to unlock it? And if so, would she be nosy enough to read all the messages between Nui and me, or worse, from Channon? Since I had Nui's phone, it was entirely possible Duen would know how to access it. I had to get it back somehow, before she could start asking awkward questions. I wished I could hurry along Nui's arrival.

81

NUI

KHUN SUSAN WAS SPEAKING INTO HER HEADSET WHEN I walked into her office. "She's here, Mark. Let me put you on speaker." She nodded for me to sit down. There were papers all over her desk that must have piled up in the weeks she'd been away.

"How are you feeling, Luna? Any lasting effects from last night?" Khun Mark asked.

"No Dad. I'm completely fine. Thank you."

"That's good. So, I spoke with our company's legal counsel and asked him what he thought."

"And?" Khun Susan asked.

"He's not an expert on this issue, but he said it's up to the police to decide if they deem it necessary to proceed with an investigation. I put a call through to Jake at the Embassy. Maybe he or his staff can recommend a lawyer who could help us. I want to be prepared if it comes to that."

I swallowed. "I am so, so sorry." The idea of having to face the police left me shaky. Why did I assume this couldn't happen to me? Was I really so naïve to think the rules wouldn't apply to expats?

Both parents were silent for a beat. "I have to get back to work. I'll call you as soon as I hear from Jake," Khun Mark said.

"Bye honey. Speak later." Khun Susan hung up, then turned to me.

"Do you finally understand how serious this is?" Her tone wasn't angry. In fact, it was remarkably calm, but it was a far cry from our warm conversations the day before. Maybe she was very focused in a crisis and didn't let her emotions run away with her.

"Yes Mom. I get it. I don't know what to say besides sorry."

"I hope you learned your lesson," she sighed, turning back to her papers.

"Trust me, I have. I won't ever do anything so stupid again." *At least not here in Thailand,* I silently amended.

"Are you ok for me to see Nui, then? I'm really worried about her." There was nothing I could do at home, and if I went early, I should be able to avoid Yumi and her suspicions. If she even decided to visit.

"Let's wait until lunch. If we haven't heard from Dad by then, you can go. I'm pretty sure you have some studying to do, don't you? I called BIS to let them know you wouldn't be in today. Can you get your homework from Yumi?" Khun Susan asked.

"Sure, I'll text her. I'll just do some reading now. Thanks, Mom."

While I had plenty of study material, I wasn't sure I'd be able to concentrate with the potential investigation hanging over me. I also wondered if I could find some information online on the side-effects of astral projections.

82

LUNA

A KNOCK ON THE DOOR WOKE ME UP. KHUN YAA AND KHUN Bpoo were quietly talking near the window, but turned as Duen walked in. She wai'ed to her grandparents.

"Hey, Nui. How are you doing? You ok?"

Blink. As ok as I could be. I checked the clock above the TV mounted opposite the bed. Someone must have turned it on during my nap, but it was set to mute. Duen was early for a regular school day.

"Grandma, do you want to get something to drink and eat while I'm here?" Duen asked.

"That's alright, Duen." Khun Yaa replied, but Khun Bpoo hooked her arm through his.

"Let's walk a bit, otherwise we'll get rusty," he said, nodding at Duen and me before escorting his wife out the door.

"Where's Mae?" Duen asked, then grinned. "Sorry, I mean, is Mae coming back soon?"

Blink.

"You need anything?"

Blink.

"Hmm, how do you want me to figure that out?" Duen pursed her lips, then smiled.

"How about we play it like tai chai, ok?" I didn't know what tai chai was but assumed it was similar to *Twenty Questions*.

Blink.

"Something medical?"

Blink, blink.

"Something personal?"

Blink.

"Something to do with the family?"

Blink, blink.

"Something to do with your friends?"

Blink.

"A person?"

Blink.

"That's easy. It's Channon, right?"

Blink, blink.

"Hmm, not Channon? Oh, Luna?"

Blink.

"What about her?"

Stare.

"Sorry, I mean, you want to see her?"

Blink.

"She said she was coming, but I don't know when. Want me to call her?"

Blink.

Duen rummaged in her bag and pulled out my phone, just as I had suspected. She tapped out the code. Shit, so she'd known it all along, with me being clueless and careless.

"Wow, Nui, you have a lot of new alerts. Why are you

following all those weird sites? There are a few messages from someone called Yumi. Who's that?"

Stare.

"Is she in your school too?"

Blink.

"Ok, let me just text Luna. She's probably still in school."

Please use SMS and not WhatsApp. I said a silent prayer.

She typed something but suddenly went still and just stared at the phone, using her forefinger to scroll, then she glanced up at me with a stunned expression.

"No way, Nui. You lied! You weren't at Luna's at all. It says here she wasn't even home. And why is she calling you Luna?"

I closed my eyes in misery.

83

NUI

I SHOULD HAVE SAVED MYSELF THE RESEARCH. NONE OF THE websites I found yielded anything useful about physical side effects of out-of-body experiences. At noon I checked in with Khun Susan, but still no word from Luna's dad. We ate a quiet lunch.

"Is it ok if I go to see Nui now, Mom?"

"Go ahead, but keep your phone handy in case Dad needs to speak with you."

"Will do."

On impulse, I grabbed Luna's favourite lip balm and hand lotion to give to her. Even if she wouldn't be able to apply it herself, maybe it would make her feel a bit better. The little teak elephant, *Chang,* I had given her when we explored Bangkok during the early days of our friendship went into the same pouch. Going by Skytrain and moto-taxi was faster than using a cab. On the way, I texted Duen to find out what room Luna was in. The neurology department was on the first floor of Building C. I was about to ask directions at the nurse's station when I saw my grandparents enter a room a few doors down. I followed, briefly knocked, and walked in. My eyes immediately turned to the bed and my body in it, and I instinctively recoiled at the lines and tubes poking out from beneath the covers. I almost backed out, but I was there for a purpose. When I finally forced myself to look directly at Luna, I was shocked at the pure despair in her eyes. Not a single muscle moved in her face, only the eyes kept tracking me. I couldn't even begin to imagine what it must feel like to be fully aware, yet helpless. A tremor went through me.

"Hey Luna. How are you?" Duen asked.

"Hi Duen." I wai'ed to my grandparents. Khun Yaa looked terrible, aged beyond her years. Then she gazed at me with distinct displeasure. That almost hurt as much as seeing my still body.

"I don't think you should be here, Luna. Nui's mother is very upset with you about the drinking." Khun Yaa moved around the bed, blocking my view as if she wanted to protect 'me' from 'Luna'.

I could have set the record straight but that would have exposed Luna, and by extension me, as having lied to my family. I wasn't sure which was worse. Duen prevented me from having to make that decision.

"She didn't drink with Luna, Khun Yaa," Duen said, waving Luna's phone at Khun Yaa. "They texted yesterday, but Luna wasn't even home. I think Nui went to someone else's house. Do you know a Yumi, Luna?"

I nodded. "Yes, Yumi is a classmate of ours. Nui was supposed to come to our house yesterday, but my mom had made other plans and I didn't have time to call Nui to explain."

Khun Yaa visibly softened towards me. "I'm sorry, Noo Luna. I shouldn't have accused you like that."

"Mai pen rai, Khun Yaa, don't worry. Can you tell me what is going on? What's wrong with Nui?" I was still standing by the door, not sure if I wanted to come closer to my motionless body. It was creepy to see myself as a zombie in a hospital bed. Khun Yaa moved back to the other side of the bed and stroked my hand, summarizing pretty much what Duen had told me already.

"And what can they do about it?"

"The doctors said there are some treatments, but nothing specific." I had never seen Khun Yaa so beaten down. I almost teared up myself, but I couldn't; I had to come up with a reason to speak to Luna alone. If I could somehow communicate with her, we might get some answers.

Sometimes the direct approach was also the easiest. "Khun Yaa, would it be ok if I speak to Nui alone for a few moments? I have something personal to tell her."

Grandma looked slightly taken aback, but considered my request for a moment.

Finally, she nodded. "We'll take Duen to the cafe. We'll be back in fifteen minutes."

Maybe she felt she had to make amends for accusing me about Luna's drinking.

"Thank you very much." I wai'ed again.

"Hey Duen, would you mind leaving Nui's phone here? I need to show her something."

Duen frowned.

"Why? Why can't you show her on your own phone?"

"It's a new app she'll need for some school stuff." I ad-libbed.

Duen looked at Luna. "You ok with that, Nui?"

Luna blinked.

Duen sighed, then unlocked and handed the phone to me.

"Here, the code is 1103."

Damn it. How did she know that? I would have to change it.

As soon as the door closed, I sat on the chair next to the bed and looked at Luna.

"You did this, didn't you?"

Luna blinked.

84

LUNA

I WANTED TO FADE INTO THE MATTRESS OR THIN AIR—
anything to avoid the upcoming 'chat'. How was I going to
explain to Nui what I had done, or more importantly, that I
needed her help to unlock me? She had good reason to be
furious seeing me hooked up like this, lines and needles
sticking out of her body. I only had fifteen minutes to come
up with a way to make her understand. I felt so powerless, but
I had to try.

"Duen said you can blink for yes or no?" Nui started.

Blink.

"So I'll just keep asking questions and you blink?"

Blink.

"Did you try to force me from your body?"

Bam! Nui went right for the throat. I should have seen it
coming, especially as she'd speculated before about the
connection between her seizure and my comment about not
having to be in the same room for a swap. I stared at her and
finally resigned.

Blink.

"I knew it!" Nui jumped up. "I just knew it. How could you? Do you have any idea what you did? It was bad enough that I fainted and had to go to the hospital, but look at you… you paralysed my body. You are such a…" She stopped mid-tirade and took a deep breath. "Shit, Luna, why the hell did you do that? We had agreed to switch back. Why did you have to force it?"

I stared at her. My tears had tried up. Nui could hardly pretend she was completely innocent.

Somewhat chagrined, she understood. "Ok, fine. I get you were angry and must have assumed I'd backed out, but really, Luna, you knew how dangerous this could be. Ajaarn had warned us about it. And admit it, this isn't the first time you tried, right? The first seizure… That was you too, wasn't it?"

Blink.

Nui took a deep breath.

"So, what now?"

Stare.

"I don't know what to suggest. Any ideas?"

Blink.

"You do?

Blink. *Come on, Nui, isn't it obvious?*

"You think it can be reversed?"

Blink.

Wait.

Blink.

Two very deliberate yesses.

"But how?"

I wanted to shake Nui for being so dense.

She glanced at her phone.

"I better change the code."

Come on Nui, the code is unimportant right now. But

equally I didn't want Duen or Mae to read any of my texts either.

She fiddled with the settings, wasting precious minutes until Khun Yaa's return.

"Ok, it's now 1412, Khun Yaa's birthday, ok?"

Blink.

Nui looked back at me. The phone must have helped her to focus. "You think if we try to meditate together and connect out-of-body, we might be able to unlock you?"

Blink.

Wait.

Blink.

Wait.

Blink.

I knew she would get it. The immensity of my relief almost surprised me.

Nui looked at me as if she was weighing her options. *Options?* There was no other option! If she didn't agree to help, I'd be truly stuck. *And you only have yourself to blame, Luna.*

"I need to think about it." Nui said. "What if we swap but can't break the paralysis? That would work out fine for you, but I'd risk being stuck because of something you did."

Ouch! That hurt. On some level, I understood her hesitation, but I couldn't contemplate her saying no. Would she really leave me like this? *Don't forget who started it.* The little voice in my head wouldn't shut up.

"Besides, how would we do it? I don't think I could concentrate here. There are too many people around."

Stop looking for excuses, Nui. They won't let me out of here while I'm in this state.

Nui finally looked me in the eye as if she'd decided something. "I need to think about this, but there are a few things you need to know about what happened at your...."

Before she could finish, the door burst open.

"Nui! My God, what happened to you? This is awful." Yumi stormed in, speaking at full volume and speed, as usual. "Luna told me you were here. I brought you some flowers." She waved a bunch of beautiful Thai orchids at me. "I figured you can't eat chocolates or anything, otherwise I would have brought some."

The interruption was frustrating, but Yumi's enthusiasm, as usual, made me want to grin. I tried to convey my thanks with my eyes. She must have come straight from school if her dress code was any sign. Today she was wearing a frilly pink mini dress with a red cherry and rose print, and a triple strand of pearls draped around her neck. A white boxy leather jacket and cowboy boots rounded out the outfit, and a big red purse, large enough to be sufficient as a weekend carry-on bag, was slung over her shoulder.

She turned to Nui. "So, what happened to Nui? Did they say? Is she going to be ok? And by the way, you still haven't answered any of my questions from last night."

I didn't know what that was about, but Nui squirmed, clearly uncomfortable with whatever they had discussed.

"Yumi, please could you give Nui and myself a few more minutes?" Nui asked. "I need to tell her something personal."

Yumi glanced from me to Nui and back again.

"Are you still being weird? Are you avoiding me? I know it wasn't a coincidence that..."

A polite knock on the door interrupted her.

The door opened and Channon poked his head in.

"Hi, can I come in?"

I closed my eyes and wished I could beam myself somewhere else.

85

NUI

"Hey Channon, how are you?" Yumi bounced over to him and extended her hand.

"Hi. Yumi, right? Nice to see you again." Channon grinned, but then glanced over at Luna and his smile faded. Luna had her eyes closed, as if she couldn't bear to look at him.

"Can she hear us?" Channon asked, walking closer to the bed.

"Yes, and she can communicate by blinking." I replied. The room was too crowded, and Khun Yaa and the rest would be back in a few minutes. I really needed to get everyone out so I could finish my 'conversation' with Luna.

"Hey guys, would you mind giving Nui and myself a few minutes? I just need to bring her up to speed on something private."

Yumi narrowed her eyes, but apparently decided this would be her chance to get to know Channon better.

"Channon, want to grab a coffee?"

Channon glanced at each of us and finally shrugged. "Sure." He turned back to Luna, and softly touched her hand. "I'll be back in a few minutes." Luna kept her eyes closed, but I could see a single tear rolling down her face. It made my heart squeeze painfully.

"Thanks guys."

If Khun Yaa and Khun Bpoo were going to be punctual, we only had a few minutes left. I sat on Luna's bed to look her directly in the eye so she'd understand every single point I had to tell her.

"Erm, this is kind of awkward, but I have a confession to make."

Luna looked confused.

"You know about the site, pinkelephant, right?"

Blink.

"I'm not sure how to say this, but I wrote that blog. I mean, it's technically anonymous, but really, it's my site. I wanted to use it to build a portfolio for my Uni application." I swallowed hard and forced myself to sit still. "The problem is… I mean, that last post was a bit controversial and, erm… so, it turned out, that the police got hold of it somehow and they shut it down."

Luna still looked confused. My rambling explanation sounded daft even to me.

"The thing is… they kinda could make a case for lèse majesté, not that I think they will, but I guess they could, and the problem is, the site kinda leads back to you. I mean, your name and IP address." I locked my hands, but then forced myself to face Luna again. I owed her that much. "So, there's a possibility of me going to prison. Except, they think you wrote it, so actually, you could go to prison. If we swapped back, I mean."

'Eyes are the windows of the soul.' The random thought

popped into my head, and Luna conveyed lots of different emotions with just one look. Her expression ran from confusion to shock to disgust to worry to something like rage. It was too fast to pinpoint exactly what she was telling me. I had to divert my eyes for a moment to gather myself.

"So, we're in a bit of a bind. We both screwed up. I guess we need to decide which is the lesser of two evils for both of us. Being stuck in a body or stuck in prison."

I glanced at my watch.

"There's one other thing, Yumi keeps asking really strange questions. I think she's convinced there's something strange going on. She's asking some very specific stuff. It's almost like she guessed about the swap, somehow. It's really weird." Luna didn't blink at all, but kept staring at me.

I cleared my throat.

"So, I think we need to decide what we're willing to risk. I mean, of course, there's also the best-case scenario we get you unlocked and there won't be an investigation. We will both know more later today, then we can figure out the next step. Does that make sense?"

Blink.

I glanced at my watch again.

"Khun Yaa will be here any minute. I'll come back tomorrow and we'll decide then, ok?"

Blink.

86

LUNA

MY HEAD WAS SPINNING. NUI'S REVELATIONS HAD HIT ME like a freight train. Her duplicity, her going behind my back and putting my entire family at risk, was unbelievable. And every time we had an argument she had pretended to be the wronged party. *You traitor.* Yet, had I been any better? Jeopardizing our bodies carelessly was how I had ended up like a zombie. We had both wanted something different, but navigating the other side wasn't so easy after all. Nui was right. We had to consider what was at stake. Was I willing to go to jail for something I hadn't done? Would I be able to deal with it? What would it do to my family? And would Nui be willing to risk being paralysed? My thoughts gridlocked having to decide something this huge. I wished I could just switch my brain off. The thought reminded me of an old family joke when Mom had said exactly that, and Luke, serious in his innocence, had asked, 'But if it's switched off, how do you turn it on again?' The memory triggered another round of tears, and a decision. I wanted my family, no matter what, and I would risk everything to make it happen.

The return of the grandparents and Duen interrupted my thoughts. Khun Yaa looked at Nui and me with trepidation, as if she sensed that something big had happened. She walked over and gently wiped my tears.

"What have you done, Luna? Why is she crying?" Khun Yaa asked Nui.

"Maybe Luna talked about school and Nui knows she may not be going back," Duen suggested.

Shit. What was it with Duen today? She kept dropping one bombshell after the other.

"What do you mean, Duen?" Nui asked. "Why wouldn't she go back?"

"She didn't tell you? Mae and Paa need the money to renovate the shop next to ours and convert it into a cooking school. So, Nui won't be able to go much longer. But she couldn't really go back like this, anyway. "

I would have throttled Duen if I could have gotten my hands on her. The big blabbermouth! I looked at Nui and saw her go white with shock. She groped her way to the chair next to Khun Bpoo to sit down.

"Duen! Stop talking about our private affairs! You should be ashamed of yourself," Khun Yaa scolded Duen.

"Sorry, Grandma," Duen said, only half apologetic. I never realized she was such a big gossip.

"First, Nui will get better. And second, your parents haven't decided anything yet about the shop. Just because you want the cooking school doesn't mean it's going to happen, Duen," Khun Yaa stated firmly.

"You want a cooking school, Duen?" Nui asked. "You never… I mean, I'd never guessed."

Come on, Nui! That's the least of the issues right now. I

felt like screaming my head off. Had the entire world gone mad?

"But it would be terrible if Nui had to leave BIS. She loves it there," Nui said.

"Yeah, but Mae said Nui has lost her focus, so she thinks they're wasting money on the school fees."

"But that's not really fair, is it?" Nui asked desperately. "I mean, maybe she has been a bit distracted, but to take her out of school seems rather drastic."

"Nong Luna, I think you need to let us decide what's best for the family," Khun Yaa interrupted.

Nui immediately caved and wai'ed to her grandmother. It was probably reflexive.

"I think I'd better go. I'll come back tomorrow," Nui said, standing up.

She came over to look at me.

"I'll see you later, ok? Think about what we discussed."

Blink.

Nui turned to leave when the door opened again, and Yumi and Channon appeared.

Frying pan–fire was the phrase that immediately jumped into my head.

NUI

THIS WHOLE SITUATION WAS INSANE. I NEEDED TO GET OUT OF here and think.

"You're leaving already, Luna?" Yumi asked.

"I gotta get home, Yumi. There's something I have to do," I said.

"Oh, you're Yumi?" Duen pounced. "You're the one who got Nui drunk."

Yumi turned around to glare at Duen.

"Yes, I'm Yumi and no, I didn't get her drunk. I offered her a drink, and she accepted. That's different." I silently applauded Yumi for not letting my brat sister get away with her constant interfering.

"How is Nui, anyway? What did the doctors say?" Channon jumped in to relieve the building tension.

Khun Yaa gave Yumi a critical side glance, but then told Channon about the diagnosis. I translated for Yumi who was the only one who didn't speak Thai.

Hearing the status again didn't make it any easier to process. I was almost at the door when Duen stopped me.

"Where's Nui's phone? Do you still have it, Luna?"

Damn. I had meant to take it with me to clear all messages relating to our swap. My little sister was way too inquisitive for her own good. At least I'd had the foresight to change the access code.

"Sorry, almost forgot. Here." I handed the phone to Duen, who stuck it in her back pocket. Thankfully, she didn't check it immediately, so I wouldn't have to explain the changed code.

"I'll be back tomorrow, ok?" I turned around but remembered at the last minute. "Yumi, can you text me our homework, please?"

"I'll walk out with you," Yumi said, before casually adding, "Channon, are you coming? You could show me the pet hospital now if you like."

WHAT?! I could almost hear Luna and me scream in unison. I bit my lip to stop myself from giggling. If it wasn't for Luna's condition or the threat of prison, I would have fallen over laughing at the sheer absurdity of it all. A quick glance at Luna snapped me out of it. Whatever Yumi was up to, I had more important things to consider, including finding out if I needed a lawyer.

In the corridor, I leaned back against the wall, closed my eyes, and took a few deep breaths to steady myself. I could hear Channon telling Luna that Chone was fine, that he was waiting for her to come back and visit him. Yumi chimed in that she would pet Chone for Luna, even though that was probably the last thing Luna wanted her to do. I shook my head and pushed off the wall. As I turned to leave, I saw Mae hurrying down the corridor and got another shock at her pinched look. Same as Khun Yaa, she seemed to have aged overnight. I felt a sudden deep anger at Luna for having made my family suffer. As soon as Mae saw me, she stopped. I automatically wai'ed to her, but I could tell she wasn't so easily appeased. She didn't know I hadn't been drinking with Luna, but my brat sister would clear that one up. The door behind me opened and Yumi and Channon walked out. Mae nodded at Channon and, without a word to me, walked past and straight into the room. Ouch. That hurt.

Yumi hooked her arm through mine. "I feel really sorry for Nui. It must be horrible what she's going through right now."

You're not helping, Yumi, I wanted to say, but a look at her arm through mine reminded me of Yumi's own struggles.

I felt deflated and drained. I had troubles of my own and couldn't worry about everyone else at the same time.

"Let's go. I have to get home. Are you really going to the pet hospital?" I asked Yumi.

"Sure. Channon told me about the great work they are doing, so I wanted to see for myself."

I wonder what Channon is up to? At least it prevented Yumi from asking me more awkward questions.

88

LUNA

GRAND CENTRAL WOULD HAVE FELT LESS CROWDED THAN MY hospital room today.

"Any change?" Mae asked as she walked in.

Khun Yaa shook her head.

"How did Channon know Nui is here? And who was that other girl?" Mae asked.

"I texted Channon. I figured he would want to know," said Duen. "And the other girl is Yumi. She's one of Nui's classmates and *she's* the one who got Nui drunk. It wasn't Luna," Duen said.

"Oh," Mae said. I couldn't tell what was going through her mind. Mae was difficult to read at the best of times, and right then, she seemed to have closed herself off completely. *To protect herself, perhaps? Maybe that's what it takes for her to handle this?* I wasn't sure where that thought came from. My mom was more upfront, and I rarely had to guess what she was thinking.

"You go home, Duen. You have homework to do and Joey needs to go out," Mae said to Duen.

"Can't I wait for Khun Yaa and Khun Bpoo? I don't have a lot of homework today. I want to hear what the doctors have to say," Duen replied.

I let their conversation wash over me as I replayed Yumi's casual remark about visiting Chone with Channon. Was she trying to move in on Channon while I was out of commission? I'd never thought Yumi was mean, but maybe that had changed in the three years since I had seen her. Sure, I knew she found Channon attractive, but would she really go that far? And Channon? I thought he and I had a special connection. How could he so casually invite another girl to visit the dog I had practically adopted? I felt betrayed, especially since I was helpless to do anything about it. *Stop it, Luna, don't fabricate stuff.* He probably only wants to show her the hospital. There's nothing wrong with that. After all, that's how you guys started out. *Exactly. What if he wants to start something new?* My head was going to explode. There was no room for another drama or crisis. I had to concentrate on getting out of this bed.

As if my thoughts had conjured them up, Dr Sunchawee and Dr Chomploy entered the room, a nurse trailing behind holding a clipboard that she handed over as they all gathered around my bed. Another standoff with the family on one side and the medical staff on the other. The family wai'ed and again, only Dr Sunchawee was too rude not to reciprocate. *He probably thinks he's God.* The way he behaved towards the family was offensive to me, but I was glad for any distraction from the whirlwind in my head.

Dr Sunchawee cleared his throat. "We have the test results, but we're not one hundred percent clear on what they mean." *Wow, big admission. So, you're not all-knowing after all.* The running commentary in my head kept me from going completely crazy. Or maybe it was a sign I had already crossed that line.

"While the symptoms are very similar to locked-in syndrome, there is no corroborating evidence as to what caused it. We now believe there must be a psychosomatic cause."

"What does that mean?" Khun Yaa asked.

Dr Sunchawee turned to Dr Chomploy as if it was beneath him to explain the disorder.

"Psychosomatic is a psychological condition that leads to physical symptoms, often with no medical explanation." Dr Chomploy said. "It can affect almost any part of the body. Stress or a chaotic lifestyle or substance abuse or depression could cause it."

Stress—check.

Chaotic life—check, check!

We'll leave the alcohol out for now.

"That can't be it. Nui doesn't have any of this," Mae said firmly.

As if.

"But what can you do about it?" Khun Yaa asked.

"I'd like to consult with a colleague about her case. He's a psychiatrist," Dr Sunchawee said.

"A psychiatrist? You believe this is all in her head?"

Gosh, Mae really could be blunt. But, looking at her face, I realized she was actually being critical of the doctors for coming up with such a silly theory. *She's actually defending me! Wow!* I couldn't decide if I should be shocked or pleased —or both.

It helped that Dr Sunchawee's diagnosis matched my assessment that the cause wasn't a physical condition, and it gave me hope that I actually could reverse it.

"So, Nui has to stay here?" Mae asked. "Until when?" Her tone was more subdued now.

Dr Chomploy answered. "Because she can't function on her own, we need to keep her here under medical supervision. Should the psychiatrist be able to discover an underlying reason, it will help us determine the treatment."

Ha! As if! No one but Nui and I know the reason. Besides, how is he going to assess me, anyway?

"What can we do?" Khun Yaa asked in a small voice. That she was hurting because of me made me feel horrible. I'll try to get out of this as soon as possible, Khun Yaa, I promised her in my head.

"Keep doing what you're doing now—visiting her, offering support. Dr Pompetch, the psychiatrist, may want to speak with you as well. He'll want to know if there have been any changes in Nui's behaviour that might give us some clues to what is going on," Dr Sunchawee said.

"She has been kind of acting strange the last few weeks," Duen piped up.

"Duen!" Mae scolded her.

"But she has! You said so yourself. Maybe the idea of having to leave BIS was too much for her." Either Duen was on a roll today or I hadn't paid enough attention to her before.

"Duen, that's enough." Khun Yaa was clearly unhappy with Duen's disrespect. Mae's face had gone white. Did she think Duen had a point about BIS?

Though I had been more than ready to leave Nui's family behind, I didn't like seeing all the distress my condition was causing, especially as they were not the primary reason for it. I wished everyone would leave so I could focus on what Nui and I had to do.

"I suggest you all go home and get some rest. Nui is in excellent hands with us, and we know where to reach you if there's any change. You can come back tomorrow morning and speak with Dr Pompetch."

Thank you, Doc.

The doctors walked out while the nurse took my blood pressure and made some notes on her clipboard.

"I'll come back in half an hour to get Nui ready for the night, alright?" The nurse asked.

Khun Yaa and Mae nodded.

"I'd rather stay." Khun Yaa said.

"You heard what the doctor said. You should get some rest too. Nui will understand, right, Nui?" Mae looked at me.

Blink.

Yes, please. Go home. I need to think.

89

NUI

I LEFT CHANNON AND YUMI OUTSIDE SAMITIVEJ AND HEADED in the opposite direction. Luna's parents hadn't texted or called, so I assumed there was nothing new on the investigation. Back on the Skytrain, I mulled over Duen's bombshell about my potential withdrawal from BIS. How could Luna have kept this from me? Did she really think I wouldn't find out eventually? She probably wanted to wait until after we completed the switch. She must have been really worried that I would back out of our agreement. Though I had flirted with the idea, the police investigation had put a new spin on things, and going home was more tempting now. But what would I risk by initiating the switch? Would Luna even be able to meditate? Her physical state had not affected her mind, but what if we couldn't break through the lock, or worse, what if I ended up like her? Which was the better outcome? Prison or prisoner in my body? And even if everything went according to plan, I'd still be stuck in Bangkok, especially if my parents made good on their threat. *Caught*

yourself between a rock and a hard place, Nui, haven't you?
My eyes started tearing, but I refused to give in to self-pity.
*You don't have all the information, so no point freaking
out—yet.*

Luna's mom was in her office when I got home.

"Hi, Mom, any news? Did Dad speak to a lawyer?"

"Hi, honey. How's Nui? Will she be ok?"

"They don't know yet. It was really freaky to see her so
helpless. She can blink to communicate, but nothing else
moves."

"That's horrible. I wonder what caused it."

I could tell you, but you wouldn't believe me.

"They don't know. The family said they were waiting for
more test results. So, what about the lawyer? Did Dad say
anything?" I asked.

"He only mentioned that Jake gave him a recommendation, and he was going to call them. He'll be home soon and
we can talk about it then."

"Ok."

"How are you feeling, honey? Everything alright?"
Luna's mom asked.

"Yeah, I'm fine. No problem." *Besides my world falling
apart.*

Back in my room, I checked my phone. Nothing from
Yumi, even though she had promised to send me the homework assignments. Guess she was too busy hanging out with
Channon. That was just another powder keg waiting to
explode. I wondered if Yumi would have moved in on
Channon if Luna hadn't been paralysed. It was mean of her to
take advantage of the situation so shamelessly.

*Hang on, Nui, you don't even know that's what she's
doing. Maybe she really only wanted to see the hospital.
Yeah, right, when pigs fly.*

It reminded me to check if Yumi had posted anything online about her thirteenth birthday party, in case she asked me again. She was Luna's friend, so I found her details easily enough. Her birthday was coming up in February, but there was nothing about prior parties. I wasn't sure why that day had stood out so much that she'd ask about it specifically. Unfortunately, I couldn't ask Luna, but maybe her mom would remember. I made a mental note to check with her.

I tried to catch up on my reading, but my mind kept drifting. I was imagining different scenarios in my head, trying to fit them all together like puzzle pieces. Maybe writing them down might make the situation clearer.

- Investigation and conviction—yes/no?
- BIS withdrawal—yes/no?
- Unlock Luna and swap back—yes/no?

It was like having too many cooking ingredients and deciding how to best put them together. The outcome would taste fantastic or disgusting.

It was crazy-making. My stomach was tangled up in knots. No one ever said I would have to make life-changing decisions when I was sixteen. *Yeah, and how many people deliberately mess up their lives like you and Luna have?*

This was getting me nowhere. I started pacing the room, then went to take a shower while waiting for Luna's dad to come home.

I was brushing my hair when Luke knocked to summon me for dinner. Khun Bo wasn't in the kitchen, even though it was a Monday night, which was odd. Even more odd was seeing Khun Mark already sitting at the table. He rarely made it home so early. The table was loaded with takeaway from the hotel restaurants.

"Hi honey, how are you doing? Any after-affects from yesterday?" Khun Mark asked.

"All good, Dad. Thanks." I sat down and put a few pieces of food on my plate to pretend everything was normal. I was on tenterhooks to find out what the latest update was.

"Did you speak with the lawyer, Dad?"

"Why do you need a lawyer, Dad? Something wrong?" Luke asked.

"Just needed some advice, Luke." His dad answered and then turned to me. "Yes, Jake recommended a lawyer who has dealt with a few cases involving foreigners who have run into similar problems. I told him the background and how we found out it might be an issue. He recommended we wait to see if the police contact us." Khun Mark took a sip of his wine.

"So, we really know nothing new, do we?" I asked. I had hoped for a more definite answer, but apparently it was going to be a waiting game.

"What did you do, Luna? Did you break the law?" Luke held his fork in mid-air, eyes wide.

"No, of course not." I said, aiming for a confident tone.

"Hmm." Luke didn't quite buy it and neither did I.

I turned back to Khun Mark. "What do you think? When will we know that it's over, Dad?" This sounded petulant, even to my own ears, but the uncertainty was killing me.

"What do you want me to say, Luna? I have no experience with this kind of thing, and I need to take his word for it. At least he knows what happened, and we can call him if there's indeed an investigation," Khun Mark replied.

Luna's parents were amazing and so pragmatic. My own parents would have at least threatened lifelong house arrest. But then I remembered Mae's haunted face as she looked at my body in the hospital and I realized I wasn't being fair. My parents just had a different way of showing they cared.

"Thank you both so much. I'm gonna do some homework, ok?"

I walked back to my room and fell back onto the bed, staring at the ceiling.

Now what?

LUNA

AFTER THE NURSE FINISHED HER EVENING CHECK, SHE TURNED the light low and put the TV on mute. Everyone had left, and the solitude felt calming rather than lonely. I could finally hear myself think, and I had plenty of issues to focus on. First, I had to find a way to unlock my body, with or without Nui's help. Since meditation had been the trigger for the switch and my locked-in state, it was logical that it might also be the way to rectify my condition.

Duen had taken my phone, and in my paralysed state, I wouldn't have been able to access Ajaarn's meditation recordings, anyway. But I wondered if I even needed them. Nui and I had practised often enough that the words and mantras were clear in my head and I knew the breathing exercises inside out. I thought maybe I could meditate to clear my head and decide what I wanted. The priority was to get me unlocked. But what about the switch? After Nui had told me about the investigation, I wasn't so sure I dared put myself at risk of going to prison. Yes, I wanted to get back to my family, but what would happen if there was indeed a conviction? *For once, Luna, make up your mind and stick to it.*

As always, that sounded easier said than done. So much hinged on making the right decision. *Right decision for whom?* My brain snagged on the thought. True, the right decision for me might not be the right one for Nui, but who gets to decide? I had to do what was best for me, and Nui would have to do the same. Hopefully, the end results matched or were at least compatible. I realized I kept making the same stupid mistakes, trying to make things happen instead of letting them develop naturally.

And what about Channon? I thought I was being fair telling him about the switch, but that had backfired. Not only did he not believe me, but he probably thought I was so messed up, he preferred to hang out with other girls. Yumi! What the heck was that all about? Did she really only want to see the pet hospital, or was it because of Channon? Would she do this to a friend? *Don't forget, she thinks you're Nui and you're not actually friends.* Still, given our conversations, I would have expected her to have more integrity. And, no matter how much I hated the thought of losing Channon, ultimately it was his decision whom he wanted to date. Right now, I had more immediate issues to deal with.

Meditation is meant to calm your mind so you can become mentally and emotionally clear. Ajaarn's introductory words to our class flashed into my head. I thought, if I could meditate, maybe it would stop the merry-go-round in my head, and perhaps I could even find out how and where my body got stuck. The room was quiet, and being unable to move, I was already in the perfect position to focus. And with everyone gone, there would be no interruptions. I closed my eyes and started the breathing count.

NUI

I WAS IN LIMBO, MY LIFE ON HOLD, UNTIL I HEARD FROM THE police. I wished Yumi would hurry and send me the homework assignments so I could avoid another evening of brooding. Patience had never been my strong suit and my hands were itching to do something. I decided to delete the original blog documents from my laptop, and even though it was like closing the barn door after the horse had bolted, at least I was doing something. At the last second, I changed my mind, and instead copied the articles onto a USB stick, thinking I could at least keep the inoffensive ones for future use, whenever that might be.

A message pinged.

'Man, that pet hospital is something. I'm going to volunteer there. I'm on my way home. Will send you the stuff then.'

So Channon got another convert. Do all the foreign girls fall for his charms? Maybe he gets a commission from the hospital for bringing in volunteers. I knew I had no reason to be spiteful, especially since I wanted Luna to forget about him all together, but it annoyed me how easily he had agreed to Yumi's request. *Concentrate on your own business instead of fussing about Channon and Yumi.*

I looked around the room. I liked Luna's home. I liked having my private space, and I liked Luna's parents and how they were dealing with the crisis, supporting me. Even Luke wasn't so bad as a little brother, certainly no more annoying than Tum.

Not that I didn't love my own family, but I resented that my parents thought they could decide what I should do with my life. Why couldn't they see that my ambitions were totally different from theirs? I had zero interest in studying law or something equally boring. I always felt that a lot of what my parents did was with an eye towards our community, or the temple, or what our neighbours thought of us. Maybe that wasn't fair, but I didn't give a damn if someone thought I was ambitious or 'aiming above my station' for wanting something different. How was I supposed to use my potential if I had to stay within the boundaries of what *they* thought was acceptable?

I groaned and wrapped my hands around my head to keep it from exploding. *Why does this decision have to be so difficult?*

If I stayed in Luna's body, I would get everything I wanted delivered on a silver platter. Why shouldn't I just take that? *You won't get any of it if you end up in jail.* Should I switch back to avoid the risk of going to prison? But what if the police just let the matter drop, and I'd swapped back for no reason? Dammit. My thoughts were chasing each other like spinning carousel figures; round and round going absolutely nowhere.

The front doorbell rang, and I heard Khun Mark talking to someone. A minute later, there was a knock on my door.

"Luna, can you come to the living room, please?" Khun Susan sounded odd.

She grabbed my arm as soon as I walked out and whispered into my ear, "The police are here and they want to talk to you. Dad's calling the lawyer to find out if we should wait for him. Don't say anything. Let Dad handle it."

My knees weakened, and the blood drained from my head.

Oh my God, oh my God, oh my God. It's happening.

"Come on, let's not keep them waiting." Khun Susan linked her arm through mine and more or less dragged me to the dining room.

There were two guys, one middle-aged, wearing a dark blue suit, and a younger man wearing a tight-fitting brown police uniform, sitting with Khun Mark at the table. The first thing I noticed was that neither police officer had taken off their shoes, which was bad manners. It was such a silly thing to focus on that I almost burst out laughing. *Nui, get a grip.*

All three looked up as we entered. I automatically wai'ed, but neither returned the gesture. Luna's dad pointed to the chair next to him. Khun Susan sat on my other side, our hands interlinked under the table.

The older guy spoke first, in halting but passable English.

"I'm Colonel Songpol with the technology crime-suppression division of the Royal Thai police. This is Lieutenant Pimpilai." He gestured towards the younger officer. "I believe you know why we are here?"

He was addressing me, but Khun Mark immediately answered, drawing their attention to him. "Yes, we understand you had questions about the blog my daughter was working on for her university application."

Luna's dad said it pragmatically, as if it was the most normal thing in the world to have police officers come to your house on a Monday night to question you.

The colonel ignored Khun Mark's answer and looked at me again. "My division handles inappropriate content and computer crimes, including crimes which insult the monarchy. Do you understand?"

"But then, surely, there must be a misunderstanding. My daughter has shared the content of her posts with us and correct me if I'm wrong, but there was no reference to the monarchy at all." Khun Mark was super polite but firm. My teeth were going to break if I clenched them any harder. Khun Susan squeezed my hand under the table.

Again, Colonel Songpol snubbed Khun Mark and turned to me. "As you know, we have put a block on the site. It is our responsibility to investigate any inappropriate content." Khun Mark opened his mouth to respond but the colonel pre-empted him this time, holding up his hand like a traffic stop sign. "Mr Taylor, I need to speak to your daughter and I must ask you to let her answer for herself." His tone had sharpened.

"In that case, I believe it's best if we wait for our lawyer to arrive. I can't allow her to be interrogated without legal representation." Khun Mark straightened up and pulled back his shoulders. I could feel the tension in the room thickening. My heart galloped in my chest. Colonel Songpol sat completely still, and I couldn't read his facial expression at all. The lieutenant however, didn't hide his animosity. My stomach coiled into a tight ball and I felt on the verge of throwing up. I squeezed Khun Susan's hand harder to anchor myself. A quick glance at her face surprised me. She appeared completely relaxed, but her grip on my hand told a different story.

Finally, Colonel Songpol cleared his throat. "Mr Taylor, this is not one of your American TV shows, but if you insist, then you can come to the police head office tomorrow at nine o'clock sharp with your so-called legal representative for a recorded interview. Lieutenant Pimpilai!"

The lieutenant produced a business card that included a map of where the police head office was located. Ironically, the station was right across from Wat Pathum, the temple where Luna and I had done our meditation training with Ajaarn Anurak. Some might call it coincidence, but to me, it felt like I had come full circle to where it all had started.

Colonel Songpol stood, and the lieutenant followed his lead. I wai'ed automatically, before Khun Mark escorted them to the front door.

I slumped down in my chair, covering my face with my hands. "No, no, no, no."

Luna's mom quietly rubbed my back until Khun Mark came back into the room.

"I thought you handled that really well, Mark."

"I'm not so sure. I hope I didn't make it worse by insisting on a lawyer." He sighed.

"No, I think it's completely reasonable to have legal counsel, and they should have expected that."

"We'll see. I'm going to call Stephen Clarke again and make sure he's available for the appointment. We need him to be there." He turned towards me. "Go to your room, Luna, and try to get some rest. We'll leave here by eight."

I simply nodded, afraid I was going to cry if I opened my mouth, then I got up to hug both. I managed a muffled 'sorry' before escaping.

Outside the living room, I stopped for a moment to take a deep breath, and overheard Khun Mark talking softly.

"I'm worried, Susan. I think this was just the opening and

they'll be a lot tougher at the station. I just hope they're not trying to use our case as a warning to others—foreigners or locals."

My blood pressure went into freefall, and my vision blurred. *Don't faint, don't faint.* Holding my arms out like a sleepwalker, I slowly made it to my room and dropped into my chair, putting my head on my knees. Gradually, the dizziness faded. I sat up.

My list of hypothetical scenarios stuck out from under my laptop. I stared at it until my eyes became blurry with tears, then ripped the paper into tiny pieces. If the police were determined to make a case against me, I wouldn't stand a chance to defend myself. *You've really only got one option left now, Nui. You can't go to prison.*

LUNA

THE DOCTORS HADN'T WANTED TO INTUBATE ME SINCE I could breathe on my own as long as I wasn't congested. Instead, they had clamped a mouth prop between my teeth and put an oxygen mask on top. It was only meant to be a back-up, but it strangely exaggerated my breathing rhythm as I consciously had to bypass the plastic piece with every exhale. *Inhale to a count of four, hold, exhale to a count of eight.* I envisioned myself in the temple with Ajaarn's voice repeating the count.

My heart rate settled into a slower rhythm than it had all day. The steady drone of the air-conditioning unit provided the perfect white noise to drown out any other sounds coming from the corridors outside.

Feel your breath flow through your body in one continuous cycle as you inhale and exhale.

Locked-in… Mom… Dad—thoughts and pictures flashed through my mind, but I deliberately turned the focus back to my breathing. This meditation was all about giving my mind a rest.

Imagine a ball of pure, warm light, of love and compassion, just inside your chest. The light is pulsing in time with your heartbeat. Inhale and feel the light expanding, covering your whole body in a white bubble.

Chan… Focus!

Feel the light expand even further to cover this building, the city, the country, and now you can see the entire planet covered in this warm light radiating out from you. Feel your connection with every person, creature and animal on this planet. Be at peace.

My lower back and abdomen began tingling, which was a sign I was coming into synch with the life stream again.

Cho… Focus!

Energy started coursing from the top of my head through my entire body, down to my feet and out into my fingers and toes.

Yu… Focus!

Wave after wave of electrical pulses ran through my body.

Para… Focus!

My body felt weightless. The surge now carried me along effortlessly, like an avalanche gaining speed and power. I felt amazing and full of vitality, despite lying immobile in a hospital bed. Rather than directing my point of view outwards and to the connections with the other spirit threads, I kept my concentration on the energy ripples flowing through me.

Harnessing the intense current, I slowly directed it towards parts of my body. Left leg, right leg, hips, stomach, chest, left arm, right arm, neck, face, top of the skull and all the way back down to my feet.

On the third circuit, I could feel it. My right big toe wasn't just tingling, it was twitching. My left knee jerked involuntarily, but I didn't want to break the cycle. Instead, I concentrated even harder to complete the loop.

One by one, I felt my muscles responding as if they were waking up from a deep sleep. Not the prickle I would normally get if my foot fell asleep, but a warm pulsing that relaxed each muscle.

I wished I could stay in that state forever. And I created it with just my mind. Amazing. I realized I was grinning. Grinning by myself. My muscles were responding to my thoughts.

The awareness shocked me right out of my bubble. My eyes flew open.

Afraid it was just a fluke, I lay stock-still trying to decide what to do next. *Ok, only one way to find out, Luna. Try to lift your right thumb.* Big inhale and my thumb moved up. Feeling bold, I aimed to move my entire hand, and again, it worked. My grin was back, and I lifted my right arm to look at my hand, turning it this way and that. That I was still looking at Nui's hand didn't change my sense of empowerment, relief, and sheer gratitude. Unbelievable. I had done it!

Overwhelmed, my eyes became blurry, and I felt tears dripping onto the pillow. But this time I could actually wipe them away with my fingers.

Next, I took off the oxygen mask and mouth prop to run my tongue over my dry lips. An alarm shrieked and made me jerk. I turned towards the monitors and one of them was blinking red.

Feet pounded in the corridor outside. The door flew open and the night nurse rushed in, turning up the light. I waved at her, grinning, and she slammed to a sudden stop, plastic soles squeaking, her eyes wide.

"Arai…What?" She stammered, clearly shocked, but then rushed forward to check all monitors and lines either out of habit or to collect herself.

"Can I have some water, please?" My voice sounded raspy. The nurse looked back at me as if she was afraid I was playing a trick on her. She said nothing but took my blood pressure, then pushed a button to lever up the bed and handed me a cup with a straw. The water tasted amazing. My first drink in two days.

"I'll page the doctor," she said, shaking her head in amazement. "It's a miracle."

I laid back and closed my eyes. *Now what, Luna? You're still in Nui's body.* I refused to let my ongoing problems diminish my sense of accomplishment. Besides, I realized, now I had proven to myself that I had much more power than I'd given myself credit for, there was no limit on what else I could do with enough determination and focus.

NUI

I HAD A MISERABLE NIGHT, TURNING AND TOSSING, NEVER falling asleep long enough to rest properly. My eyes felt dry and gritty when I dragged myself into the shower. This was going to be one of the few times when I needed Luna's coffee kick to wake me up enough to deal with the day ahead, even if my heart already beat erratically at the thought of the police interview. I dressed conservatively in dark blue slacks with a white blouse and a light blue jacket. Ballerina flats completed my demure outfit. Anything and everything to show that I was an ordinary, boring, law-abiding teenager.

Luna's parents and brother were having breakfast in the dining room.

"Are you going to prison, Luna?" Luke normally didn't talk in the morning until he finished his soggy cereal, but nothing about today was normal. His eyes were wide with worry.

"It's all a misunderstanding, Luke. I'm sure everything will be fine." I tried to put on a brave face, but I was shivering inside. Was it possible I wouldn't see him again? Could they throw me into jail immediately?

I changed my mind about the coffee. I was too jittery already.

"Eat something, Luna. It might be a long day," said Khun Susan.

I managed a dry piece of toast and washed it down with some lukewarm tea. Anything more and I'd throw up.

Luke argued for staying home, but the parents were adamant he should go to school as usual. Soon after he left, the doorbell rang and Khun Bo escorted a gentleman to the dining room. He was about Khun Mark's age and height in a light grey suit, white shirt, and red striped tie with a Thai flag lapel pin on his jacket.

"Mr Clarke? Good morning." Khun Mark stood to greet the newcomer.

"Stephen, please." He shook hands but declined any coffee.

"Luna, your dad shared what you wrote with me, and the details of when and where it was posted. You need to understand that the police have quite some leeway in interpreting content they deem inappropriate. So, I'd like you to think carefully before answering their questions. Most of all, don't get drawn into a debate about the content itself. That's a no-win situation because they're allowed to interpret it any way they want to. Understand?"

I bit my lips but nodded.

"If you're not sure about something, say so. Don't make things up. I will stop you if I think something requires clarification."

He turned to the parents. "They haven't specifically mentioned lèse majesté yet, have they?"

"Not directly, it didn't get that far." Khun Mark answered.

"Let's hope they won't bring it up today. It would put the interview into a whole different ballgame. Right now, it looks like it's a preliminary investigation. Also, it's important that Luna answers herself. Since she's written the articles, they may question her directly. You're only there as observers, both of you." He waited until both parents nodded. "I'll intervene if I think it's necessary." He glanced at his watch. "I think we should get going. We don't want to keep them waiting."

Five minutes later, the four of us were in the car with Khun Pak driving. Morning rush hour traffic was heavy and slow. The adults chatted about something but I tuned them out, watching the cars, motorcycles and tuk-tuks around us as if it was my last chance to see a normal street scene. I was rehashing potential outcomes along the same lines as those that had kept me awake the night before with the same unproductive results. Khun Pak pulled up outside the station fifteen minutes early. I looked over my shoulders to the orange rooftops of Wat Pathum across the road. This was where it had all started. I wished I could set the clock back to early December before Luna and I came up with our crazy experiment. With a deep sigh, I turned around and followed the adults into the station.

94

LUNA

MY MIRACULOUS RECOVERY MUST HAVE SPARKED A MINOR uproar in the hospital. The only saving grace was that it had happened during the night, when there were fewer medical personnel around to bother me. All night long, I kept flexing my hands, legs and feet, and turning my head side-to-side to make sure I could still move. I would have loved to walk around, but I was still attached to the infusion lines. Instead, I kept playing with the handset to adjust the back of the bed up and down. I was exhausted and I could have used the sleep, but even small movements were worth the peace of mind they gave me. As soon as morning dawned, a steady parade of nurses and doctors came through my room to see the medical 'miracle' for themselves. Dr Sunchawee kept asking questions I couldn't answer, even if I had wanted to. I was feeling petty towards him because of his arrogant behaviour towards me and Nui's family, and I was almost sure he'd chalk up my recovery to his own skills. It didn't really matter. The most important thing was that now I could leave the hospital and meet with Nui to make the final switch.

Khun Yaa, Mae and Paa rushed into the room around eight. I had expected them last night, but the staff had held off telling them about my recovery until the doctors had completed their initial assessment.

Tears were streaming down Khun Yaa's face as she hugged me. Even Mae looked relieved and squeezed my shoulder and kissed my forehead. Paa kept nodding and smiling.

"You gave us such a fright, Nui. What did the doctors say?" Khun Yaa asked, using a paper towel to wipe the steady flow of tears from her eyes. Her relief made me cry too until we were both choked up and had to blow our noses, smiling at each other over tissues.

"They don't really know what happened, Khun Yaa, only that everything is ok now and I can go home." They hadn't said that in so many words, but since I had managed my recovery, I felt entitled to decide about leaving, too.

"I'll get the paperwork and see if there's any follow-up to be done." Paa said to no one in particular, probably just glad to be doing something.

Mae nodded and bustled around the room to collect what we needed to take home. While she picked up Yumi's flowers, Nui's elephant and some magazines Khun Yaa had been reading during her vigil, she kept checking over her shoulder as if to reassure herself that I was indeed well again. Khun Yaa laid out some clothes they had brought for me, and I ducked into the bathroom to change out of the hospital gown. It had hurt when they had disconnected the IV line, but that didn't compare to the sharp sting of the catheter removal. I was almost afraid to pee in case it still hurt, but every twinge was a reminder that I was back in charge of Nui's body.

Coming out of the bathroom, I looked around for the most important thing—my phone. If Duen still had it, at least she wouldn't be able to snoop any more now that Nui had changed the access code. But I needed to call Nui to set the time for our switch back. Now that I was no longer paralysed, she had absolutely no reason to delay the swap. I wanted to get home to my parents and put the whole mind switch episode to bed for good. I'd deal with any fallout later.

95

NUI

KHUN STEPHEN SEEMED TO BE FAMILIAR WITH THE POLICE station procedure. After a brief conversation with a receptionist, they escorted us to an interview room. It looked like a plain meeting room, except there were no windows or items of furniture besides a metal table with some built-in buttons and six black plastic chairs. The walls were dull grey and the fluorescent lighting made us all look sickly. Luna's parents sandwiched me between them. Khun Stephen sat at the head of the table, leaving the other side for the police officers.

Colonel Songpol and Lieutenant Pimpilai kept us waiting. If their goal was to make me even more anxious, it was working. When the door opened, my breath hitched. *Here we go.*

Both officers nodded briefly and sat down opposite us, spreading a few files on the table. Colonel Songpol looked at Khun Stephen, who stood and handed him a business card with a slight bow. The colonel passed it on to his colleague and then leafed through some papers.

Lieutenant Pimpilai pressed a button on the table and

stated the time, day and people present in Thai. Khun Stephen activated the recording function on his phone on the table in front of him, which drew a dark look but no comment from the lieutenant.

Handing me a piece of paper, Colonel Songpol asked, "Is this your article?" His tone was neutral, but I was wary of him, especially after the comment I had overheard between Luna's parents the night before. It was a print-out of my blog entry with a date stamp in the upper right-hand corner. Knowing they had tracked it to my IP address, there was no point in pretending it wasn't mine. I nodded.

"You must say it out loud, for the record," Colonel Songpol said.

"Yes," I replied softly.

"Speak up," Lieutenant Pimpilai said.

"Yes, this is my post," I confirmed.

"What was your intention when you wrote this? And your plans for distribution?" the colonel continued.

"Intention?" I swallowed and glanced at Khun Stephen. "I wanted to write an essay like the ones we're writing in school. That's all. Just asking some hypothetical questions."

"Why?"

"What do you mean, 'why'?"

"Why did you write a blog? Why did you make your personal opinions public?" Colonel Songpol stared at me without expression.

"Because…" I was getting uncomfortably warm, though the cold draft from the air-conditioning was hitting my back.

"Yes?"

"I… I'm interested in writing and I wanted to see what people thought of what I had to say, you know, my content and style."

"How many people did you send this to?"

"I didn't send it to anyone directly. The link is only on our alumni page. I thought they were the right audience, since this is the type of essay we do at school." I felt clever for having come up with that.

"So you were planning to ask other students to question the political system as well?"

"What? No, of course not." I almost shouted. The colonel was twisting my words. Khun Stephen coughed.

"Sorry, no, that's not what I meant." I softened my tone.

"You said you wanted to ask hypothetical questions. What did you mean by, 'Do political systems change out of natural evolution? If so, what, and who prompts it, and when does the old outgrow its viability?'"

God, I was so glad I had amended my original wording, which had been much less generic than this.

"We, um, we were discussing what happened prior to the fall of the Berlin Wall and Arab Spring in school, and that was the base for my question. You know, why do people decide it's time for change?"

I hoped they didn't decide to check our school curriculum as we had discussed those topics a year before—not recently.

"How long have you been in Thailand?" Lieutenant Pimpilai asked.

"Since last August." I was pretty sure he could have looked that up himself.

"Khun puut pa-sa-thai dai mai?"

"Dai kha."

"Tum mai rien rew mak?" What did it matter how fast I had learned to speak Thai? I shrugged.

"You must be very interested in Thailand?" Lieutenant Pimpilai asked.

"I live here, and it makes it easier if you speak the

language." I deliberately answered in English and pretended he only referred to the language.

Colonel Songpol had been flipping through some pages, and now he picked up his interrogation again.

"How many articles did you post on your blog? Did you write all of them yourself?"

My mind went blank. I had had so many ideas for topics, but right now I couldn't remember if I had actually written about them or not. I started mentally ticking them off.

The room was silent while everyone waited for my answer.

"Three, I think. Or four?"

"You think? Let me refresh your memory." He held up a page. "I quote: 'Rules, standards, guidelines, and laws govern every aspect of our lives. First, our parents tell us what we can and cannot do and what they expect of us. Next it's the school and teachers. Then the job and your bosses. Religious leaders, judges, politicians, police, the list is never ending. And above all, the government, elected or not. Who gets to decide what we should and shouldn't do?'" He put the page down, but kept his eyes locked on me. "Can you confirm that this is one of your posts?"

Oh shit. An icy shiver went down my back. I had been so focused on the *Traditions* post that I completely forgot about the full *Who's life is it, anyway?* article. Now that he put the posts next to each other, I realised how bad the combined questions made me look. I could feel the blood draining from my head. My blouse stuck uncomfortably to my back.

Colonel Songpol waited. I felt cornered.

Khun Stephen cleared his throat at the same time as Khun Mark nudged my leg under the table.

"I…" I coughed. "Yes, this is my post."

"So, two out of your four posts question the authority and government. Are you still telling me that there was no purpose behind this?" The colonel made it sound like he already knew the only plausible answer to that question. My eyes started tearing up.

"I'm so sorry. I really didn't mean it the way it sounds."

"Then what did you mean?" he asked. Khun Susan pressed her hand down on my knee to still my bouncing.

"I… I just wanted to open up a conversation about some topics that interest me. Nothing more." I finally croaked out. Khun Susan pressed a tissue into my hand and I wiped my eyes.

"Who paid for the blog?" Lieutenant Pimpilai asked.

"I did, from my allowance." At least that was a straight-forward question.

"And your parents gave your allowance to you?"

"Yes."

"So you were using your parent's money to set this up? Do you realise they can be held responsible too?" Lieutenant Pimpilai hammered home.

"What?" I nearly shouted. "No, they had nothing to do with this. I swear." I wished I could just crawl into a hole and die.

"That's not how the law sees it." I realised the lieutenant wasn't as inept as I had interpreted his earlier passivity. Why wasn't Khun Stephen saying anything? Surely he had reason to speak up now. I threw him a pleading look, but he shook his head. It probably meant that the officers were within their rights. It felt like we had been in the room for hours, but a quick glance at my watch said only thirty minutes had passed. Could I ask for a toilet break, anyway? Before I could speak, the colonel started up again.

"Since you're so interested in Thailand, I suppose you do you know that *lèse majesté* is a crime in this country?"

"I…" My mouth went dry, and I glanced at Khun Stephen. The colonel waited. I cleared my throat. "I… yes, I understand that it's illegal to speak ill of the monarchy, but…"

Colonel Songpol didn't let me finish. "So, what did you mean by, 'when does the old outgrow its viability?' Or, 'And above all, the government, elected or not?' Are you asking for the removal of our monarch?"

"No, of course not! I didn't even write about the monarchy." That, I could say with absolute conviction. Khun Stephen cleared his throat. I looked at him and he gave a tiny shake of his head. I'd forgotten I wasn't supposed to argue the content of the post, but how was I going to defend myself if I couldn't say that at least?

"I'm sorry, but no, this is definitely not what I meant." It came out meeker than intended.

"Then, what did you mean by 'the old' in relation to politics?" Colonel Songpol didn't give me a chance to regroup.

"I…"

"Yes? Are you suggesting the monarchy has served its purpose?"

The colonel kept looking at me, expressionless. I could feel my face heating, but I looked down at my hands, sweaty and clenched in my lap. The room fell silent for what felt like an eternity. Abruptly, Colonel Songpol gathered the papers and pushed back from the table.

"I will write up a report and pass it on to my superiors. We will let you know the outcome. I ask that you do not attempt to leave the country until you have heard from us."

Khun Stephen rose at once and bowed slightly. After the officers left, I blew out a big breath.

"I'm so…"

"Not here, Luna. Let's go," Khun Stephen interrupted, shooing us out of the room. Outside, Khun Susan tucked my arm under hers. I leaned against her, grateful for the support. My legs felt weak, as if I had run a marathon.

"Overall, I thought it went ok," Khun Stephen said once we stood outside.

"You think *that* was ok? It was horrible." Aware of police officers coming and going into the building, I tried to keep my voice down.

He didn't answer. "We'll have to wait for their final decision. It's hard to judge something like this. It all depends on what else they have going on, and/or if they are trying to make a statement to others. I'll let you know as soon as I hear from them."

"Thank you Stephen. I really appreciate it. Do you want us to drop you somewhere?" Khun Mark asked. He sounded subdued. Not only had I jeopardised myself and Luna, but inadvertently, I'd also put her parents at risk. Luna would never forgive me for this.

"That's ok. I'll take the train back to my office. Try not to worry too much," he said, then he walked off towards Siam station.

"Honey, I'm gonna walk from here to the hotel. I could use the exercise," Khun Mark said to Khun Susan. "Why don't you have Khun Pak take you home? And Luna, I think you should still go to school." He kissed his wife, hugged me and then started walking towards Erawan Shrine while Khun Susan texted Khun Pak to collect us.

"Dad's right. There's still enough time for you to go to school, and it'll take your mind off things. Let's go home and get your stuff, then Khun Pak can take you to school."

"Sure Mom." I felt nauseous, but craved some normality after the horrible last few days. Also, I had to figure out how to tell Luna about the latest development. She and I had a big joint decision to make.

96

LUNA

BY THE TIME THE FINAL PAPERWORK WAS DONE, I WAS ITCHY
with impatience. This was taking way too long. The doctors
insisted I come back for a follow-up visit the next day and
reminded me I still had to complete the course of rabies shots.
Those would be a piece of cake compared to the days of
paralysis, and they'd be Nui's responsibility, anyway, after
our switch back.

Khun Yaa insisted the parents drop us off at the house and
continue to the store. Khun Pop had been manning the shop
single-handedly for them while they were in the hospital with
me. Unexpectedly, it almost felt like a real homecoming
walking into the house, and Joey's yappy welcome dance
made me laugh out loud. Khun Yaa asked what I wanted for
lunch and suggested I rest while she prepared some of my
favourite dishes. I couldn't wait to taste her delicious food
again. I hugged her, simply happy to physically be able to do
it. It was wonderful to be out of the hospital bed and moving

about on my own. Every step and touch was a confirmation of what I had accomplished.

I sat on my bed and looked around the room that had been my home for the last few weeks. Sure, it wasn't as big or comfortable as my own, but not so bad either. Even sharing it with Duen had been manageable. Though I had just changed at the hospital, I wanted to wash off the reminder of my stay there and after two days of sponge baths, a shower was definitely in order. As I grabbed shorts and a t-shirt, my thoughts wandered. *What should I wear for my first proper date with Channon?* Maybe I'd get a new dress, something blue that went well with my hair and eyes. I felt a bit more daring now that I had worn Nui's tighter clothes for weeks, so perhaps something more fitted. Mom had taken Nui for a manicure/pedicure and a facial, so I'd be all set on that. A delicious little shiver went down my spine. Right now I felt invincible, and I was determined to make the date happen, no matter what Yumi was planning. I was sure I'd be able to convince Channon that I was still the same girl, just back in my own body. But first, I needed to set up the time for the switch with Nui.

Thankfully, Duen had left my phone plugged in to charge on my nightstand. I closed the door and tried to call Nui, but it went straight to voicemail. She probably had turned it off for school.

97

NUI

LUNA'S MOM AND I WERE QUIET, LOST IN OUR OWN THOUGHTS on the drive home. Drained of energy, I shuffled like an old woman into my room to change for school and grab my bag. How I was supposed to pay attention in class was beyond me, but hopefully it would distract me for a while from the investigation.

Replaying the interrogation in my head, I gradually became disgusted with my meek behaviour. Crying in front of the police! *You're such a coward, Nui.* How could I expect to become a tough reporter if I couldn't even handle one interview? *Yeah, but if I was a reporter, I'd be doing the interviewing. I wouldn't be the subject. And it wouldn't be an interrogation.* My brain was scrambling for excuses, but deep down, I knew there was no justification. I had deliberately and intentionally started the blog, only remotely considering how it could backfire. But worse, I had dragged Luna's family into my mess as well. This wasn't the person I wanted to be and I could clearly imagine Mae's fury and Khun Yaa's disappointment if they knew of my behaviour. My emotions were all over the place—angry, scared, resentful, discouraged, overwhelmed.

Startled, I realized I was crying again, tears dripping down my nose and onto my hands. I'd been standing in front of the bathroom mirror in a stupor. A chime from my phone on the bed announced a missed call and reminded me I needed to get going. I blew my nose, then splashed some water on my face, hoping to hide the tell-tale signs of my crying. I knew I had to go to the hospital to see Luna and tell her truthfully about the trouble I was in. It was only fair that she knew what was at stake if we made the switch. Hopefully, by then, she would also have some answers from the doctors and if not, we'd try the meditation she had insisted was the only way to reverse the paralysis. I definitely couldn't leave her like this and not at least give it a go. We had no guarantee that the 'unlocking' would work or that we could switch back at the same time. It was all a gamble. *And if you get locked in instead of Luna, maybe that's your penance for what you have done.* I shivered.

98

LUNA

WHEN I GOT BACK TO MY ROOM, I SAW I HAD A MISSED CALL from Nui. I FaceTimed her, wanting to see her reaction when she realized I had fully recovered.

"Guess who!" I giggled when I saw her eyes go wide and her mouth drop open.

"Luna? Oh my God. You're back. Wow! That is…". She blinked as if doing a double-take. Looking closer, though, I thought my eyes were suspiciously red, like she had been crying and my skin was awfully blotchy.

"Pretty amazing, huh?"

"Yeah, I thought it was Duen calling to tell me something else had gone wrong. But this is fantastic! How did you manage? Wow! I don't know what to say." Nui kept staring at me, shaking her head. "When I saw you yesterday…" She didn't have to complete the sentence—I knew how scary it had been.

"I know. In the end, it was almost easy. I thought I'd meditate to stop myself from going crazy. Remember how it feels when we have an out-of-body experience, calm but also empowering? Well, I figured I could try to use that energy to see if I could unlock myself, and it worked! It was mind-blowing." Even I was still surprised by how natural it had felt to have that power.

"Wow. That sounds awesome. I'm so glad it worked, and this is over!"

"Well, yeah, I'm unlocked, so *that* is over, but we still have to switch back." Maybe I should have let her absorb the news first, but I was too eager to move forward and straighten out our messed-up lives.

"No, you're right, of course."

I waited, but she volunteered nothing further. Odd.

"So, when are we meeting? By the way, why aren't you in school?" I could see my room behind her. Nui looked away, and I saw my lips trembling. "And why have you been crying? Is everyone ok?"

"I, I mean we, just got back from the police station and your mom said I should go to school now."

"Police station? They called you in? Shit. What did they say?"

"They asked a lot of questions, but then they only said they would let us know." Nui looked down again and said in a low voice, "I'm really sorry Luna. I didn't mean for this to happen. I really didn't expect them to take this so seriously, or act so fast."

"Duh. I read your posts, Nui. Even I know you can't just question the status quo here. How are my parents? They must have freaked out. As if my mom didn't have enough to worry about already."

"I know. But do you think my parents weren't worried when you were paralysed? And Khun Yaa already has a weak heart." Nui rallied a bit.

"So, you mean there's a real chance I could go to prison?" I could hardly believe my question. The injustice of it was just too much. I had done nothing wrong to deserve that.

Nui shrugged. "Maybe, but I honestly don't know."

"So, basically for you, it's all easy-peasy. We switch and you just get your old life back while I could get arrested? Thanks a lot, Nui! You really screwed up my life!" I didn't know if I should be angry or scared.

"But it could all turn out to be ok too." Nui countered. "And it will not be the same life for me either, especially if my parents take me out of BIS."

"Ha, going to another school is hardly the same as going to prison. And I had nothing to do with your parents' decision. You know that it's about the money they want to use for the shop."

"Duen said it was because Mae was angry that you hadn't been focusing enough on your studies."

"As if! We haven't even had any tests yet, so they are just using it as an excuse. And likewise, it could all turn out to be ok for you, too."

We were going round and round with our arguments, but our swap back wouldn't work unless we made a joint decision.

"You know, Nui, I've been thinking. What in the world possessed us to consider a switch such a good idea? I mean, if I was meant to live your life, wouldn't I have been doing that it in the first place? We could have avoided this entire mess if we had stuck with our original plan and switched back immediately."

"Maybe, but why then were we even able to switch? I mean, if everything is set in stone from the beginning, then we shouldn't have been able to do that, no?"

Now it was my turn to contemplate her argument.

"Hmm, not sure. But you know what's really ironic? Channon said that I was having an identity crisis if I couldn't decide who I was or what I wanted to be. It pissed me off, but actually I think he was right. If nothing else, at least now I know what I want. This whole thing about trying to be someone else only caused more problems than we started with, right?"

Nui sighed. "I know."

"Ok, here's what I think. I want to go home and I'm willing to risk whatever happens with the police. What about you? Honestly. You heard what Ajaarn said. We need to be one hundred percent clear and agree." I tried to keep my expression neutral.

Nui stayed silent for a long moment, then sighed again. "I agree. I think it's the right decision for us both."

"Can you skip school and come here? Your parents are at the shop and only Khun Yaa and Khun Bpoo are here, so it's quiet."

Nui let out a long breath. "Let me see if I can ditch Khun Pak. He's supposed to drop me at school. I'll text you, ok?"

"We're having lunch soon. I'll tell Khun Yaa you're coming to catch me up on school stuff."

"Fine, see you in a bit," Nui said, then hung up.

I couldn't wait to be home in a few hours, but felt a sliver of apprehension. Was I being naïve, hoping that the police situation wasn't as bad as Nui made it out to be, or that my parents could protect me in any case?

99

NUI

Ditching Khun Pak was easy, and bad traffic helped. I told him I'd walk, and though he protested a bit, I left him no choice and jumped out at the next red traffic light. Instead of heading downtown, I took the Skytrain to Thong Lo.

I'd been home only a few days earlier to see Luna after the dogfight, but it felt like a lifetime ago. Joey greeted me at the door with his usual exuberance when Luna invited me in. Khun Yaa smiled when I wai'ed to her, but she still looked way too pale and seemed to move slower. I wished I could hug her. *Later*. At least she had forgiven 'Luna' after Duen had straightened out the drinking issue.

Lunch was earlier than normal, but Khun Yaa must have needed the routine of cooking to calm herself after the hospital ordeal. By unspoken agreement we didn't talk about that, but I pretended to want to know more about Thai customs and ceremonies to distract her. Khun Yaa was planning to go to the temple in the afternoon to give thanks for 'Nui's' recovery. I mentally promised to go with her. It would be good to get back into a routine with her and I definitely should make merit for myself after the mess I had created.

I suggested to Khun Yaa that Luna and I would do the washing up so she could rest. When she readily accepted, it was the clearest sign yet of how much the episode had taken out of her. It also cleared the way for Luna and me to meditate in peace.

We went to the boys' room and sat opposite each other on the beds, leaning back against the wall.

LUNA

"Ok then, let's do it. No games, right?"

"No games." Nui confirmed.

I hit the taped recording and Ajaarn Anurak's voice filled the room.

NUI

IT HAD BEEN EXHAUSTING BEING ON GUARD CONSTANTLY AND after the added stress over my blog; I was ready to let go. My breath deepened, and I drifted off into a meditative state much quicker than I thought possible. I sensed Luna opposite me, breathing to the same pattern. A wave of energy coursed through me, waking up nerve endings until I became acutely aware of every cell in my body. The last two times I had felt my source energy as intensely as this was when I had to fight off Luna's attacks, but that didn't compare to the elation I experienced in this moment. I could even forgive her for trying to push me out of her body. Though I had said I was ready to switch back, I still felt conflicted. *Go back home or live the life I had dreamed of? Take a risk or play it safe?* During the police interview, I had been one hundred percent sure I needed to return home, but now I questioned that decision again. Maybe Luna was right, and we were only meant to live our own lives. But that was easy for her to say, since she got everything she wanted. Why shouldn't I take this opportunity and create my own future instead of doing what everyone expected me to do? *Because you'd be living a lie, Nui.* I hesitated to bond with Luna's spirit thread, afraid she would recognize my inner struggle.

LUNA

LIFTING OUT OF MY BODY HAD BECOME EASIER WITH practise. The sense of peace and freedom was as blissful as before. For a moment, I just revelled in that joy and happiness. Then, casting around, I tried to locate Nui's spirit thread. I knew we were both tethered to the life stream, which I liked to compare to a tree trunk with us being the branches and leaves. I sensed her nearby, but for some reason when I reached towards Nui, I couldn't click in with her like in the past. We had to be connected for the swap to work. By now, we should have formed a solid link with strong vibrations running between us, so we'd be able to make the exchange. After my ill-advised earlier attempts, I didn't dare push her. *Come on Nui! You agreed that it's the right decision. Where are you? Why aren't we connected?*

NUI

Make a decision. Trust your instinct. Do what's right for you. Everything will work out. I couldn't tell where these thoughts were coming from. Was it my inner being urging me on, or was I trying to talk myself into something? *You can't back out of your deal now. You promised Luna. It's the honourable thing to do. You can't just leave her hanging.* My guilty conscience fought for primary position. *But look at all the opportunities you'll miss out on if you go home. It's not right, Nui. But what about your family? Are you really ready to just leave them?* This meditation was turning into the opposite of calm and peaceful for me.

LUNA

THIS CAN'T BE HAPPENING. SOMETHING IS SERIOUSLY WRONG. Why can't I connect to Nui? We committed to switching, so why isn't this working? Our spirit threads didn't link up like they should. Did we wait too long? My serenity was unravelling. *Wait!* Don't lose it now. Focus. This has got to work. There was no other option. I had to try again.

NUI

DECIDE! YOU STILL HAVE TIME TO CONNECT TO LUNA. YOU promised her. Yes, but…. I was trembling with tension. *I can't do this.* I exhaled sharply and slowly opened my eyes to look at Luna.

'*On the count of five, you will open your eyes and feel refreshed and calm. One, two, three, four, five. Take a deep breath in and release. Open your eyes.*'

LUNA

The recording had stopped. I felt like crying. We had failed. I coughed out a breath and looked at Nui.

"What happened? Why didn't we connect?"

Nui stayed silent.

"Come on Nui. We have to try again. I know we can do it."

Still no response. She didn't look at me, but rubbed her nose and bit her lip.

"Nui? What's wrong? Let's try again."

"I can't." I barely heard her.

"What? What do you mean, you can't? Of course you can. You promised."

Nui sat up straight, her expression shifting from guilt to… resolve? "I'm really sorry Luna, but this is my only chance. I have to take it."

Blood rushed to my head as her meaning dawned on me. My ears were ringing as if a giant gong had been struck inside my head.

"You never intended to switch back, did you? You planned this all along?! How could you?!" I was shaking, my body on fire, about to combust. "You will not get away with this Nui. I'm not going to let you."

THE END

TO MY READERS

Thank you so much for choosing to read Eek-Daan, whether you have been waiting for Luna's and Nui's story to continue or you have stumbled across this book by chance. If you had fun reading Eek-Daan, I'd appreciate it if you'd help others enjoy it too.

Recommend it: Just a few words to your friends, your book groups, and your social networks would be wonderful.

Review it: Please tell your fellow readers what you liked about my book by reviewing Eek-Daan on Goodreads or on whatever site you bought the book from. If you do write a review, please send me a note at maria@mariakuhnbooks.com so I can thank you with a personal e-mail. You can also stop by my website www.MariaKuhnBooks.com to keep up to date with the final instalment of this trilogy. Sign up for my newsletter and as a thank you, you will receive the companion short story 'Yumi'.

Thank you for your support. I hope to see you next time!

Maria Kuhn

GLOSSARY

Ajaarn - *Teacher (title)*
Chai (kha/krub) - *Yes*
Chai mai kha? - *Right? Isn't that so? Isn't that true? Is that ok?*
Da man - *Damn it*
Farang - *Foreigner*
Kha (female version) Khrup (male version) - *commonly added to a sentence to make the sentence more polite and formal*
Khanom Khrok - *small sweet and savory pancakes mostly eaten in the morning*
Khun + First name - *form of address i.e. Khun Susan, Khun Mark, Khun Bo (In writing often only 'K' + name)*
Khun Bpoo - *Grandpa (paternal grandfather)*
Khun Yaa - *Grandma (paternal grandmother). Khun Yaa and Grandma can be used interchangeably*
Klong - *canal*
Kluai thot - *deep-fried bananas*
Khun puut pa-sa-thai dai mai? - *Do you speak Thai?*

Lèse Majesté - *A crime. Any person who defames or insults the monarchy can be imprisoned*

M.L. or Mom Luang - *Hereditary royal title*

Mak-ku-tet - *Guide*

Mae - *Mom*

Mai pen rai - *Isn't that so?; whatever; right?; Never mind; Oh, don't worry.*

Mai roo - *I don't know*

Miang Kham - *salad wraps/snacks*

Ni Hen Wu Li, Ni Ying Gai Geng Jing Sheng, Ni Bu Hui Zhi Dao Shui Zai Shuo Tong Yi Ge Yu Yan - *That was very rude of you You should be more careful. You never know who speaks what language.*

Nii laaw-len chai mai? - *Are you kidding me?*

Nong - *form of address for a younger person*

Noo + name - *endearment: Little Mouse*

Paa - *Dad*

Pi' - *form of address for an older person*

Pen arai? - *what happened?*

prik jinda - *extra spicy chilli*

Sabai di - *I'm well*

Sabai di mai? - *How are you? Casual among friends*

Sawasdee khrup/Kha - *Hello/Goodbye*

Soi - *Street*

Soi dog - *feral street dogs*

Tai chai - *Twenty question game*

Tuk-tuks - *three wheeled open-sided motor taxis*

Wai - *hand gesture (hands together in prayer form in front of the body) as a greeting or show of respect*

Wat - *Temple*

Zen Yang Cai Ke Yi Rang Ta Xiao Shi? Wo Xiang Dan Du He Ni Liao Liao? - *How do we get rid of her? I want to talk to you alone*

STAY IN TOUCH

Readers Club Download offer

A Family Torn Apart – Impossible Choices – New Beginnings

FREE DOWNLOAD: SHORT STORY

If you'd like to find out more about Yumi, simply go to www.MariaKuhnBooks.com and sign up for my Reader's Club. As a gift you will receive the free companion short story 'Yumi'. I will also let you know when the final instalment of this trilogy is coming.

ACKNOWLEDGMENTS

When travel is restricted in real life—travel in your mind! This was never more true than during the pandemic years when I had to rely on my memories or helpful tips from my Bangkok friends to conjure up the City of Angels.

Writing is a solitary exercise but producing a book certainly isn't. Eek-Daan would not have seen the light of day without my trusted writing group with their inspired and spot-on comments and suggestions. A big thank you especially to Hannah for her patience with my endless questions afterwards, Nickie for, yet again, correcting my mangled Thai phrases and any distorted cultural habits, Laura for adapting my vision of the cover and Victoria at The Word Tank, for cleaning up the manuscript.

Thank you also to my beta readers for the early feedback. Every single comment helped. The story has evolved over time, so any remaining errors are, of course, entirely mine.

A special thank you also to the Alliance of Independent Authors for being an indispensable resource for newbie authors. I learn something new every day.

And to Ziggy and Yoko for making sure I didn't stay glued to my desk for too long. Special treats are in order.

ABOUT THE AUTHOR

Maria grew up in a tiny village in the German countryside. She now lives in London after thirty years of criss-crossing the world working in five-star hotels. Along the way she made wonderful friends, met quirky characters, tasted delicious cuisines, experienced diverse cultures, enjoyed bustling cities and awe-inspiring nature. All of these deserve to have their own stories told—eventually.

Eek-Daan is her second book in the Krung Thep trilogy.